JAMILA GAVIN

When I am asked if the Surya trilogy is autobiographical, the answer is yes and no. Yes, that I couldn't have written it had I not been born in India into the period leading up to the Second World War, independence and partition; yes, that as a child I lived both in a palace in the Punjab and in a drab flat in a war-damaged London street; yes, that music, sea voyages, schools, friends were all part of my rich Anglo-Indian experience. But no – in any accurate sense to do with the plot or events described in the books. Everything I experienced simply became material with which I could overlay a complete fantasy. As a child can turn a table into a house or two chairs into a train, I turned my life into a fiction in which any resemblance to characters living or dead is purely coincidental – as they say in the movies.

Also by Jamila Gavin

for younger readers

Contents

Part Three: Just as in the Wheel

'The Body is the chariot,
Reason is the charioteer,
Mind is the reins.
The Horses are the five senses,
Their paths the objects of sense.
So the one whose chariot is driven by Reason
And holds the reins of his Mind,
Reaches the end of the journey.'

The Upanishads

PART ONE
Swift and Shining

'Swift and shining is the great God Surya,
Maker of light,
Illuminator of the universe;
Traversing the heavens in his twelve-wheeled chariot,
With flying sparks and seven horses.
Creating day
Ensuring birth
With the rays of his all-seeing sun.'

The Rig-Veda

ONE

The White Road

'Jhoti! That little brat of yours is stealing Ajit's tin! If you don't come right now and sort it out, her bottom will feel the back of my hand!'

A woman's voice screeched harshly across the yard. It penetrated the inner courtyard where Jhoti crouched outside the kitchen door, grinding spices on a block of ribbed stone. She had been at her job an hour or more so her arms ached and her fingers were all red with rolling and mixing the spices into a paste.

She jerked back on her haunches and sprang to her feet; too quickly, for as the blood drained from her face and a sharp pain jabbed through her stomach, she swayed with dizziness and had to lean up against the wall. She should remember that she was pregnant and not make these swift movements; but she was so used to reacting instantly to the sound of her sister-in-law Kalwant's voice, that it had become a reflex action. So she only paused long enough for the dizziness to pass and the pain to subside, before she hurried across the courtyard and out into the compound beyond.

An ancient, knuckly, pepul tree spread a twisting shade beneath its broad, dark green leaves. Here, the infants, those that is who were too young even to herd goats or follow the buffalo, tumbled and played under the baleful eyes of the male village elders, who sat smoking on their string beds, or sipping tea and playing cards at an old wooden table.

Usually there was no need to interfere. Even infants can sort out their own problems if left to it. But today, as Kalwant was passing by on her way to fetch water from

11

the well, she had noticed her son, Ajit, struggling to gain possession of a tin from Jhoti's daughter, Marvinder.

'It's mine!' raged Ajit. 'I found it.'

'It's mine!' insisted Marvinder. 'Ma gave it me.'

When Ajit saw his mother, he fought harder, shouting, 'Ma! Marvinder's trying to take my tin away.'

'No, I'm not!' screamed Marvinder. 'You took it from me. It's mine, I tell you,' and she tugged even more fiercely.

However, determined that no snip of a girl would get the better of her son, Kalwant yelled for Jhoti.

As Jhoti hurried into view, Kalwant pointed accusingly, and shrieked, 'Do you see?' as Marvinder now had Ajit flat on his back and was sitting astride his chest. 'That child of yours is a little snake! Look how she attacks my son! Stop her at once, or I'll . . .'

Jhoti turned hesitatingly towards the battling children. Marvinder was winning. She held the tin grimly between her fingers while Ajit kicked and punched in his efforts to regain it.

Jhoti knew it was Marvinder's tin. It was a Bournville chocolate tin which she had retrieved from the Chadwicks' rubbish tip. When Marvinder saw her mother, she cried indignantly, 'Ma, Ma! Ajit says this tin is his. But it's mine, isn't it? You gave it me! He's trying to steal it!'

'Did you hear that?' Kalwant's voice peaked with self-justified outrage. 'Did you hear?' she appealed to the world at large. 'Marvinder is calling my son a thief! This is too much!' She plonked down her water vessels and with threatening hand outstretched, she strode towards the children.

Jhoti broke into a clumsy sprint, but could not reach her daughter before Kalwant snatched her up, tipped her upside down and began slapping her bare bottom for all she was worth. Marvinder's screams echoed round the compound. The old men paused in their gossiping, turned round and frowned. The other children froze their actions and stared in awe.

'Stop it, stop it!' begged Jhoti, crying herself. 'She's only a baby. Leave her alone!' She grabbed her daughter's head and managed to clasp her under the shoulders. For a moment, it looked as Marvinder would be torn limb from limb as the two warring mothers tugged at each end of her.

Then another voice rang out from within the low, flat-roofed dwelling. It was a voice cracked with age, but authoritative. 'For goodness sake!' Madanjit Kaur berated them. 'Can't an old woman get any peace around here?'

Mother-in-law shuffled out. Her unmade grey hair hung loosely down her back. She stood surveying the scene with hands on hips, her narrow, black eyes glaring vehemently. The baggy folds of her pyjamas beneath the full, green cotton tunic, could not disguise her powerful, stocky figure, or the strength of will with which she presided over her domain.

'Yes, Jhoti! I know it's you.' She wagged an accusing finger. 'No good dropping your head in that shamefaced way. There's been nothing but trouble from you ever since you entered this household, and it's not as though you came with much dowry either. How could we tell, when we arranged this marriage, that you had been so badly brought up? And now we see you doing the same with your own child, wilful and disobedient girl! *Arreh Baba*! I guessed as much as soon as I laid eyes on you, but no one would listen to me. The old man is too fond of a pretty face, that's the trouble! You all are!' She aimed her recriminations at the old men, but they just shrugged and turned away bending closer over their cards, not wishing to be drawn into any womanish disputes.

'Get on back to your tasks, Jhoti, and take your brat with you!' she commanded.

Kalwant smirked, and dropped Marvinder's legs which she had been clutching all this time. Jhoti staggered as the full weight of her daughter swung against her body.

Marvinder's sobs pierced the air. 'Ma, Ma! It's my tin. You know it is!'

13

Kalwant, under the full protection of Mother-in-law's gaze, reached out and extricated the tin from Marvinder's grip. 'There you are, my precious,' she held it out to her son. 'Now it's yours again!'

Ajit snatched it gleefully and ran round proudly displaying it like a trophy. Marvinder's mouth opened wider as a protesting wail gathered in her throat, but Jhoti hastily stuffed the end of her veil into the child's mouth, and heaving her up on to her hip, ran from the scene.

'Hush, darling!' she entreated. 'Or Grandmother will have us both beaten. I'll find you another tin, I promise.'

Only when she reached the privacy of the inner courtyard, did she set her child down on the ground. Then she unstuffed the veil from her daughter's mouth and wiped away the tears from both their faces.

'Come and help me finish grinding the spices. You like that, don't you?' she whispered, hugging and kissing her.

Marvinder nodded, weeping quietly now as her mother held her tightly. 'Oh, darling baby,' Jhoti whispered, 'who else would I have to love, if I didn't have you?'

Living as she did with her husband Govind's family, Jhoti was at the very bottom of the pecking order. Not only was Govind the youngest of three sons, but he was always away. She had met him for the first time when he had come home for their marriage, and then a week later, he had gone again; back to Amritsar. In due course they sent him word to say that she was pregnant, and he said he would come home in time for the birth. But Jhoti gave birth earlier than expected, and when he heard it was a girl, he didn't hurry back. It was another two months before he saw his daughter. But at least Jhoti had been in her own home then. She stayed as long as she dared, relishing in the affection which her mother and sisters lavished on her. How they cared for her and her baby; each day her mother would come with oils and massage her belly, her limbs and her feet; her sisters washed and combed out her hair, rubbed and oiled her scalp and then talked and joked and laughed for hours with her, taking it in turns to rock the infant.

When she finally returned to her in-laws, she wondered if the pain of homesickness would ever pass; and in the evening, when all the chores were done, when the men got tipsy on home-brewed rice wine, and the women welded themselves into tight little gossipy knots from which Jhoti was usually excluded, Jhoti would soothe her baby to sleep, then slip away and walk through the dark fields, and climb the steep dyke to the narrow, straight-as-a-die, long white road; turning her face towards home, she looked and looked until the gleaming road disappeared over the dark horizon.

Jhoti's life began on that long, white road. Only six miles further down to the south, she had been born in another small farming village. A village so simple, that a casual eye would barely have distinguished it from the well-ploughed earth and the dappled shade of eucalyptus trees.

She was taken to her new home along this same road, aged thirteen, a child bride. Every time she came and stood on the edge of the road, she remembered that day; remembered the train of bullock carts, all festooned with garlands of flowers and overburdened with too many wedding guests. How flamboyant the men had looked; her father, her uncles, her cousins and brothers, like peacocks with their turbans of turquoise and blue and green and vivid pink. Then there were the women, glittering like tinsel. How they loved weddings. What an opportunity to get out their finery; their thick, chunky jewellery, their satin *kurta* pyjamas, their tinselly veils glittering with silver and golden threads, so dazzling the eye that they looked as if they might burst into flames in the heat of the sun.

They had chosen the pure white bullocks to pull the carts. Usually, the bullocks would have been pulling a plough, or winding a dreary path round and round and round a well, all day, drawing water to irrigate the fields. But that day was her wedding day, and their thick white

15

skins had been lavishly painted with rich colours, to defy the brown summer arid landscape, and their horns, like arched spears, were wrapped in gold.

Later, the men sang at the tops of their voices and whipped the lean haunches of these silent beasts. Whipped them till they galloped down the road towards her husband's home. Too fast, too fast! Jhoti had wept inside. Were they in such a hurry to wrench her from her mother and her sisters? Were they in such a hurry to hand her over to a stranger, whose mother must now become her mother, and whose brothers and sisters must become more to her than her own siblings?

Only her younger sister seemed to notice the tears in her eyes. She leaned closer to her and squeezed her hand. 'Don't cry, Jhoti,' she pleaded, almost crying herself. 'Don't cry, Didi, dear elder sister, or else the charcoal round your eyes will run, and you will ruin your beautiful bride's face. Don't be sad. We'll come and see you.'

But Jhoti knew they wouldn't; knew they couldn't. She would go home to them once, for the birth of her first child, for that was the custom; but life was hard; too hard for the luxury of family visits. No, from now on, her life must be Govind's life; his mother and father must become her parents, his brothers and sisters, her brothers and sisters.

During the wedding ceremony, she had had the sensation of separating from her body, and like a ghostly stranger found herself looking on at her own marriage.

Was that really her? That slight figure, dressed all in crimson, so that all she surveyed was through a crimson glow? And the man next to her, his head bowed so low that his face was buried from sight in his garland of golden marigolds; who was he? Oh, she knew his name: Govind Singh, they had told her. The youngest of three sons of a farmer whom most people considered quite wealthy. Of course, being the youngest, he wouldn't inherit much, which was probably why they didn't mind the fact that he had married beneath him. But who was he really? What was he like? After all, he was only sixteen, barely older than her eldest brother.

She had heard some talk. People said he could read and write like a scholar. That's why he went away to the city of Amritsar. A local English teacher, Harold Chadwick had discovered the boy's aptitude for learning. He persuaded Govind's father to allow his son to continue his education after primary school, rather than move on to the land to work, as would have been expected. Mr Chadwick flattered Mr Chet Singh on having produced a son with brains; a son who could be a clerk or a teacher or even a lawyer!

Mr Chet Singh was impressed, but possibly more relieved that perhaps he need not sub-divide the family land to take account of his youngest son. If Govind took up his share, too, the plot would be barely sufficient to produce a living.

Sitting cross-legged on a carpet surrounded by all the wedding guests, she had tried to look sideways at Govind's face, but somehow, she couldn't make out his features between the low rim of his turban, and his face down in the marigolds.

This man – this boy – was to be more important to her than her father. Her father, who owned her, would give her away, and she would belong instead to this stranger.

As Jhoti stared down the road towards home, the tears fell again as she remembered how they placed the garland around her neck; how, as the hoarse chanting of prayers rose higher and higher, her father pulled her to her feet, and taking the end of Govind's scarf had tied it to the end of her veil. Thus joined together, she was led four times round the priest and his sacred book. She had wanted to cry out, 'Oh, Father! Are you glad? Is this what you've been waiting for since the day I was born? Just waiting to give me away, to get me off your hands? Do you feel liberated? Is your burden lessened? If it is, then I shall feel comforted.'

How red everything was, red as the first drops of blood

which had fallen from her body. Then she knew that her childhood was over; that the next blood to fall from her body would be on the bridal bed, and the old women would be sure to come and take note, and then they would click their tongues with satisfaction as they announced that her honour was upheld and the bride had indeed been a virgin.

For the next seven days, Jhoti had had all the attention of a new bride. People had come to visit; to scrutinise her; form an opinion about her. They had examined her dowry and her gifts, assessed her jewellery and held up her sarees to see whether they were of silk and how many were shot with gold thread. They had pinched her cheeks and admired her beauty, but none of it was for her sake. She was being looked over as Govind's property, and whatever compliments were showered on her, they were for his benefit, not hers.

Soon he would be leaving for college in Amritsar, then she would become a nobody; only with him was she a somebody. On the day of his departure, Jhoti stood by helplessly, while Mother-in-law took over. She stormed about the place, handing out orders, packing his clothes, assembling his food for the journey and, deliberately, it seemed to Jhoti, ignoring her attempts to help, brushing her aside as if she were a useless infant.

And when they heaved Govind's rusting trunk on to the bullock cart, she watched as they fussed and kissed him and showered him with freshly strung garlands still wet with dew, and only then, just before he climbed into the cart, did he seek her out. He came towards her, awkwardly, without meeting her eye. She knelt and kissed his feet. When she rose to her feet, her head stayed bowed and she backed away. Their bodies stayed formally apart, still strangers. 'Be a good daughter to my mother and father,' he murmured. Then he was gone.

The road looked white, even in the pre-dawn darkness. When the bullock cart had come to take Govind to the railway station, it was glaringly white; dazzlingly white.

Jhoti had stood a long while, watching and watching until the bullock cart, carrying her husband away, had diminished to a speck. Then a rough voice had yelled, 'Hey, Jhoti! Come now, girl! You can't stand there pining all day. There's work to be done; spices to be ground; rice to be sifted.' Her mother-in-law summoned her to the kitchen.

That was three years ago, yet even now as she stared down the long white, gleaming road it still seemed to beckon her home and her heart ached. Pregnant again at last, for the second time, she worked her hands over her swollen belly as if trying to mould the embryo inside her. 'Please be a boy,' she murmured, 'be my son.' Perhaps then, she would attain some status in the family and gain some respect and affection from Govind.

All around her from the height of the dyke road, Jhoti could see the glows of charcoal fires like low stars, flickering through the trees. She could hear the faint drone of voices, and the smell of tobacco colliding with the scent of jasmine flowers.

And reaching her ears, as if radiated outwards on the steady beam of electricity which lit up the sky at the mission bungalow, came the sounds of a violin and piano. The English sahib and his memsahib were making their nightly music.

Mozart soared through the darkness like a strange spirit bird.

Tomorrow, Jhoti thought, she must go over to the Chadwick bungalow and try and find another tin for Marvinder.

She forced her memories back into the inner recesses of the mind and like a ghost, wandered, unseen, back to her home. She splashed herself quietly, at the courtyard pump, then crept into the kitchen. That's where she and Marvinder had a space in a corner on the floor for sleeping, except when Govind came home. Then they were allowed their own room off the verandah. Feeling her way in the pitch darkness, she knelt down beside the mattress on the floor where her daughter lay. The child didn't even stir, as Jhoti eased herself under the thin sheet, and drew the little girl into her arms; then she too fell deeply asleep.

TWO
Dora

Dora Chadwick had got to know Jhoti by sight. She had often noticed the girl slipping discreetly up the side of the compound and disappearing round the back to the servants' quarters. At first it had annoyed her, and she'd called Arjun, the bearer and asked him about her.

'Who's that girl who hangs around here from time to time? Is she anything to do with us?'

Arjun clicked his tongue with irritation. 'That's Jhoti, Memsahib, Govind's wife. She's always hanging round here. I'll get rid of her.'

'No, no! Don't.' Dora restrained him. 'I was just curious. She doesn't bother me at all, and if she's Govind's wife, well of course I don't mind her coming here. I just wondered!'

'She's friendly with the cook's wife, Maliki,' Arjun told her. 'She comes for gossip and company. They say she's not too happy what with Govind being away, they treat her badly. But I'm always telling her to clear off.'

'I don't mind,' said Dora, 'so long as she doesn't interfere with the servants' work, so leave her be.'

'As you wish, Memsahib,' Arjun shrugged, as if disappointed that he couldn't go and make a display of pulling rank.

She watched Jhoti now as she meandered along lazily, clinging to the shade of the hibiscus hedge, while her little girl selected pebbles from the ground with microscopic precision and added them to the collection loading down her veil. Such a quaint doll-like child, Dora thought, and about the same age as her own little Edith; but where Jhoti's child had a hard, thin sparse brown body, already

21

worked and shaped like a piece of carved wood, Edith was soft and plump and white and golden, looking vulnerable and breakable; two more different children could not be imagined.

The two figures, mother and daughter, moved like patterns of light, almost strobing, as they passed in and out of the yellowy shade of lemon trees. Suddenly, Jhoti noticed a swing made of rope and a plank of wood, hanging loosely from one of the branches. Harold Chadwick had rigged it up only yesterday for Edith. Her body suddenly animated, and clasping Marvinder on her knee, Jhoti jumped on the swing and pushed away, urging it up and up, her head tossed back in ecstasy and the child's laughter pealing through the still afternoon.

'Why on earth did Govind have to go and get married so soon?' Dora sighed with frustration. The two of them were still just children. It was ridiculous.

Harold, of course had minded for other reasons. Govind was his protégé, a symbol of everything Harold believed in for India, and he was afraid at first, that marriage would mean the end of all his ambitions for the boy.

Harold had found his home in India. Originally, he had gone over to visit an uncle of his who was a tea planter. 'Just for a break,' he'd said. 'See the world before I get trapped for ever in some job in the city.' But somehow, India struck a deep chord. He travelled it from one end to another, and found it hard to leave. The experience had been almost spiritual. He could only describe it as a feeling of having found his true home. He knew he must return; that this was where he wanted to spend the rest of his life, and he came back to England only so that he could qualify as a teacher and pursue that one goal.

It was at the teacher training college in London, that he and Dora met. They both loved music; she a pianist and he a violinist. They often played together and, of course, went to as many concerts as their meagre student funds allowed.

Dora was intending to go back to the Midlands from

22

where she came originally. Like a good middle-class young woman, she would take a respectable teacher's job until a suitable husband came along, and then she would join the ranks of housewives and give birth to more good little middle-class children. But then Harold asked her to marry him, and for a while she went into a state of total confusion and indecision. She found herself loving a man whose plans didn't in the least fit in with her own.

Of course, she went back home to discuss it with her parents. They were not at all pleased with the proposition. The idea of her going to India to live and make a home there seemed foolhardy, risky; had she considered the consequences for their children, if they had any? There would be the separation, for of course, nobody kept their children in India beyond infancy, but sent them back to boarding schools, doomed, in many cases, not to see them for years at a time.

Worst of all was when they actually met Harold. It was his enthusiasm which really galled them. The way his eyes shone when he talked about the people of India; their wisdom, the customs, the beauty, the poverty, the hardship, and his absolute belief that one day, this 'noble' people would rule themselves. 'After all,' he reminded Dora's parents, 'Indians were one of the most civilised and cultured people on earth at a time when we Britons were running around in woad.'

It was at this point that Dora's father could contain himself no longer. Already red in the face from mounting irritation, he exploded with 'rubbish!' and retreated into the garden to light up his pipe.

Later, when Harold had returned to London, Dora's mother had come into her room that night, and sat by her bed.

'Dora darling,' she had said in the soft, anxious voice which had become her hallmark over the years, 'Dora, your father and I, well, we don't really consider this young man to be very suitable for you. I mean . . . he is a bit . . . immature. One of these idealists. A socialist too, I wouldn't be surprised. We, er . . . really can't allow you to throw yourself away on a man like that.' She gazed pleadingly into her daughter's eyes silently begging her not to rebel or make life difficult.

Dora was indeed full of doubts, but for different reasons. It was not at all what she had planned. She had wanted first of all to experience the independence of having her own profession and income: then, in her own time, when she felt ready, to marry some nice steady respectable man – a banker maybe, or even a vicar. She imagined herself leading a small town life, accompanying local singers or instrumentalists in a purely amateur way; perhaps giving little soirees in their comfortably off suburban home, and gaining some kind of minor fame as a talented and much sought after hostess in the locality.

When Harold was offered a teaching job in India and asked her to go with him, she refused, and for a while, did everything she could to dismiss him from her life. Harold, always the eternal optimist, declared that he was sure she would come round to the notion of marrying him one of these days, but in the meantime, he would go on ahead. 'I'm sure we're right for each other,' he said. 'Perhaps when I'm established out there and have found us a home, you'll come and join me in India!' Then he was gone.

Without Harold, the world suddenly seemed a greyer place. The pavements were harder and the weather bleaker. Nothing seemed to matter the way it did. Dora trudged on with her training; became a teacher and tried to merge into the provincial life of her small town. Her parents hoped she would marry 'that nice young doctor,' but neither the nice young doctor, who did indeed propose, nor the other suitable bachelors in the district, with their respectable jobs and comfortable houses, were able to quell a choking feeling of loss.

Harold wrote often. He had been sent to teach in a tiny rural village in the Punjab called Deri. He was learning the language and was full of idealism about bringing education to the villagers and persuading them to send their children to school, before putting them to work on the land. He wrote in particular about a boy called Govind.

'Govind is just the son of an illiterate peasant farmer, but he is one of the most intelligent boys I've ever come across anywhere. I'm sure I can help him go far. I wish you would come out here and see for yourself, Dora. I could do with you by my side. I could do with your good sense to talk over my day, to discuss and make plans. Most of all, I could do with a good accompanist. I get tired of the sound of a solo violin, and God knows what these people make of it. I can get hold of a piano, you know . . .'

'Get hold of a piano,' Dora wrote back at last. 'I'm coming!'

Now, standing here, thousands of miles away on an Indian verandah Dora smiled, remembering her incredulity and joy.

As she relished her own happiness, she wondered about Jhoti swooping up and down on Harold's garden swing. She began to feel linked to her in some peculiar way. While she and Harold were being married in All Souls Church, Jhoti was having an arranged marriage to Govind in her village down the road. When Dora became pregnant, Govind told Harold that his wife, too, was expecting a baby. They both produced girls, although Harold remarked, 'I don't think Govind will be half so pleased with a daughter as I am.'

Suddenly, feeling both amazed, yet strangely perturbed, Dora realised that she and Jhoti were both pregnant again at the same time. She watched the young girl as she stopped swinging, heaved Marvinder off her lap and stood up, smoothing out her tunic.

She curved her hands round her stomach and, for the first time in her life, felt that she wasn't entirely in control of her own destiny. Her happiness gave way to melancholy.

As Jhoti and Marvinder moved slowly round the back of the bungalow and out of sight, Dora felt two arms clasp her round her knees.

'Mummy. Swing. Let's go on Daddy's swing.' Little golden-haired Edith, still tousled with her afternoon's sleep looked up at her with demanding blue eyes.

'No, baby.' The ayah came and extricated her. 'Leave Mummy. I'll swing you.'

'That's all right, Shanta. I'll do it.' She took Edith's hand and jumped her down the verandah steps. They walked, the two of them, along the winding path, between the carefully created geometrical flower beds which Harold had carved out of the red earth.

Suddenly Dora was gripped by an overwhelming sense of helplessness; a feeling of plunging downwards as in a bad dream, without power, without knowing where and how and if she would land. She stopped in her tracks as Edith ran on to the swing. She felt afraid. If after all, one had no power; if there was no such thing as free will, that everyone was simply part of some divine purpose, then how could she control anything? How could she protect her child or plan for the future? Perhaps nothing she did amounted to anything, because it was all pre-ordained anyway.

The ayah squatted on the verandah watching her. Dora felt uncomfortable. What was she thinking? Did she mind serving this white foreign woman, who had the audacity to come and claim ownership of this land; who expected to be in command and who claimed superiority in all things just because of an accident of birth?

Suddenly, rarely, Dora was overcome with homesickness. 'England.' She spoke the word out loud. She turned her eyes westwards, beyond the compound gate, over the long, white road, on and on over the fields of mustard seed aflame with yellow flowers, till her eye settled on the simple, rounded oblong shape of the Hindu temple. The sun was halfway down the sky, and by nightfall would set just behind the temple.

Impatient with waiting to be pushed on the swing, Edith came running. 'Come on, Mummy. Push me. Come on.' She tugged her mother's arm.

26

'Edith,' Dora said, picking up her child. 'Do you [see?] that temple far away over there, where the sun is beginning to drop through the sky?'

Edith nodded, putting her thumb in her mouth.

'If you could go over there, and keep on going west, do you know where you would come to?'

Edith shook her head, mystified by her mother's strange mood.

'Edith, you would come to England. England is over there, and one day, I'll take you.'

'Swing, Mummy, swing me!' Edith wriggled out of her arms and forced her mother to put her down.

Unsure how to quell this sudden sense of desolation, Dora took a few moments to fight back her tears. Then with a bright shout, she called out, 'Hold tight now! I'm coming to push you!'

THREE

The Birth

'*Aloo, okra, baigan ho,
Chaaval, Channa, Bhoona lo.*'

Marvinder sat in the earth repeating her rhyme over and
over again. She scooped up soil with her newly acquired
tin and poured it into the bottom half of a broken clay
water pot which she had found near the village pond.

'This is for Ma, this is for Pa, this is for Ajit, this is for
Chachaji . . .' she went on listing all the members of her
extended family. Every now and then she glanced across
to a door of a side room, where her mother was the subject
of quite unaccustomed attention. Women had been going
in and out all morning looking worried. Even fierce
Grandmother had an air of concern about her.

Marvinder felt confused and afraid. She had never
before been kept away from her mother and every now
and then, she heard her mother give a shuddering cry
which struck Marvinder to the heart with terror.

'*Aloo, okra, brinjal ho,
Chaaval, Channa, Pani Lo.*'

She repeated the rhyme over and over like a magic spell as
she dug and dug into the earth.

One of her aunts suddenly emerged from the room,
pushing back the broken bamboo blind, allowing
Marvinder a snatched glimpse inside. Jhoti was lying on a
bed, her head thrust back, her hands gripping the edges of
the thin mattress on which she lay. The heat of the day and
the struggle of childbirth brought the perspiration pouring
out of her body and, as one aunt wiped her brow and

28

mopped up the moisture which trickled in rivulets down her face, another had a goblet of water, and holding her like a child, held the rim to her lips so that she could drink and drink.

'Aunty, Aunty! I want my ma!' cried Marvinder, leaping to her feet. 'Can I go in now?' She clutched at the tunic of an aunt who had emerged from the room. She was one of the younger ones, Shireen. She could be kind some times, and when she had a few moments between jobs, would often become girlish and run out to join the children in their games.

'No, *baba*,' said Shireen gently, and she picked up Marvinder and lodged her on her hip. She affectionately smoothed back a straggle of hair which had fallen across her eyes. 'You must be patient. Your ma is soon going to give you a brother or maybe a sister and if you get in the way, it will make it all the harder for us to help her. Do you understand?' Marvinder nodded silently and Shireen put her down again near her precious tin and broken clay pot. 'Play now. I have to go and find Basant,' she said urgently, and set off running.

Some older children who were just coming in from school heard Shireen, and couldn't resist coming to tease Marvinder.

'Is Basant coming to see to your mother? Oh dear. Basant is a witch, didn't you know?'

Marvinder looked up at them with large, terrified eyes.

'A witch?' she exclaimed with a shudder. 'What do witches do? Will she hurt my mother?'

'Witches come out at night and go round looking for people so that they can suck their blood,' said one child sticking out his fingers at Marvinder, as if they were claws.

'Witches cast spells on babies about to be born so that the baby comes out with two heads, or with a devil's tail or sometimes with horns, and the babies are witches too, and suck their mother's blood. Whooo . . .' and the child lunged towards Marvinder making sucking noises with his lips.

Marvinder backed away with horror. 'Will Basant do that to my ma? Will she do that to my baby?'

'Oh yes!' chorused the children malevolently. 'Just you wait and see. Your baby will be a monster. A green monster with snakes round its neck, and goat's feet and a tongue dripping with blood like Kali,' and they all rushed at Marvinder with their tongues sticking out and their arms outstretched as if to tear her to pieces.

Marvinder broke into desperate screams and began running.

Sobbing and gasping, she ran and ran until she reached the road. She wanted to go to the Chadwicks' bungalow and find Maliki. Perhaps Maliki could save her mother from the witch.

In the distance, a cyclist was coming towards her, his shape shimmering out of the heat haze. Like some strange bird, with blue turbaned head, white shirt puffed up with the wind, and thin, cotton trousers flapping to the sides, he came closer and closer.

Marvinder hardly saw him what with the tears in her eyes, and her concentration on running. He passed her. Stopped and looked back. 'Marvi?' the man cried.

Marvinder didn't stop running. 'Hey, Marvi . . . Marvinder! Stop! It's me, your father.' He whirled his bike round and pedalled a few turns to catch up with her, then jumping off, he dropped his bike to the ground and lunged out to grab the child.

At first Marvinder struggled and screamed. 'Let me go, let me go! I must rush to Maliki and tell her that a witch is going to put a spell on my mother and turn my baby into a monster.' She wriggled violently, trying to free herself.

Govind knelt down on the dusty road so that he was at eye level with his daughter and gripping her chin in one hand, turned her face towards his. 'Marvi, look at me. Who am I?'

Marvinder looked at him, blinking through her tears.

'Who am I, Marvi?' he asked again as she quietened slightly.

He slackened his grip on her face and with a thumb, wiped away a tear from her cheek.

'*Papaji*?' she asked with amazement. Marvinder recognised her father, although he was home so little. Until now, he hadn't taken much notice of her and he was more like a stranger.

She looked into his pale, almond eyes, she touched his cheek in recognition. She was too young to note how her father's face had changed. He was no longer a boy; callow, broken-voiced and a mixture of shyness and insensitivity; now, his voice had deepened, the skin of his face toughened, and his hair had grown sufficiently for his beard to be bound up under his chin.

Marvinder clasped her arms round his neck and pleaded with him.

'Pa, Shireen has gone to fetch Basant, the witch, and our baby will be born a monster and will suck Ma's blood. How can we stop her?'

'Who told you Basant was a witch?' demanded Govind angrily.

'The other children. They told me she makes babies to be born with two heads and goat's feet . . . and . . .'

'Stop, stop!' shouted Pa. 'If I catch hold of the children who told you that nonsense, I'll give them such a thrashing . . .' Marvinder started crying again.

'Listen to me, Marvinder, Basant is no witch. She is the best healer in the world. You don't know how many lives she has saved. There's nothing Basant doesn't know. She helps to bring babies into the world too. They say, if you want your baby to be born safely and alive, then get Basant. She's the best midwife there is. She brought me into the world, and am I a monster?' He pulled a face and growled fiercely into her neck making her burst out laughing. 'That's better,' smiled Govind. 'Now don't let me hear you ever say a single bad word against her. Those children were just having fun making you scared, and I tell you, I'll give them such a fright they'll never be so cruel again.'

With that, Govind lifted Marvinder on to the crossbar of his bicycle. 'Hold tight,' he ordered, then turning round pushed off and headed for home as fast as he could.

When they left the road and swooped down the track to their village at a terrifying speed, Marvinder shut her eyes fearfully. She opened them again when, with squealing brakes, they came to a standstill, and she found that they were outside their home.

People began calling out at the sight of her father. 'Eh! Look! Govind's here! Govind's come home.'

'My son! How did you know when to return?' cried his mother, excitedly pushing her way out of the labour room. Govind knelt on the ground and kissed his mother's feet respectfully.

'Quick, bring water for Govind,' she ordered turning round to one of her daughters-in-law.

'I knew Jhoti's time was near and decided,' Govind explained, getting to his feet and touching his head and heart in greeting. 'Mr Chadwick sahib was visiting the school in Amritsar and he suggested I travel back with him. The memsahib, his wife, she too is very near her time. He has already taken her to their mission hospital.'

'Humm,' grunted his mother. 'Well, they have their ways and we have ours. Shireen has gone for Basant. She should be here soon. I hope she hurries. Jhoti's pains are coming very close now.'

Someone brought a pitcher of water. Govind held out his cupped hands while the woman poured. He tossed it first into his face and round his neck; she poured again and he wetted his arms up to his elbows, and finally, she poured again, several times over while he bent his mouth down to his hands and drank till he felt refreshed.

For a while, the attention was diverted from Jhoti as the women flocked round Govind, clucking and fussing; and it was Govind who said, 'Come, come, enough of all this. How is my wife?'

'She is doing well, brother,' they assured him. 'It will not be long now.'

When the women told Jhoti that her husband had arrived, she felt a sudden rush of tears to her eyes. Till then, she had maintained a reserved stance, never admitting to the intense discomfort she felt; nor sharing with anyone her puzzlement as to why her second confinement had been harder to bear than the first.

With the news that Govind was here, Jhoti gave a deep sigh of contentment. Suddenly she felt she could bear anything . . . if only . . . if only she could present him with a son.

It seemed an age before Shireen appeared, clutching Basant at the elbow and guiding her at a snail's pace towards the house.

When Marvinder saw her, she shrank into her father.

'Are you sure Basant isn't a witch?' she whispered. Basant looked in every way what she imagined a witch to be like, she was so bent and wizened; her skin hung on her thin arms like wrinkled brown paper and her fingers, which hooked round a staff, were like the scaly claws of chicken's feet. Worst of all were her eyes. They stared ahead as if seeing all things, and yet, Marvinder shuddered; although they appeared to penetrate even into her very soul, they were the creamy, sightless eyes of the blind.

'No, *baba*. Basant isn't a witch. Just you wait and see. Soon we will have a baby; the finest baby the world has ever seen; a baby for you to take care of and be a good big sister. Will you do that, Marvinder?' her father asked. 'Will you protect your little one; make sure he never runs into any danger; guard him with your life? Do you promise?'

Marvinder returned his gaze. Her father looked so serious; as if what he had asked her was very important. It made her feel suddenly grown up.

'Yes, *Papaji*, I promise.'

33

The day ended abruptly. The sun went down like a rapidly sinking ship and suddenly it was dark. Basant dismissed all the women. Now there were just she and Jhoti alone in the room. The only light came from a weak, kerosene lantern which hung on the verandah outside. Its useless beams barely struggled through the narrow iron-barred window, to cast pale stripes on the dung-smeared walls.

'Could we have light in here?' asked Jhoti fearfully.

'What do we need light for?' rasped the old blind woman.

She came towards Jhoti, her hands spread out in front of her. Jhoti shrank away, unable to control the repugnance she felt at being touched by such a creature. She stiffened with horror as the hands hovered over her face. She rolled her lips together, sealing her mouth so that no cry would escape her. The hands came down, down, steadily, without trembling. They enveloped her face. The fingers traced the outlines of her features; her brow, nose, eyes, cheeks, chin and jaw-line.

'Here's a pretty one to be sure,' murmured Basant in a low voice. Her hands continued their exploration over her face, head, neck, chest, soothing and massaging as she worked her way down towards her abdomen. Her touch was the touch of a potter, working the clay, softening it, manipulating it, moulding it, with all the years of experience and craftsmanship pouring through her fingers and palms. She worked her hands over the young woman's belly, pressing deeper this way and that to feel the shape of the baby inside.

'Ah!' she whispered. 'That is why you feel discomfort. Your infant wants to greet the world with his bottom!'

By this time, all Jhoti's resistence had dissolved away. She lay beneath the old woman's hands, pliable, relaxed and completely trusting.

'Don't be afraid,' murmured the old voice, 'I will turn him round so that he can face the world like a man.'

'He?' asked Jhoti softly.

'Perhaps,' Basant chuckled. Then suddenly her

movements became fierce. She kneaded into Jhoti's belly, grunting with the effort as gradually she eased the infant round in the womb until its head faced the exit it must use to emcrge into the world.

At last, Jhoti gave one cry and it was done.

'Now we'll have a better time of it,' said Basant.

Jhoti slept. It was as if the baby quite enjoyed its new position and had changed its mind about being born. The contractions diminished to the softest of sensations, squeezing and letting go, squeezing and letting go.

Outside in the courtyard, Govind squatted, wide-eyed in vigil. Marvinder lay asleep, outstretched across his knees. He stroked her forehead. The glow from the nearby brazier outlined her high cheekbones and her straight nose; her long eyelashes seemed tipped with flame, fluttering rapidly from time to time as dreams enveloped her brain. He ran a finger along her lips and chin, yet hardly noticed her determined mouth, for all his senses were strained towards the room where Jhoti lay. Being a father made him feel important, especially if, he hardly dared pray, this new baby was a boy.

'Madanjit Kaur! Shireen! Come now and give me a hand!' The shadows tipped wildly as kerosene lamps were snatched up and hurried towards the room.

Govind lifted Marvinder into his arms and stood up, his eyes staring intently at the bamboo blind and the shadows passing back and forth within. Marvinder sighed sleepily and snuggled her face into his beard. 'Papa, have we a new baby?'

'Nearly, nearly,' murmured Govind. A faint wind suddenly rattled the leaves of the tree like drumming fingers; it caught the scent of night flowers and filled the air with perfume. Marvinder, with her ear pressed against her father's neck, heard a song welling up in his throat – but it barely escaped before a cry of joy splintered the silence of the night.

'Govind! You have a son.'

FOUR

The Swing

Edith stood in the middle of her room. It was darkened by the blinds which had been drawn against the ferocious glare of the sun. Any light which managed to prise itself between the thinnest slit or a pinprick of a hole, scissored through the gloom, sharp, blinding and silver as mercury.

She had awoken from her afternoon sleep and, just from habit, waited for someone to come. But no one did.

She got out of bed and stood in her white petticoat. She stretched her arms and legs akimbo, as she would have done for ayah, who would then slip a cotton dress over her head, and buckle her open sandals on to her feet. But ayah didn't come to attend to her.

She stood alone. Hearing but not listening to the faint sounds of babies coming from her parents' room, and the low murmur of voices – her mother, father and ayah. All she was aware of was the persistent croo, croo, croo of the dove, whose never-ending, monotonous cry tightened her throat, she didn't know why.

She pattered, barefooted from her bedroom, through the cool, intervening bathroom to her parents' room. The door was partly ajar and she peered inside. Her mother was in bed, propped up by a mountain of white pillows to an upright position. Crooked into each arm was the small, bald head of an infant, each with its face turned into a breast and seeming to devour her mother with loud sucking noises, and pig-like grunts.

Ayah knelt at the side of the bed, massaging her mother's feet, while Father fussed around, stroking his wife's head, and administering sips of water to her.

Edith looked at them with hatred. No one had prepared

her for this. She hadn't got the words; she couldn't identify or understand the emotions which gripped her body. She had been cut adrift and was floating away, but no one seemed to see her.

When her mother first came home from the hospital, Edith thought everything would be the same as before. She had tried to climb into bed with her each morning as usual, but there wasn't room any more. These two little babies seemed to have everyone in their power. They had taken over her mother, father, and even ayah.

Before, there had always been someone to keep her company – from morning till night; but now, games were left unfinished and bedtime stories interrupted. Even at mealtimes, she could find herself abandoned to sit all alone in the dining room, at the long, dark, oak table, waited on by Arjun, who padded in and out with her meals, gentle but silent.

It was becoming apparent to her that nothing would ever be the same again.

She went out on to the verandah. Great clay pots hung along the length of the roof, overflowing with ferns and trailing ivy and casting intricate shadows like pencil etchings, over the grey stone.

Edith squinted into the sun and looked across the compound. In the distance, she could see her swing.

Someone else looked at the swing, too.

It was Marvinder. She looked at it, hanging there, motionless in the still afternoon, dropping out of the pale, yellowy shadows of the lemon tree. She had gone with her mother to the Chadwick bungalow, so that Jhoti could show off her new son to Maliki. She had been sorting rice. She pushed a tray of it in front of Marvinder and begged her to pick it clean of stones, so that she could be free to admire the baby.

Marvinder squatted on the edge of the verandah where she could see the swing, and even as she picked and sifted and tossed the grains, she kept the swing in the corner of her eye.

'So, Jhoti! Have you a name for your son, now?' asked Maliki.

'It was chosen yesterday!' announced Jhoti proudly; and she described how they had all gone to the gurdwara, where the priest had opened the Guru Granth Sahib, their holiest book. He had opened it at random, as was the custom, and called out the first letter of the first hymn. 'It was the letter J. The same initial as me!'

'J!' cried Maliki impatiently. 'What did you call him?'

'His name is Jaspal!' Jhoti sighed with happiness.

When Marvinder was sure that she had picked out every single stone and husk from the rice, she casually eased herself off the verandah and stood for a while, just close by, picking up pebbles between her toes. Jhoti and Maliki took no notice of her and carried on gossiping.

But Marvinder's eye was on the swing. It hung there from the tree, empty and inviting. Slowly, slowly, she drifted, imperceptibly towards the hibiscus hedge. No one called her back. Maliki had now taken the infant into her arms and was cooing over it with delight.

'Seems you had a better time of it than the poor memsahib,' said Maliki in a low voice. 'She had twins, I tell you! And would you believe, the English doctor didn't even know! What kind of doctor wouldn't know a woman was having twins, I ask you? Wouldn't Basant have known – blind and all that she is?'

'How did you hear all this?' asked Jhoti, shuffling closer on her haunches, and wide-eyed with curiosity.

'Arjun heard the sahib telling someone. Memsahib was in the mission hospital. First one baby was born, and what a time she had of it, and they thought that was that. But then the nurse said, "Doctor! I think there's another!" He didn't believe her, can you imagine? "Don't be silly," he says. "There can't be."

'But the memsahib went on pushing, and sure enough, out came another!' Maliki rolled her eyes with perplexed disbelief at the stupidity of some people.

'What did the doctor say?' asked Jhoti.

'The babies were lying in the womb one exactly behind the other, so when he felt her, he couldn't tell that there were two! That's what he said. What an excuse! I ask you!'

'Were they both boys?' asked Jhoti.

'First one a girl, the second a boy,' answered Maliki.

'That sounds nice,' murmured Jhoti. 'Nice to enlarge your family all at once. What names did she give them?'

'Oh some strange English names,' laughed Maliki. 'Grace – that's the girl, and Ralph, the boy. I don't know why those names!' She shrugged. 'I expect they will soon go to their church and have a naming ceremony too.'

Marvinder edged closer to the swing. She was only yards away from it now.

Suddenly, a figure came rushing out of the front of the bungalow. Edith Chadwick, all alone, ran across the garden and flung herself on to the swing. She looked sulky and cross. She proceeded to struggle and jerk, angrily tossing out her bare legs in a desperate attempt to get some momentum.

If Marvinder was disappointed at having her plan thwarted, she didn't give the slightest hint of it. Indeed, she still continued her casual, indifferent progress closer and closer. Finally, when she was near enough to be noticed or ignored at will, she came to rest, squatting down in the shade and twisting the stems of hibiscus flowers into a nosegay. She watched Edith wriggling hopelessly as she tried to get the swing moving. Suddenly, their eyes met. This was the first time they had been close enough to acknowledge each other.

At first, Edith just scowled and continued her struggle and Marvinder edged a few inches closer without getting up. But then Edith caught her eye again. Marvinder tipped her head to one side, and with a questioning look on her face, mimed a push with her hand.

The silent message was received and understood. Edith, unsmiling, gave a curt nod. In a second, Marvinder had leapt to her feet and grasped the seat of the swing from behind. She dragged it back and back and back with all the strength of a mere four-year-old, then let go.

'More, more!' ordered Edith as she swooped away.

So Marvinder pushed and pushed till her arms ached. Edith would have let her push forever but, exhausted, Marvinder finally stopped and went back to twisting flowers by the hedge.

'Are you going?' asked Edith petulantly.

Marvinder shrugged a 'maybe'.

'Would you like a turn?' asked Edith, instinctively bargaining to keep her new companion.

Marvinder looked at her with a big grin and ran over to the swing. But when Edith pushed her, she pushed with such ferocity that Marvinder began to feel afraid. She could feel the hands thudding into the small of her back. She could hear the hissing of her breath and the enraged grunt which accompanied each push of the swing. She wanted to get off.

'Stop! I've had enough!' cried Marvinder.

At first, Edith took no notice. She thrust the swing forward as hard as she could, sometimes tugging at the rope to make it twist and spin. Marvinder thought she would be flung off.

'Stop! Please stop!' Her voice rose in panic.

As if awoken from a dream, Edith stopped.

Marvinder dragged her feet on the ground to slow herself down, then jumped off. The two girls stared at each other, like strangers, unsure of themselves. Marvinder lowered her gaze. 'I'm going back to my ma,' she murmured, and walked away.

'Goodbye then,' said Edith coldly. She eased herself back on to the swing, and began her fruitless wriggling as she tried to get it going on her own.

Somewhere across the compound, the dove continued its soulless cooing. 'Cru croo, cru croo, cru croo.'

FIVE

Govind

One day, Govind returned home unexpectedly. They already knew in the village that he had arrived. Someone had seen him getting off the train, and then another noticed that instead of coming straight home, he had first called in at the Chadwick bungalow. At last, when he did appear at his father's door, it was, he said, with important news.

Everyone waited till evening, when his older brothers got home from the fields, the buffaloes had been milked and supper eaten.

Then they congregated round his father's charpoy, which had been pulled out into the courtyard. The old man, Chet Singh, sat in the middle of the bed solemnly sucking on his hookah. Madanjit Kaur took up a position of importance, cross-legged on the top right-hand corner of the bed. Govind was made to sit at the foot, while his brothers and their wives squatted in a semicircle on the ground chewing betel nuts and waiting with curiosity.

Only Jhoti preferred to stand. Rocking Jaspal in her arms, she looked on from outside the circle. Her face had an anxious expression as if she dreaded what she might hear.

Marvinder watched them from the edge of the pond. She had been washing dishes; but although her hand automatically dipped into the little hollowed-out crater of charcoal ash, which she smeared and scoured round the metal plates and pans, her eyes were fixed on Govind's unsmiling face.

What was he going to tell them?

Feverishly, she scooped up the water, sluicing the dishes

41

clean, anxious to be finished so that she could creep nearer and listen.

'I am going to England,' she heard him say.

Marvinder didn't know where England was, but judging by the consternation his words produced, she knew that it was somewhere extraordinary.

At first there was a babble of excited voices, while everyone talked at once. Jhoti stopped rocking her baby and looked dazed. Marvinder gathered up the clean dishes and carried them to the kitchen, her eyes hardly leaving her father's face as she went. Then she came back and stood by her mother. 'Ma!' she whispered. 'Where is England?'

'It's where the Chadwicks come from,' Jhoti replied.

'Mr Chadwick sahib always wanted me to go, you know,' Govind continued. 'I didn't say anything before, because I didn't want you thinking too much when it all depended on my getting a B.A. in law.'

'B.A? What is B.A?' asked one of his brothers.

'A degree,' replied Chet Singh, knowledgeably, although he wasn't quite sure what that was.

'Yes, that's right,' nodded Govind proudly. 'I now have a B.A. from Punjab University. In fact, I came top in my year.' He spread out his hands with triumph, but when he saw their blank faces, and knew that his family had no understanding at all of his achievement, he dropped them helplessly to his side.

'Look! I have something to show you.' He opened up his worn and battered attaché case, which had lain at his feet, and carefully drew out a large, framed photograph.

Everyone craned forward with fascination. No one in the family had ever been in a photograph before.

'Govind, is that you, Govind?' they cried in amazement.

Staring out of the picture, with a look of stiff importance, was Govind. His turban was neatly bound and his beard waxed and shaped into his jawline. Instead of white, cotton, Indian pyjamas and waistcoat, he wore a smart, western-style suit with shirt and tie, and flowing over the top was a black academic gown edged with ermine. In his hands, which he held prominently up to his chest, was a rolled-up scroll, tied with a ribbon.

He pointed triumphantly. 'That's my degree! With that, I will be able to get a good job and earn a lot of money,' he said.

Madanjit Kaur couldn't resist a regretful glance at Jhoti, as though she thought, Huh, we married Govind off too soon. A man with a B.A. might have got himself a much higher wife than her.

'Then why do you need to go to England?' asked his father.

Govind leant forward, his face flushed pink with enthusiasm. 'You must know what's going on in the country. You must know that very soon, in a year or two, we're going to kick the Britishers out and we will be independent. Armritsar and Lahore are seething with it, I tell you. The whole of India is seething with it. There is even talk of new homelands. Perhaps we Sikhs will get the Punjab back as our homeland. This man Tara Singh – you should hear him! What ideas he has, I tell you. And then there is the Muslim League! It is talking about a new country for Muslims which they will call Pakistan. They march around shouting, "Pakistan Zindabad!" The Britishers send out troops to crush riots, and hundreds of people are in prison, but it's no use. We're going to throw them out!'

'What kind of rubbish is all this?' demanded old Chet Singh, frowning. 'Is this what you have been learning in the cities with all your books and education? What use is a B.A. if you are going to tear the country apart?'

'India was full of separate kingdoms once!' retorted Govind. 'It was just the British who forced us all into one piece just to suit themselves. Now we have to kick them out and do what's best for us.'

'I thought Mr Chadwick sahib was your friend and patron,' cried a brother. 'You speak as if he is your enemy.'

'No, no! He is my friend. He is a friend of India. That's

43

why he wants me to go to England. I will go to an English university, just for a year. He says that I must learn the ways of the Britishers, so that when they leave, people like me will be able to take over all the jobs and help to run the country.'

The photograph was being passed round and intensely scrutinised.

'Eh! Govind *bhai*! What a handsome man you are in this photo. You look like a proper sahib.'

Govind sighed. No one in his family seemed to comprehend what he was saying.

'There have been marches and demonstrations all over India,' he continued. 'I've been on some of them myself. I've seen Gandhiji, and I tell you, that man walks round like a villager, wears nothing but a dhoti and is thin as a begger, yet he talks to all the high-ups. He's even talked to the king over in England. Would you believe it?' Govind's voice cracked with excitement. 'There are big things happening. Just you wait and see.'

'You look very high up yourself,' cried Kalwant looking closely at the photograph. 'You should talk to the king, too.'

Jhoti had sunk back into the darkness. Her heart was heavy as lead. After Jaspal was born, Govind had told her, that once he got his degree he would get a job and money, and be able to afford to bring her and the children to Amritsar. The thought of having her own home, away from the petty tyrannies she suffered here, had sustained her through all the misery of separation from him. But now?

'Ma?' Marvinder looked up at her anxiously, and gripped her hand. 'Is it bad, Ma? Shouldn't papa go to England?'

'And what about Jhoti?' Madanjit's voice broke in. She sounded harsh in the soft evening. 'We have all these extra mouths to feed, what with Marvinder and now Jaspal too. They must pay their way. Be prepared to work – eh?' She looked round resentfully at them. 'All this sneaking away

44

to see her friend Maliki over at the Chadwicks' bungalow, we'll have no more of that.'

'Wait a minute, Ma,' Govind restrained her gently. 'You are too hard on Jhoti. Anyway, Mr Chadwick has a proposition. He wants Jhoti to come and work at his bungalow. Memsahib needs extra help, what with having twins and all.'

'The memsahib already has an ayah,' snorted Madanjit Kaur, pursing her lips disapprovingly. 'What does she want of a chit of a girl like Jhoti, eh? Besides, Jhoti's got her own babies.'

'Their ayah is old,' said Govind. 'You know – that Hindu woman, Shanta. She's not too well either. Suffers from rheumatism. The Chadwicks won't get rid of her because she's a widow and has no son to care for her. Her daughters are married and moved far away. Sahib is content to keep her on so long as a younger woman comes in to help.'

Chet Singh puffed the hookah and passed it to Govind. Then he observed, 'It sounds like a good job and it would be a welcome addition to the family income.'

'Huh!' exclaimed Madanjit Kaur. 'It's a good job all right. Too good for Jhoti. They would do better to take on Kalwant or Narinder,' she gestured towards her two other daughters-in-law. 'They are older and more experienced. Or even your sister, Shireen, would be better.'

'It's Jhoti they want,' insisted Govind. 'They feel responsible for her. It's due to them that I'm going to England and leaving her.'

'Do you think we wouldn't take care of her?' protested his mother. 'Has she ever complained? Ever lacked for anything? You should tell them, Govind.'

'Yes, tell them. I am a better person for the job. More experienced, and anyway, my children are older than Jhoti's, so I am freer. You should recommend me,' Kalwant insisted.

'I tell you, it's Jhoti they want,' repeated Govind. 'Language is no problem. She'll learn. She's not so stupid.

45

Anyway, they speak good Punjabi. I want her to go, if you have no objection. After all, it gets her off your hands.'

Jhoti clenched her fist and closed her eyes. If Govind must go away, then she desired to work at the Chadwicks' more than anything else. 'Please!' she almost cried out loud. She opencd her eyes and found herself looking straight at Chet Singh. He winked at her, an old, grey, whiskery wink, then took back the hookah for a long puff.

'Let her go,' he said at last. 'I have no objection. If she's no good, they'll soon find out, then we can offer them Kalwant or Narinder.'

'It seems all wrong to me,' muttered Mother-in-law, 'but I suppose a pretty face gets to go places in this household.' She gave her husband a sneering glance.

'Well, Jhoti,' she turned to her. 'You needn't think it lets you off your duties here, or that working in the sahib's bungalow gives you any special privileges,' she warned.

'Yes,' agreed Kalwant, 'and I hope you don't start putting on airs and graces either. Just remember your place in this household.'

Jhoti bowed her head, and drew her veil across her face.

'The matter is settled!' cried Chet Singh, waving his hand dismissively. 'Now leave me in peace to smoke and play cards. Will you join us, Govind?' he asked slapping his youngest son on the back.

Marvinder asked again, 'Ma, where is England? Is it very far away? Farther than Amritsar?'

Jhoti took her daughter's hand and wandered down to the edge of the pond. A new moon was reflected sharp and silver in the still, flat water. It looked like a farmer's sickle floating there, almost solid enough to pick up. She wiped her eyes with the end of her veil and coughed to clear the sobs from her throat.

'Do you see this water?' she asked softly.

Marvinder nodded, leaning her body into her mother's thigh.

'Imagine this water stretching out bigger and bigger and

bigger, so that whichever way you looked you wouldn't see land. Do you remember that story about Manu? How God sent a flood and washed away all the land? Manu had to build a boat, and he floated and floated for years and years until one day, he came to land again? Do you remember that, Marvi?'

Marvinder said, 'Yes, yes! Was that land England?'

'No, but your pa, he will go to the edge of the ocean, almost as big as that flood. He will get on a boat, and he will sail and sail for days and days. The land will disappear and then they will be all alone with nothing but the sea. And then, at last, after a very long time, they will see birds flying and wood drifting and seaweed floating on the water, and they will know that they are near. Then one day someone will shout, "Land Ahoy!" and they will see a long, cold grey line of shore between sea and sky and that will be England.'

'How do you know all this, Ma? Have you been there?'

Jhoti laughed. 'Of course not. But there was an old man in my village who got taken away to the sea and put on a ship, and he went across the big ocean to Africa, and sailed all round the world. He was away so many years that when he came back, no one recognised him. Not even his wife. He used to tell us all about the sea.'

'Will that happen to my pa? Will he go away for so long that we won't know him when he comes back?'

'If it's only for a year . . .' Jhoti's voice faltered, 'then you'll know him.'

It was late when Govind finally came to bed. Jhoti awoke, but said nothing as she lay watching him undress by the last, low light of the kerosene lantern hanging just outside the window. She stared at him, his arms circulating around his head as he unravelled his turban. He was still a stranger. His shadow rose like a giant up the wall and bent across the ceiling above her head. Suddenly, the lantern flickered and went out. Instantly, it was as if Govind, too, was extinguished.

47

That night Marvinder had a dream. She dreamt that she was walking with her father down the long, white road. On and on they walked, till suddenly, they found their feet were being submerged. The land all around was disappearing beneath a vast expanse of water. The water rose higher and higher, and she thought they would all drown, but suddenly, a big ship came sailing up. Govind clambered on board, but when Marvinder reached out her hand, he turned his back, and didn't seem to hear her calls. The boat began to sail away.

'Pa, Pa, Pa! Take me too! Save me!' she screamed, as the water rose up her chest and now was lapping over her face. But the boat sailed on, and he never even looked back.

'Wake up, Marvi! Wake up!' Jhoti was bending over her. 'You're having a bad dream.' She hugged the child closely. Somewhere in the darkness, Jaspal began crying, and Govind grunted crossly at having his sleep disturbed.

'Pa will never come back,' said Marvinder after a while, then she rolled over and went back to sleep.

SIX

The Snake

After Govind had departed for England, his degree photograph was placed on a ledge next to a faded bazaar portrait of the Sikh spiritual leader, Guru Nanak, and regularly draped with garlands of flowers. Each day, Jhoti, Marvinder and Jaspal sent up a little prayer to Guru Nanak, and asked God to protect their father and send him safely home again.

Govind didn't write often. Anyway, Shireen was the only member of the family who could read, and that at a simple level because she had only attended school till she was nine years old. He wrote more fully to Harold Chadwick, and Harold would then bring Jhoti up to date with Govind's progress.

Friends of the Chadwicks had found digs for Govind in a part of London called Whitechapel, the sahib told her. He had one room with a sink and a cooker in it and was learning to look after himself. He had started his courses at the university and was coping well, but hated the food.

'He'll have to learn to cook!' joked Harold, trying to bring a smile to Jhoti's sad face.

But it only bewildered Jhoti to imagine her husband grinding spices or kneading *chapatti* flour, and she became convinced that he would starve. She would stand silently while Harold read parts from her husband's letters, waiting for something that she could understand, some sign that he missed her and his children; that he looked forward to coming home. But there was nothing like that in any of the letters. He wrote of things she knew nothing about and countries she had never heard of, such as Germany, France and Poland.

'There's talk of war in Europe,' wrote Govind. 'The fascists often come marching round this area. They're a tough bunch, I tell you. Behave like thugs half the time. I get off the streets when they're around. Anyone that's a Jew or a foreigner, they beat them up! You wouldn't believe it!'

Harold frowned and looked worried at those words. 'That doesn't sound like the England I know,' he murmured sadly. 'They can't have another war. It's not possible,' he wrung his hands with despair. 'Yet fascism seems to be everywhere, and this man, Hitler . . . how is he to be dealt with?'

For a moment, he was lost in his own thoughts, then he turned back to Jhoti with a reassuring smile.

'And you, Jhoti. What shall I tell Govind about you?' he asked.

'Tell him his son is well; he is beginning to walk and most of his milk teeth have come through. Marvinder is getting tall, and now she's been put in charge of the buffaloes. She herds them out to the fields each morning, and brings them in for milking at dusk. Tell him that his parents are both in good health, as are his brothers and sisters.'

'But you, Jhoti?' said Harold, kindly. 'What shall I tell him about you?'

'I am well, too,' answered Jhoti simply.

'Is it wise to let your child mix with the servants?' Miss Alcott was visiting Dora about the forthcoming church bazaar. They sat on the verandah sipping tea. She stared disapprovingly at Edith and Marvinder playing at house beneath the low branches of the temple tree.

'Isn't it time she was at a school?'

Dora repressed a sigh of annoyance, and said politely, 'Harold and I decided that we would educate her ourselves for a little while longer. The world is such an unsettled place at the moment, we felt loath to part with her. I mean, England is out of the question now that there's talk of war.'

'There may not be a war. Chamberlain seems determined to find a compromise of some sorts,' said Miss Alcott.

'But India, too, is in so much turmoil,' sighed Dora. 'They want independence, and oh! I can understand it. We have no right to be here. But I'm worried. Only Gandhi's stopping them from all-out rebellion.' As she spoke, Dora frowned and her mind seemed to wander away from her guest. Then abruptly, she returned. 'Anyway,' she said firmly, 'Edith's too young for boarding school.'

'I think you're being far too sentimental,' Miss Alcott stated frankly. Her position as sister and secretary to the Reverend Cyril Alcott, vicar of All Souls and her advanced middle age, obviously made her feel entitled to speak her mind when and where she pleased, especially to the lower orders, which included people such as Dora Chadwick, the young wife of a mere schoolmaster.

'You don't want your child getting too familiar with the natives. It can lead to problems later on. I've seen it happen. People must know their place in life, and if you don't mind my saying, I believe it's idealists like you, with a misguided desire to promote equality, who have helped to fuel these disgraceful aspirations among the Indians. Independence, my foot. How can they rule themselves, I mean look at them. The vast majority haven't progressed since the invention of the wheel.'

She looked pointedly towards the road, along which a bullock cart laden with sugar cane creaked and laboured its way towards the town.

'And if we did leave, you know what would happen? They'd be at each other's throats. I mean they are already. There's no love lost between Muslim and Hindu. There was trouble in the town just the other night, and Superintendent Lincoln had to go and sort it out.'

Dora said nothing and nodded in a polite if non-committal sort of way.

Miss Alcott heaved a weighty sigh and shifted herself in the cane chair. It was hot, and her flowery cotton dress was sticking to her skin. 'Then of course there's the Sikhs. If you ask me, I think they're the worst of the lot. They'll go for both their throats. If we leave India, they will all fall upon each other like hyenas and tear the place apart. It would be a tragedy, an absolute tragedy.'

She got up and straightened out her damp skirt. 'If you'll take my advice, I think you should consider sending Edith to somewhere like Auckland House School for Girls in Simla. It's as good a place as you'll get in this country. They have a kindergarten section. She would soon get used to being away from home. She needs proper friends; girls of her own kind, not servants' children. And if you don't mind my saying, I wish you would take more part in our affairs. You keep yourself too much to yourself. People notice, you know. Why don't you come along to the Mothers' Union or the Women's Institute; the club is doing a Gilbert and Sullivan this autumn. You and Harold should get involved. I hear you're a pianist. We're going to need a pianist. Shall I tell Major Pocock? He's producing it.'

'I'm not sure,' replied Dora, reluctantly. 'I'll think about it, and let him know myself.'

Miss Alcock shrugged. 'Please yourself,' she said through pursed lips.

She went over to her bicycle, which was leaning against the verandah steps, and put on her topee.

'Hey you! Girl!' She hailed Marvinder who turned automatically at the commanding voice. 'Open the gate!'

Marvinder, who had Jaspal on her hip, began to hurry up the drive, but Edith overtook her calling out, 'I'll go!'

Frowning, Miss Alcott pedalled through on to the road. 'Thank you, Edith,' she said primly, 'but I think you should have let the girl open the gate.'

'Oh, but I like opening gates,' cried Edith. 'Come on, Marvi!' she called. 'Come and swing!'

'She's turning into a heathen, there's no doubt about it, poor child,' muttered Miss Alcott as she cycled away. 'I must ask Cyril to intervene.'

*

It came from under the toy cupboard, the snake. Edith saw its eyes first of all, like bright beads, glinting in the dusty darkness. Then as it ventured further into the room, its head swayed from side to side, like a scout examining the lie of the land. Every now and then, its tongue flashed from its mouth like lightning.

The lizard on the wall froze, still as an ornament, and even the sunlight, falling in warm dappled patches across the carpet, seemed to cool.

Edith watched it from her rocking horse. She only paused for a moment with surprise, her mouth opening instinctively to exclaim, but shutting it again without a sound.

Ayah had got her ready for church. Like a passive doll, Edith had allowed herself to be dressed in her hated pink frock with the white smocking across the chest; had allowed her feet to be imprisoned in white socks, and the white, leather shoes with a fold-over strap which buttoned and pinched.

Now she sat on the rocking horse while old Shanta brushed her hair. It was one of the ayah's favourite tasks. She loved trapping the long, golden tresses in the bristles and lifting it outwards, like a river, a river which then became a cataract, streaming down as she gradually released it from the brush.

When Edith briefly stopped rocking, Shanta was pleased. It gave her a chance to thrust the brush close to the scalp and pull through the tangles which had gathered in the night. But then Edith casually resumed her motion, her eyes never leaving the snake, as it edged its way along the fringe of the carpet, head reaching forwards, then that slight pause, while the rest of its body caught up in a swift S.

The playpen stood in the middle of the carpet. Jhoti had just bathed and changed the twins. They rolled around like little buddhas, chubby arms and legs flailing among the teddies and wooden bricks. Ralph saw it first; chortled with delight at the undulating patterns on its scaly back;

reached out a hand through the wooden bars of the playpen, longing to grasp its writhing body.

Edith went on rocking. She didn't say a word, though her eye was fixed on the snake.

At the sight of Ralph's hand, the creature halted. It lifted its narrow head, its tongue flickering with curiosity. Edith stopped rocking a second time. In the pause, Ayah took the comb and rapidly divided her hair with a parting and began plaiting with deft fingers.

The room, the lizard, the older sister stopped breathing. How long is a moment? Then somewhere in the universe, a god blinked and life started again. The snake moved on, sliding away towards the watery coolness of the bathroom beyond. Ralph withdrew his hand, disappointed, and Edith went on rocking.

Edith always accompanied her parents to church. They cycled the mile down the road, Edith riding in front of her father on the crossbar. He in his smart, light brown suit with topee on head, and Dora in some suitable, long-sleeved cotton frock, with one hand alternating between keeping her billowing skirts in check or hanging on to her white, panama hat.

Now that Jhoti helped Ayah to look after the twins, Marvinder was given charge of Jaspal for long periods of time. It was rare to see Marvinder without Jaspal growing out of her hip like a second torso. On Sundays, she too made her way to the church. It was by a different route, across the fields and through the mango groves. Today she went as usual, picking her way among the gravestones, round the back of the tall, grey walls of the stone church to the east door. Here, old Ram Singh crouched like a gnome, toothless and rheumatic that he was, and pumped air through the bellows into the organ, while Mr Austin, the organist, produced music which made the wooden floors vibrate.

Often, Marvinder folded her veil, put it on the ground and laid Jaspal on it so that she was free to have a go at

54

pumping the organ. Ram Singh didn't mind. It gave him a break to have a smoke. Just so long as she pumped evenly and didn't jerk the bellows.

> 'O God, our help in ages past,
> Our hope of years to come,'

Marvinder sang along with the congregation. She knew the words without knowing the meaning, and she loved the shudder of the organ when Mr Austin used his feet and produced the loud, deep vibrating chords for the last verse.

When at last it was time for the sermon, Edith was always allowed to flee the tedium of sitting through the Reverend Alcott's droning voice. Her leather shoes would echo with relief down the stone aisle as she hastened out in search of Marvinder. They would play hide and seek among the graves, sometimes their laughter reached the older members of the congregation who looked accusingly at Dora. Or the girls would simply wander about looking with awe at the kindly, stone faces of guardian angels, and trace their fingers over the inlaid words on the headstones.

That Sunday, the Sunday of 3 September 1939, Mr Austin was playing the hymn, 'There is a green hill far away without a city wall'. When it ended, there was the usual pause, while people closed their hymn books and shuffled themselves into some kind of comfortable position for the sermon. Marvinder waited for Edith to come out, but she didn't appear. Getting impatient, she left Jaspal lying on her veil near Ram Singh, and crept up to the organ loft. Noiselessly, she peered down through the balustrade at the congregation all splashed in different colours with reflections from the stained glass windows.

The vicar was speaking in a solemn voice, but somehow, today it seemed different. Everybody had their eyes on him, even Edith. No one fidgeted or dozed; no one's eyes wandered around the church. Then suddenly, they all knelt down with bowed heads and clasped hands and began to pray. Someone hurried up into the organ loft and among anxious whispers, Mr Austin flicked through the hymn book looking for a change of hymn. Then when the vicar had stopped speaking, they all sang 'Abide with me', in a very slow, sad way.

Marvinder went back into the churchyard and waited. At last, the service was over, but when everyone emerged from the church, they came out silently. No one was talking. The vicar stood as usual at the door, shaking hands, but no one smiled.

Edith emerged holding her mother's hand. She looked ill at ease. On seeing Marvinder she detached herself and ran over to her.

'What's wrong?' asked Marvinder. 'Why is nobody talking?'

'We are at war,' said Edith. 'The vicar told us. He got a telegram right in the middle of the service.'

That evening, Dora didn't leave it to Jhoti and the ayah to put the children to bed. Dora was filled with a terrible dread. She wanted to clasp all her children round her. If she had only known of one sure, safe place in the world to escape to, she would have gathered them all up and run. As it was, she fought down her panic by helping to undress them, finding excuses to clasp them in her arms and smother them with kisses.

Jhoti was going to and fro between the kitchen and the bathroom carrying big kettles of hot water for their baths. Suddenly, she gave a fearful shriek. They heard the crash of a kettle, and Jhoti ran out in terror. '*Sāp*, Memsahib! *Sāp*!'

'Snake!' Dora went white with horror. 'Harold! Harold!'

Edith climbed on to the rocking horse. Her face was blank and cold as marble.

Jhoti had flung the kettle of near boiling water at the snake and helped to stun it, so when Harold and Arjun came rushing in, it didn't take long to club it to death and fling its body outside into the dust.

Later when Dora examined it, to satisfy herself that it

would no longer be of any danger, she suddenly felt remorse and foreboding. Why had they killed it? Why had they allowed mindless panic to destroy such a beautiful creature?

She wandered back into the nursery and checked each of her twins.

Then Dora went into the smaller annexe off the nursery, where Edith now slept. As she peered at her daughter through the mosquito net, she was shocked to find her lying awake. Edith stared at her unblinking. Her gaze was so fixed, so emotionless, that at first she thought she must be asleep, even though her eyes were open.

'Edith?' she whispered.

Edith stared at her a second or two longer, then without replying to her mother, rolled over and slept.

Jhoti stood in the darkness of the verandah and breathed deeply. The pungent smells of jasmine, lilies and lemons hung in the air. Marvinder crouched, dozing nearby, her head lolling against Jaspal, who was clasped in her arms. She clambered to her feet and came to her mother.

'Ma?' she whispered. 'Was the snake dangerous?'

'It was a cobra. Cobras can kill,' answered Jhoti.

Marvinder shuddered and drew closer to her mother.

'Shall we go home now, Ma?' she asked.

'In a moment,' murmured Jhoti. She could see the light come on in the drawing room. Harold and Dora entered. His arm was round her shoulder as if to comfort her. Then he took out his violin, while Dora went to the piano. This was how they always ended their day, and Jhoti liked this last invisible link with them.

Each evening, she would squat outside on the verandah, with Jaspal suckling at her breast, and Marvinder playing hopscotch on the flagstones, and listen to Harold and Dora making music together. It was like a religious ritual, and Jhoti found it strangely comforting.

She watched their blurred shapes through the wire-meshed windows and listened to sounds she would never

57

know were Beethoven, Schubert, Mozart. Even Marvinder, fidgeting around her mother, eventually became still, sometimes huddling into Jhoti to watch and listen, and sometimes even pretending that she was playing the violin too. She copied the way Harold held the instrument under his chin with his left hand, and drew the bow up and down with his right.

At last, Arjun would enter the room quietly and wait to be noticed. Then he would announce that their dinner was ready to be served. Wrapping her veil around Jaspal, and tugging Marvinder's hand, Jhoti would at last go back home along the white road.

That night, as they walked back home, there was a long, low rumble coming from the road. Had it been in monsoon, they would have thought it was thunder. But it was September, and the rumble went on longer than any roll of thunder.

From that day on, often in the night, they would hear the rumbling sound, and it was a long time before anyone knew they were army trucks moving troops. Some to go to the ports to board ships for Europe, others to go to the border areas for fear of invasion.

For no one in her village did the fact that the world was at war mean anything. Nothing interrupted their routine. There were still the fields to tend and the buffaloes to milk. It would have been possible for no one to even know, except that one day a letter came from Govind.

'As soon as war was declared, all the students went and joined up. I too have joined up and will be sent from England to meet up with a Punjab regiment in France. We are all very excited and keen to see action. You would be proud to see me in my uniform. Of course, it means I will not complete my university course until after the war.'

Jhoti and Marvinder listened in silence to Harold reading out the letter. When he had finished he said quietly, 'I'm sorry, Jhoti. It looks as though you won't be seeing your husband for quite a while yet.'

'I knew papa would not come back,' said Marvinder.

SEVEN

The Lake

Beyond the church, through a deeply shaded area of mango trees, crumbling slowly away under monsoon rain and relentless sun, invaded by the predatory embrace of weeds and vines and twisting roots of ivy, was the rajah's palace. It was Marvinder who had first told Edith about it.

'Doesn't look much like a palace to me,' Edith complained. She thought all palaces would be like the ones in her book of fairy tales; palaces with tall narrow turrets, marble domes and slanting roofs of gold with arrow slitted windows. But when they clambered through the tangle of vegetation and reached the vast sweep of grey stone verandah, she was impressed.

The building rose like a huge mouldering wedding cake, supported on great, fluted stone pillars and rising tier upon tier, terrace upon terrace until finally it culminated in a flat roof, fifty, eighty, a hundred feet up, hemmed in by stone balustrades and fierce parapets.

Edith fell silent. She was overawed, even afraid. It was so wild, so defiant. If silk-turbanned rajahs and bejewelled queens had ever looked out of those blank windows, or stood on the roofs to watch the sun go down, all trace of them had been smothered. Wherever there was a chink, a crack, a space between pillar and roof, step and verandah, wall and ceiling, a plant, a tendril, a cluster of grasses had seeded itself; long trailing weeds and brilliant flowers, cascaded precipitously; saplings reached out like new-born foals on long dangly legs, with twigs and leaves sprouting and spreading out and out into unimpeded space.

By day, pigeons and sparrows and kites and crows flew in and out of the rooms and roofs; bees, hornets and wasps built their own vast palaces of honey which hung like huge nets from the alcoves. But by night, the palace became the domain of bats and owls, stray dogs and roaming hyenas. Snakes slithered out across the cool stone and a myriad of brilliant insects swarmed in and out of their hidden kingdoms.

At first, Edith hadn't wanted to stay long. It frightened her, and she had turned haughtily, remarking that it wasn't her idea of a palace. But that was years ago. Now she was older, nearly ten. She had been at boarding school for almost two years and had become hardened.

The absence from home was long. Six months without a break, without seeing her mother and father. She blamed the twins. If it hadn't been for them, the war wouldn't have broken out in Europe, then they would have all gone back to England; they would have lived together in a house and gone to day schools. But the day war broke out was the day the snake nearly bit Ralph, and somehow she linked the two events with her despatch to boarding school. The twins required so much attention and hard work. Edith thought of them as leeches, sucking away at their mother. Even now, although they were six years old, she never saw her mother without a twin draped round her legs, or clinging to her neck, making demands, ensuring that there was no time for Edith.

At first she cried every night in her school dorm and wrote letters to her parents begging them to take her home. She thought that she would die of homesickness; thought that the lump of pain would never stop choking her, but then one morning, she woke up. The pain was gone, but it was as if a stone had replaced her heart and she had simply stopped feeling.

It was the same when she came home for the holidays. They met her off the train, her mother and father, each with a twin in hand. She felt hatred and stiffened when they kissed her. How annoying, then, that the twins adored her. Ralph and Grace followed her round everywhere, and called her Edie! And because Jaspal called his elder sister, Didi, as is the custom, the twins also called Marvinder, Didi. They loved the two sounds being so close. 'Edie and Didi!' they chanted, until it drove Edith mad.

One day, Edith remembered the palace and she whispered to Marvinder, 'Let's run away and hide from the twins. Let's go to the palace.'

Marvinder was a little troubled at leaving the twins. They had been put partially in her charge, while Jhoti helped Dora Chadwick prepare the house for a party that night, though Jhoti or Dora was always popping out to check that all was well.

'Do you think we should?' Marvinder asked. 'We were supposed to keep an eye on the twins.'

'We always have to look after the twins,' wailed Edith. 'I'm fed up. I want to play my own game. I want to go to the palace and play kings and queens. We can take dressing-up clothes. My mother has some lovely sarees and we can take cushions to sit on.'

'How will we take it all there?' asked Marvinder, getting swept away with the idea, despite herself.

'We'll take a bike. We'll take Arjun's bike. We'll put the cushions and sarees in the front basket. I'll cycle. I've ridden his bike before, and you can ride to the palace on the back seat.'

'What palace?' demanded Ralph, whose sharp ears caught the last part of Edith's sentence.

'Mind your own business,' retorted Edith rudely.

'Can we play whatever it is you're playing?' demanded Grace looking very interested.

'Yes, you can play, if you can find your own dressing-up things,' declared Edith, with a sudden cunning flash of inspiration.

'Come on, Ralph, Edie says we can play too!' squealed Grace, tugging her twin into the bungalow.

'Quick, Marvi!' hissed Edith. 'You get Arjun's bike, and I'll get the sarees and cushions. Let's get away before the twins come back.'

61

Edith flew into the house.

By the time the twins emerged with armfuls of drapes and dressing-up clothes, Edith and Marvinder were a wobbly speck in the distance.

Their high-pitched voices called out in dismay. 'Edie! Didi! Wait for us!' But Edith pedalled away with fierce determination. Only Marvinder, sitting side-saddle on the back seat, turned her head uneasily, to watch Ralph and Grace rushing up to the gate, waving frantically. Then she saw their arms drop to their sides and their bundles of dressing-up clothes tumble to the ground as she and Edith dwindled from sight.

'Hey! Ralph!' Jaspal's head appeared, peering over the wall as if he were a giant. When the twins saw him, they shrieked with amusement and went rushing over.

'How did you make yourself so tall?' asked Grace.

Jaspal grinned mysteriously. 'I ate magic beans and grew in the night.'

Ralph and Grace were already climbing the small tree which grew up against the wall, and soon they were high enough to look over the other side.

'Jaspal's standing on his buffalo!' chortled Ralph, who saw him first.

'Let me see, let me see!' urged Grace, pushing herself up the branch.

Jaspal laughed. He was in charge of this buffalo and he loved her. He named her 'Rani'. He always took her to the fields each morning where she spent the day pulling up water from the well to irrigate the fields; then after school, he would bring her back to let her cool off in the pond near the village.

'Where's Didi?' he asked the twins.

'They've gone without us,' scowled Ralph. 'They've gone somewhere to dress up.'

'To a palace, Edith said they were going to a palace!' insisted Grace.

'That's what she said, but she probably made it up. Edith makes up things all the time,' muttered Ralph.

'There isn't a real palace here.'

'Oh yes there is,' said Jaspal. 'I know where there's a big palace. It is Ranjit Singh's old palace. He was a famous king of the Punjab, my grandfather told me. No one lives there now – except ghosts, they say!'

'Where, Jaspal, where?' they exclaimed with delighted terror. 'Take us to it.'

'If you ride on top of the buffalo, I'll lead you across the fields. It's quicker that way, and there's the palace lake there where I can let Rani cool off. It's full of fish. We could go fishing!'

'Come on, let's go!' yelled Ralph enthusiastically.

'Can we really ride Rani?' begged Grace.

Jaspal nodded with delight. 'Of course! Her back is broad enough for ten children!' He reached up a hand. 'Come, you can jump down from there. It's easy.'

Jaspal helped the twins on to the wall, then bringing his buffalo close, till its great bulging sides leaned into the wall, he helped each twin to slide on to the beast's back.

'Eh, Jaspal!' Jhoti called her son from the verandah. She had just glimpsed the buffalo carrying the two English children on its back. They looked like little golden gods, with their blond sun-bleached hair streaming in the wind, and their honey-coloured arms and legs contrasting starkly against the animal's thick, dusty black skin.

'Where are you going?' she called.

Dora came out to look too. She knew she should order them back, but when she called out their names, and they looked round at her with such joy in their faces, all she could yell was, 'Be careful, my darlings! And Jaspal, don't be away too long, will you!'

Jaspal walked to the side, so upright and proud to be in charge, his hair tied up in a topknot, his legs, which emerged from beneath a pair of grubby white shorts, as thin and knobbly as the stick he was carrying to guide the buffalo. He waved and shouted, 'Back soon!'

Jhoti and Dora stood for a long while gazing after the buffalo with the children plodding across the fields, before

finally going back inside to continue laying the dining-
table.

The palace looked even wilder than ever. Edith gave a
shudder and almost wished they had after all brought the
twins with them. It seemed so lonely and so quiet. She
would have suggested going to get them, or changing
their plan and doing something else, but Marvinder had
already pulled out a saree and draped it round herself.

'Now, I'm a queen!' she cried strutting up the verandah
steps.

She swept the glittering material round her. It was
turquoise and gold and when she let it billow out as she ran
up and down, she looked like a wonderful peacock.
Suddenly, she paused briefly in a great dark doorway.
'Let's go inside!' she said, and without waiting for an
answer disappeared into the black chasm.

'Marvinder!' Edith rushed up the steps in a panic. 'Don't
go away.' She hesitated for a second in the doorway. She
could see nothing inside but an impenetrable darkness.

'Marvinder?' Her voice had dropped to a whisper.
There was no reply. She stepped a half step forward.
'Marvi! Answer me!' she demanded, hoarsely. She heard a
stifled giggle. Edith moved forward more boldly. She
couldn't see anything at first, and then slowly, her eyes
began to adjust and she saw that trickles of green light
revealed a huge empty room.

'Marvinder!' she called out loud. Her voice echoed, and
there was a rush of wings as a disturbed pigeon flapped
past her face and swooped through the door, making her
scream.

'Edith, come up here!' Marvinder's voice came from
somewhere above her head.

Edith looked slowly round, and then she saw the
opening in the far wall and the start of some stone steps.
The steps were narrow and twisting with no rail to hold
on to, and the treads were worn, as if thousands of feet had
climbed up and down and up and down, gradually

hollowing out the stone. She put one foot into the first indentation, then the next and the next, as steadily she climbed upwards.

A shock of brilliant daylight greeted her eyes at the top. She had emerged on to the first terrace. It was like stepping out on to the deck of a ship, for the whole palace seemed to be floating in a great green ocean of foliage which trembled and undulated all around.

'Edith! Look at me!' Marvi's voice came from inside the enormous room which extended almost the full length of the terrace. Edith dashed in through the large rectangle of a door.

It was a wonderful room, which must once have been furnished with huge silken cushions, magnificent rugs, embroidered hangings, low, intricately-carved ebony tables on which stood brass lampstands and ivory boxes inlaid with precious stones; a room whose walls must have been hung with the skins of tiger, leopard and cheetah and the antlers of deer decorating the doorways. A room fit for a king, a hunter, a proud ruler, a warrior, where princes and princesses rustled by in fabulous silken clothes and brilliant turbans; a room with space enough for eye-flashing dancers to whirl and stamp, and musicians with sitars and tamboura to hypnotise the night with passionate ragas, while tabla drums beat their audience into a frenzy.

Edith sensed it, though the room was stripped as bare as a rock. It was as though some strange spell had been cast over the palace; the carpets had been turned into dry, dead leaves, which tumbled lazily across the dusty, stone floors; the silken cushions had become lumps of stone; the only trophies on the walls were the lizards which streaked like lightning from one diagonal to another, only to stop suddenly, utterly motionless, as if playing some game of statues. And the kings and queens? The princes and princesses? Where had they gone? Had they turned into the shiny-backed beetles which scuttled in corners? Or the long-legged spiders which spun their own web of curtain across the windows? Or were they the ghosts the people

65

whispered about, who emerged sometimes to reinhabit their chambers and walk the verandahs and terraces?

'Look at me!' said Marvinder softly. She sat at the far end of the room on a slightly raised stone dias. She sat cross-legged with her turquoise saree swirled all around her. The sunlight caught the silver and gold threads and made them glisten. She looked like a queen.

They began to play; almost silently, almost as if they, too, were under a spell. They laid out the cushions and draped themselves in sarees and veils; they moved around making royal gestures, and began to wander up and up through the palace, till finally they reached the roof.

At this height they were level with the tops of trees and looked out over the landscape around them. They felt like gods. There was the church and the graveyard; there was the long white road, running like a shimmering thread, on and on, past Marvinder's village, on and on until it would have reached her mother's home village, except that it disappeared over the horizon.

'I can see my house!' screamed Edith gleefully.

When they crossed the roof to look out over the other side, an avenue of sky ran between the great spreading boughs of eucalyptus and mango and neem trees; it took the eye all the way down to a shining lake which Edith never knew existed.

'Look! Oh look!'

'That is the rajah's lake,' said Marvinder. 'It's where he used to fish. My uncles go there often.'

The lake was surrounded by wild undergrowth, which made the waters look dark green. In the middle of the lake was a small island with a landing stage for mooring a boat, and a cupola, which jutted out like a stone umbrella under which a king might sit and fish through a hot afternoon.

Beyond the lake on the other side, the jungle had been kept at bay by the farmers, whose fields of wheat and mustard came right up to the boundary. Across one of these fields, Jaspal and his buffalo came into view carrying Ralph and Grace on its back.

Edith leapt up and down with excitement, screaming at them. 'Ralph! Grace! Look! Over here! Oh, please look, you two!'

Marvinder, too, waved and yelled at the top of her voice. 'Jaspal! Jaspal *bhai*!'

But somehow the three of them didn't seem to hear. Perhaps they were too intent on the boat. Jaspal helped Ralph and Grace to slide off the buffalo's back and while the children ran their fingers over the battered, wooden sides of the boat, the buffalo ambled down to the water's edge and immersed its great body in the mud and weeds.

The boat was already very close to the water so when a slight breeze ruffled the surface, the stern bobbed gently as tiny waves lapped around it. All it took was a push and it was afloat.

Edith and Marvinder watched, at first still waving and shouting in their efforts to get the children's attention; then they fell silent mesmerised by the scene, which slowly unfolded like a piece of mime.

Ralph pointed to the island in the middle of the lake. Grace and Jaspal looked and nodded enthusiastically. Grace climbed into the boat and awkwardly crawled over the centre seats to the stern. She didn't notice the loose planks or the holes in the sides. Ralph and Jaspal, still on land, put their hands to the prow and began to push. The boat wobbled and they could see Grace laughing. She put her hand to her mouth as if to stiffle anxious squeals.

The boys pushed and heaved, their arms extended to the full, out in front, their legs stretched behind as they put the full weight of their bodies into the push to get the boat away from the shore. At last, with a final heave, the boat slid away with the boys plunging into the water after it.

'Oh, what fun! what fun!' cried Edith, clapping her hands despite herself. 'Look at them trying to get into the boat!'

The boys were both balanced on their tummies tipping and rocking as they pulled themselves aboard.

Marvinder didn't speak.

Ralph found an oar and wriggled it out from under the seat. There seemed to be only one. He began to plunge it into the water. Meanwhile, Jaspal and Grace were using their hands to paddle the boat along.

Slowly, slowly, the boat began to drift further and further from the shore, whether by the exertions of the children or by a faint wind which caught the craft in its grip and tugged it out towards the centre of the lake.

The same wind suddenly sent a heap of dead leaves scurrying and rattling across the palace roof, and made the girls' sarees billow out like sails. A flock of green parrots exploded into the sky with a wild screech. If only they could have leapt as easily into space from the parapets and flown down to the lake side. If only their sarees could have turned into wings and given them the power of flight. Instead, they stood, helpless and rooted.

It was like looking through the wrong end of a telescope. They saw the terror of the children as the boat began to fill with water. The children used their hands, frantically trying to scoop out the water. It was all so fast. Suddenly, the three children were up to their waists in the water, then their chests and then . . .

Edith was aware of a whimpering at her side. Marvinder's fingers were clawing at her saree and she began to run, first away then back to the balustrade, then away, then back. Her whimpers became fierce screams, squeezed out of her body in short gasps. Then suddenly she was gone. Edith was hardly aware of it, for Edith just stood as if she had become one of the hard, grey, immobile palace stones; inactive; doomed, as these stones had been doomed to be a dumb, passive witness; to see but never to forget.

They looked so small, so insignificant, struggling there in the water. Their splashes were no bigger than a dog might make as it swims after a stick. Then suddenly, there was nothing except a blank expanse of water. No boat, no children.

Edith gave a deep sigh as if she were eternally weary.

She turned away, and wrapping her saree tightly round her body wandered down like a sleepwalker to the grand chamber. Edith lay down on a cushion, her head on another and closed her eyes.

She slept.

EIGHT

Goodbye

Long after the Chadwicks had left for England, people remembered Dora Chadwick walking down the long white road between her bungalow and the Anglican Church.

It was usually at dusk, when daylight was fading; when the hooves of homecoming buffaloes and goats churned up the fine dust on the road, so that when it mingled with the still fierce shafts of light from the setting sun, it blurred the outlines of the hoarse-voiced infants who ran among them with sticks to guide them home. She walked in this milky twilight with a topee on her head and wearing one of her flowery, English cotton dresses. Her pale as paper bare arms hung listlessly at her sides, and her sandalled feet almost dragged, as if just putting one foot in front of the other took all her effort and courage. It was the routine of a ghost, haunting the road to the graveyard where her children lay buried.

The village children invented a game. They called it 'Mad Memsahib' because it was said that Dora Chadwick had gone mad after Ralph and Grace were drowned in the lake. As in 'Grandmother's Footsteps', they would stalk behind her at a safe distance, walking when she walked, stopping if she stopped and always ready to scatter if she should turn round.

But Dora Chadwick never looked back. She went through the same motions day after day. When she reached the church she walked down the gravelly path to the graveyard at the back, and the straggly procession of village children dispersed among the tombstones to spy and snigger into their hands. Always bringing up the rear of the procession was Jhoti.

It was Harold Chadwick who had commissioned Jhoti to follow his wife just in case the village children got out of hand, or she became distressed in any way. To go himself would have broken the illusion that she was putting the twins to bed; and in any case, he found it unbearable to visit their little grave. He had had no faith before their deaths and now no comfort from any spiritual source. There was only his belief in the permanency of music and his love of the violin.

So Jhoti would enter the graveyard and crouch respectfully at a distance, watching Dora as she made her way among the mounds and monuments. She ignored the ornate crosses, the stone cherubs and the sweet-faced guardian angels: they were a mockery. Where had God been when He was most needed? Where the guardian angels? When her children died, Dora's faith in God died too.

Grace and Ralph were buried in a single grave in a far corner, beneath the shade of a neem tree, with no elaborate monument or declaration of faith; just a simple cross beneath which was inscribed on a plain headstone the names and dates of birth and death. Here, Dora would come and lie casually across the mound, as if she were spreading herself comfortably over their bed.

'What shall we have tonight, darlings?' she would ask in her high, English voice. 'Perhaps it should be Ralph's favourite story, as Grace chose yesterday. Shall we have the story of Rapunzel, Ralph?'

It was so real. Often Jhoti was certain the twins were talking to their mother for she nodded and laughed and told her story with such tender intimacy that it would have been easy to believe they were in a darkened bedroom, with wafting mosquito nets and the rustling of sheets.

'"Rapunzel, Rapunzel, let down thy golden hair."'

When the story was over, there was at first a silence, as though she listened, then the faint motherly whisperings of 'goodnight' as if she stroked their sleepy heads and

71

smoothed out their limbs. Finally, she would sing. A nursery rhyme would sadly fill the air, so that even the spying, sniggering village children were pacified and would creep quietly away to their own beds.

By the time Dora had returned to her home, the lamps on the verandah would already be lit.

Each homecoming was the same. Harold would be waiting to greet his wife. As she climbed the verandah steps, he would come to the mesh door and open it for her, then putting an arm round her shoulders, draw her inside.

At this point, Jhoti knew herself to be dismissed, but she could never leave. Now was the final ritual of the day. Harold took up his black violin case which rested on a shelf near the piano and put it on the table. Standing squarely before it like a priest before the host, he reached out with his long white fingers and undid the two clasps. He lifted the lid and exposed a lush, deep, red velvet interior in which the violin lay, draped with a silk scarf.

Harold didn't remove the instrument immediately, but first unclipped the bow from inside the lid. He would always do exactly the same thing each night: hold up the bow to the light, twist a silver knob at one end which tightened the creamy horse hair; then, without letting any part of the bow's hair touch his fingers, he held the bow at arm's length with his right hand, while with his left, he extricated a block of yellow resin from a tiny compartment in one end of the violin case. Firmly, he drew the hair of the bow up and down on the resin block and then returned it to its place. Still one-handed, Harold then unwrapped the silk scarf and lifted up his rich, brown violin and tucked it under his chin.

Meanwhile, Dora had mechanically seated herself at the piano and selected some music which she propped on the stand before her. She played, as she always did, the one single note for Harold to tune to then, after he had twisted the pegs which held all four strings, he finally gave a nod of approval and the music would begin.

Jhoti wanted to be comforted by the music too. She was

bound to them and their grief. They all shared a sense of guilt. Each one of them thought, if only I had done this or that . . . if only . . . But Dora's twins were dead and Jaspal was alive. His survival was a miracle. His body, too, had been brought ashore and laid, apparently lifeless, alongside Grace and Ralph. A helpless crowd had gathered. It is bad luck to touch the dead, so no one had attempted resuscitation. Harold was rushed over from the school and, in a frenzy, flung himself over Ralph and Grace in turn, pumping at their chests and sucking at their mouths: and even in that moment of anguish, he didn't abandon Jaspal, but tried desperately to pump the water out of his lungs.

When Dora and Jhoti arrived, each frantically worked on a child, on and on until they collapsed weeping and defeated, and it was then that Marvinder, who had watched in shocked silence from the trees, came and laid her body over Jaspal and whispered in his ear, 'Live, live, live, Jaspal.' She lifted his arms up and down, up and down as if he were some dead bird which she was trying to make fly again.

Someone tried to prise her off. 'It's no use, Marvinder! Come now, child, leave him in peace.' But still she clung to her brother. 'Live, Jaspal, live!' she screamed. As firmer hands wrenched her away, Jaspal suddenly coughed and a quantity of water flooded from his mouth. He lived.

It was a long time before anyone wondered where Edith was.

Darkness had fallen; perhaps they were so used to her being away at boarding school. The Chadwicks had gone to the hospital with their dead twins and Jaspal had been carried home like a god-child. Now that he was alive, everyone reached out to touch him for good luck, especially those who wouldn't lay a finger on him when they thought he was dead. Then, in the middle of the night, a panic-stricken Arjun came beating on their door, yelling at the top of his voice, 'Has anyone seen Edith? Edith is missing.'

They awoke Marvinder from an exhausted sleep and she simply told them that she had left Edith at the old palace.

Frantic torchlight and kerosene lamps bobbed through the darkness, dazzling the moths and fireflies and casting giant, wavering shadows up the huge walls of the palace.

They found her, still asleep on the cushions. When they awoke her, she said, 'It's all my fault. I made so many wishes that Ralph and Grace would go away for ever, and now they have.' Then she closed her eyes again and they carried her home.

The music started. It seemed infinitely sad. The notes of the violin soared like a lone bird, rising and falling.

Once Edith had asked her father, 'Where does the sound go?'

He told her that it travelled on and on for ever into space, and that perhaps somewhere, in a million light years time, some being on another planet would hear Mozart and be amazed.

From her bed, Edith could hear the music and wondered if the souls of Ralph and Grace would live for ever, too. Would their last cries be, at this moment, travelling through space? What would the being on another planet think when he heard Mozart followed by the screams of dying children?

It was her fault they were dead. She had no doubt of that. She had wished it so often, even prayed for it. Now all she heard was her mother crying that she wished she was dead too, and once, Edith had passed her father's study to hear strange racking sounds coming from inside. When she secretly peeped in it was to see her father slumped over his desk, his shoulders heaving with sobs.

Edith's loneliness seemed to be without end, and lying in bed in the darkness listening to the music, she felt forever excluded and that no one could ever love her again.

Jaspal and Marvinder, too, stood watching and listening. Then, when at last their mother was ready to go home, they walked with her in silence, one on each side, back down the long, white road.

The whole world was breaking up. Somewhere across the sea in Europe, Govind was taking part in a terrible slaughter as he helped the British fight the Nazis. Some people in the village said maliciously, 'But aren't the British our enemy too? Why should Govind fight his enemy's enemy? We want the British to be defeated so that India can go free.'

Whatever the arguments, no one knew if he was alive or dead. Govind hadn't written for months and any news which Harold Chadwick received was full of gloom and even fear. There was fear that the war would reach India, that there was danger of invasion from the Japanese. They had captured Malaya, Singapore and Burma. Would India be next? More army trucks rumbled through the night, churning up the long white road as they headed for the border areas. Then there was the fear, greater than all the rest; the fear among themselves between Hindus, Muslims and Sikhs.

Neighbours looked at each other and weren't sure who to trust any more.

Somehow, the death of the twins signalled a greater death to come from which no one, no one would escape unscathed.

When Jaspal and Marvinder continued to drape garlands of marigolds around their father's portrait, it was with the same reverence that they garlanded Guru Nanak's picture. So without their realising it, Govind achieved saintliness in their eyes. He became someone they worshipped rather than remembered.

Jaspal often gazed at it with pride. 'My father is an important man,' he would boast to his friends. 'He reads like a guru and he is a soldier in England. When the war there is over, he will come home and everything will be all right.'

But when they heard that the war had finally ended, it was a long time before any letter came from Govind. When it did, it was as if it came from a stranger. Shireen read it, but it seemed so alien and incomprehensible that Jhoti took the letter to Harold Chadwick. He read it at a glance, his face giving no indication of its contents, then with a deep sigh, he sat back in his chair behind his desk, while Jhoti stood patiently nearby.

My dear wife,

The war is over and I am back in England with a painful wound in my leg. I am told I will need much treatment and that it is best that I receive it here. So do not expect me home for a long time. I will write again when I have more news.

Govind

'That's all?' asked Jhoti. 'What kind of wound? Who will look after him? How long will it take? Why does he not ask after his mother, father, wife or children? Is the letter really from Govind or is it a mistake? And why does he not give an address? How can we write to him?' She finished in tears.

Then Harold told Jhoti that he, Dora and Edith were going back to England.

'Now that the war is over, there are ships going out once more. We must visit our parents. Edith needs to go to school. I promise you that, as soon as I can, I will find Govind for you. I promise.'

Jhoti's anxiety increased. The prospect of losing the Chadwicks seemed to underline the growing fear that everything they had known was falling apart. With the Chadwicks leaving and Govind away, she would once more be at the mercy of her in-laws: bottom of the pile, at everyone's beck and call.

It was a silent, even sorrowful crowd who turned up to see the Chadwicks depart. Arjun, Maliki and Rani stood a little apart from the rest. They had been part of the Chadwick household for nearly ten years and already looked bewildered, as if they hardly knew what would become of their lives now. Clustered on the verandah steps were Jhoti and her children, and all over the compound were other small groups of people.

Edith emerged first from the bungalow. She was dressed as if going to school, in a blue, striped cotton frock, shoes, socks and gloves and her topee on her head. She carried a small suitcase and had a school satchel on her back.

She looked disconcerted by the crowd and turned as if she might run indoors again, but then she saw Marvinder. Soon after the twins had been buried, Edith had been sent back to school and the two girls hadn't seen or spoken to each other for so long. She looked at her friend as if she had just awoken and memories of their games in the palace came flooding back.

She put down her suitcase and opened it up. 'I want you to have something,' she said rummaging through her belongings. Then she found an Indian cloth purse.

'This is what I want to give you.' She held out a little silver locket on a thin silver chain and opened it in front of Marvinder. Inside was a photograph of herself.

'I'd like you to keep this to remember me by,' she said, handing it to Marvinder.

Marvinder was overcome by the gift. She held it up with shining eyes for all to see.

'It's beautiful!' she exclaimed. 'Look, Ma!' She showed it to Jhoti. Jhoti gently clasped the locket round Marvinder's neck and then kissed Edith's hands.

Without consulting her mother, Marvinder wriggled a small ring off her finger. It was only a cheap, little ring which she had bought at a gypsy fair for two annas, but she loved it because it had a very deep, glowing orange stone. Edith had always admired it.

'Take!' She pressed it into her friend's hand.

Who had noticed the last time that Edith had smiled? At any rate, when she accepted the ring and pushed it on to her middle finger, her face broke into such a broad smile that everybody else smiled too.

A large Austin Rover tooted at the gate. Jaspal sped over to open it, and the Reverend Alcott drove in looking hot and red-faced in his black cassock.

'Right! Is everybody ready, eh what?' he bellowed in a jovial voice. He had volunteered to drive the Chadwicks to the station to catch an express train to Bombay where they would board their ship for England.

Harold came out first, and with Arjun's help, heaved two great tin trunks down the steps and tied them on to the roof. There were three more big suitcases which went into the boot of the car. Soon, all their belongings were in the car and now there was just themselves.

'Edith, you sit at the back with your mother,' said Harold, 'but say "goodbye" first.' Edith went before each person; they were people who had known her all her life, Arjun, Shanta, Maliki, Jhoti and shook their hands solemnly. They in turn pressed their palms together in the traditional *namaste* and then couldn't help giving her an affectionate hug.

Then Harold went in to fetch Dora. The farewells were tearful and filled with pain. She was not just saying goodbye to her home and servants, but to the land in which her babies had been born and to whose soil she must now leave two of those babies.

Many came forward with garlands and bunches of flowers and boxes of sweets.

When the heavily-laden car drove for the last time out of the gates, a great cry went up behind them as people wept and waved, and the village children, who had once crept cheekily behind Dora on her way to the church, now ran behind the car shouting, 'Goodbye! Goodbye! Come back soon!'

Edith looked back through the clouds of dust which the wheels churned up on the long white road. Her eyes looked beyond the gesticulating figures which still raced after them, and fixed on the image of Jaspal and Marvinder standing motionless in the middle of the road. She was filled with an unexpected feeling of loss.

'Goodbye,' she shouted, suddenly winding down the window and thrusting her body so far out that her mother grabbed her in alarm.

'Are goodbyes forever?' she asked, as their image finally faded and she sank back into her seat.

Nobody answered her.

PART TWO

Fire

'The Wheel of his power made one circle
In which the human soul was wandering
Like a restless swan.'

The Upanishads

NINE

Fire

'Quick, Jaspal! Hide! They're coming!'

Jaspal's best friend, Nazakhat, came flying down the path. 'Come on!' He grabbed his arm and hauled him into the sugar cane fields. They lay, flattened on their stomachs, not daring to breathe.

Who were they this time? Sikh, Muslim or Hindu? Whose house, whose shop, whose temple or mosque would they burn? Peering through the bamboo-like stems of the sugar cane, Jaspal saw the powerful, striding legs of men as they marched by. Whoever they were, they were not of their village. They had come from outside, driving up in trucks; coming to spread terror and havoc.

There were shouts, screams, crackles and flames. Black smoke billowed up into the sky.

'Ma, Ma, Ma!' Jaspal was whimpering . . . whimpering . . .

'Jaspal! Eh, Jaspal! Wake up, wake up! You're dreaming!' Marvinder shook her brother fiercely, forcing him out of his nightmare.

'Look!' she cried. 'The sun is up. Now up with you too. You must help Uncle Pavan finish those chairs today.'

Jaspal shuddered. His heart was still thumping from the terror of the dream. He lay back on his mattress for a moment, listening to the sounds of a new day beginning. He gained comfort from the argumentative crows caw-cawing at each other, and the low raw bark of a stray dog, awakened by the ache in its starved belly.

'I'll fill the bucket for you to wash, if you like,' said Marvinder sympathetically.

He listened, while she went to the pump in the yard and

wrenched down the handle. It gave its usual protesting squeal before there was a whoosh of water into the metal pail. Up and down she heaved, until the pail was half full.

'Come on!' she called. 'It's ready for you. You'd better get going, or there'll be trouble.'

While Jaspal doused himself all over with water, old bent Grandmother shuffled stiffly out of her room. She massaged her own back with both hands as she hobbled over to the brazier outside the kitchen door. Each morning she lit the fire and began the long preparation of the day's food.

Jhoti came out, stretching the sleep from her body. 'What was all the rumpus about?' she asked.

'Jaspal was having a nightmare again,' said Marvinder. 'That boy, I tell you, he keeps me awake at night with all his mumblings and ravings.'

'It's these troubles,' muttered Grandmother. 'They're beginning to tell on all of us.'

'If only Govind would come home,' cried Jhoti.

'Well, at least he's sending you money,' Grandmother reminded her. 'Otherwise we'd all be in trouble.' She poured out a goblet of hot, scented tea to take to Uncle Pavan.

'Yes, but we need him home,' said Jhoti. 'Money isn't everything. What use is a husband when he is thousands of miles across the ocean and with all these dangers around us? He said he would come when his wound was healed. Now he says he's trying to make a lot of money there so that he can set up in business when he gets home. I don't understand. What business? I thought he was going to be a lawyer or a government man or a teacher. That is why he went to England. I tell you, Grandmother, if Govind doesn't come home soon, I will go to Britain and find him and take the children too.'

Grandmother cackled with derision. 'How could you ever do that?'

'Oh, I would find a way if I had to,' insisted Jhoti, and as if to emphasise her determination, she took down his dusty photograph, which she had brought with her from her in-laws, and began rubbing the glass fiercely with the end of her saree.

Life had become difficult after the Chadwicks left, so it was decided that Jhoti should go with her children and keep house for Uncle Pavan, her father-in-law's brother who was a carpenter in the next village and lived with his aged grandmother.

She had been reluctant at first, even bitter, for it was as though they had no place for her in the family house while there was no news of Govind coming home.

Everyone knew that Uncle Pavan was a crotchety, bad-tempered man. He was lame in one leg after it had been broken in childhood and then not set properly. Unable to work in the fields and embittered by his ill fortune, he had taken up carpentry and lived with his aged grandmother who did her best to look after him. Jaspal was to become his apprentice.

'He'll need to learn a trade,' muttered Father-in-law. 'He can't exactly follow in his father's footsteps when we don't know what they are!'

The arrangement worked better than Jhoti expected. Old Grandmother, beneath her prickly manner, was an affectionate, kind creature who welcomed Jhoti and her children. And Uncle Pavan was good at his trade and worked hard. Jaspal learned quickly by his side in the workshop. Marvinder, too. She learned to cane chairs, prepare wood and embroider cushion covers.

It could have been a good life but for the terror which hung over the land.

Jaspal finished washing and Marvinder helped to rub him down vigorously with a towel. She combed out his wet hair, sometimes tugging so hard that he jumped and squealed before she finally wound it round into a topknot and sealed it with a small, white handkerchief.

'Here,' said Jhoti, beckoning him over for a *paratha* stuffed with potato and dal. 'Eat, and be quick about it. You're late, and Uncle Pavan will be angry.'

Jaspal always worked for two hours in his uncle's workshop before setting off on a three-mile walk to school across the fields.

Well, he wasn't the only boy to be up at dawn working. Nazakhat would be up too. He was a tailor's son, and would already be sewing on buttons. 'Buttons, buttons, buttons. Sometimes, buttons dance before my eyes!' he complained.

Certainly, Jaspal didn't envy him. I'd rather be a carpenter than a tailor, he thought to himself. Today there was sandpapering to be done. A local businessman had decided to furnish his house in the western way and had ordered six dining chairs. Such good business didn't come along every day, so Uncle Pavan wanted a particularly fine job done on them.

Jaspal rubbed and rubbed until his fingers were roughened by the sandpaper, and his muscles ached from rubbing. Then he swept away the fine dust and arranged the tools for his uncle. Uncle Pavan was a strict task master and would beat him if everything wasn't perfect.

'It's time for you to go to school now, my boy!'

Grandmother stood in the doorway. She held out a napkin in which she had wrapped another *paratha* stuffed with vegetables for his lunch. He put it in the cloth bag along with his wooden writing-board.

'Go, child, go!' She gave him an affectionate hug and pushed him on his way.

He passed Marvinder, who was already sitting under a thin tree with a tray of brilliantly coloured threads at her side and needle in hand. She nodded at him enviously. She would like to have been going to school, too, but there was always too much work to be done ever to spare the girls. But whenever she could, she would hang over his shoulder when he was reading and pester him to teach her. Uncle Pavan thought school was a waste of time, even for Jaspal.

'Will reading and writing make him a good carpenter?'

But Jhoti had insisted on Jaspal going to school. In this

one respect, she had the power to insist, because Govind was sending some money regularly, and she could argue that her husband would undoubtedly expect his son to be educated.

'Don't go dawdling off with your playmates after school,' Uncle Pavan bellowed after him. 'I want you home promptly. There's a lot to get done. I've promised those six chairs by the end of the week.'

Every morning when the door to his uncle's workshop closed behind him, Jaspal felt the pleasure of freedom rush through his body and soul. It was only for a short time, the time it took to walk to school, and then afterwards, the time it took to return. These were the best times, the only times when he was free and at no one's beck and call. He and his friends could race and jump and play hide and seek, and steal guavas from the guava groves or sneak into the fields of sugar cane to hack away at hunks of juicy stem to peel and suck and chew. They could chase goats or plunge into the river with the water buffaloes.

This morning, on his way to school, Jaspal was more solemn. He met Nazakhat as usual near the well, and as they picked up their path across the fields, he told him, 'We may be going to England.'

Nazakhat looked at him with wide-eyed disbelief. 'Rubbish!' he gasped.

'No, not rubbish. I heard my mother talking. She said if my father didn't come to her, then she would go to him.'

'But England! England is . . . right across the ocean . . . across the other side of the world . . .' Nazakhat couldn't quite explain how far away England was.

'Yes, but my father is there. He has been fighting for the king. He has been wounded. He's a great warrior. He's even got medals!'

'Yes, yes, yes!' yawned Nazakhat tapping his mouth with boredom. 'You've told me that a hundred times. But the war is over now. He's not a warrior any more. I've heard he's not even a teacher, that he's probably nothing but a servant in some white man's house.'

Jaspal danced with anger. 'Why do you listen to lies?' He flung himself on to his friend and forced him to the ground.

'Hey, hey! It was just a joke, Jaspal. Stop it, you idiot!'

'Well, I don't like your jokes,' cried Jaspal grimly holding Nazakhat's shoulders down and leering into his face. 'If you say such a thing again I'll punch your teeth in!' He held up a clenched fist.

'Come off it, Jaspal! Come on, friends!' Nazakhat raised a foot, pressed it into Jaspal's chest and thrust him off with a shout of glee.

'Friends! Yes?' He had Jaspal's head under his arm and forced him towards a boggy irrigation ditch. 'Friends? Or I chuck you in!'

Jaspal struggled and fought as other children came running to join them and pitch into the fray. In the tussle, they both fell in.

'Oh, no!' Jaspal looked in dismay at his once clean shirt and shorts now all covered in a foul-smelling mud. But when he looked at Nazakhat, he burst out laughing. 'Man, you should see yourself!' he exclaimed. You look like a half-drowned dog.'

'And you!' retorted Nazakhat. 'What do you think you look like, o mighty son of a warrior! Come on, I'll race you to the river.'

They washed off the mud as best they could in the river, before carrying on to school all wet and dripping. But the sun was hot, and within the hour, they knew their clothes would be dry.

The teacher was waiting for them under the broad shade of a mango tree. He picked up a large metal triangle and jangled it fiercely with an iron bar.

The children responded dutifully, all lining up shoulder to shoulder, with straight backs and hands to their sides. Muslim stood next to Hindu and Hindu next to Sikh. This was the only school for miles around, and at least fifty children attended it.

'So, my little citizens of independence! Is everyone present and correct?' The teacher liked to call them 'his little citizens of independence'. In only a few months India would be independent, and every morning now, they started the day by singing their new national anthem so that they would learn it to perfection and never forget it.

'Jana Gana Mana Adhi Na-yake Joiahe, Bharata, Bhagaya Vidhata. The whole world praises you from the bottom of its heart o giver of all good gifts.'

Afterwards, he would call out, 'What day is it today?'

Today the children responded in a great chorus. 'The date today is Wednesday, 5 June 1947.'

Jaspal enjoyed school. He had learned to read and write without any trouble. His teacher said he was a good pupil. Sometimes, Uncle Pavan would pick up a newspaper in the bazaar and bring it home for Jaspal to read. And it was Jaspal who could write letters. Uncle Pavan grudgingly admitted that this could be of use in certain circumstances. It was he who wrote on his uncle's or mother's behalf to his father in England.

The last letter said:

Dear Dada,

We hope this letter finds you in perfect health and that your wound does not trouble you any more.

Last week, Uncle Pavan had to have a tooth pulled. It was very painful. He thanks you for the money order of five hundred rupees which you sent from England. The money is much appreciated as business these days is not too good here.

Ma and Marvinder are both well, though Ma asks when you are coming home. She misses you and often cries.

I am in very good health and doing well at school. My teacher is pleased with me. He would like me to go to the upper school in Batala where you went. What a pity Mr Chadwick has gone back to England and would not be my teacher. Uncle Pavan says further education is useless. He wants me to be a carpenter. What do you think?

I do hope you are coming home soon. There is a lot of trouble in these parts. We wish you were here to protect us.

We will remember you as usual at the temple and send up a special prayer.

May all God's blessings be with you,

Your loving son,

Jaspal

Today as he stood to attention for the roll call, Jaspal saw a worried expression on his teacher's face. Suddenly, Jaspal remembered his dream, and a feeling of uneasiness tightened his stomach.

Things weren't right with the world. He wasn't sure why. Everyone had been so jubilant and proud when the date for independence was declared. There had been processions and fireworks. Jaspal himself had taken part, sitting up on a great elephant holding a garlanded picture of their new prime minister, Jaharawal Nehru. Now they would run India for the Indians, their teacher told them. Yet almost immediately, it seemed instead as though the whole country was at war with itself.

Jaspal had noticed that men who used to be friends with each other, who used to sit in the tea shops gossiping or playing cards, now argued and thumped the tables. Strangers came into the village to march, wave banners and make speeches. There should be a homeland for the Muslims, a homeland for the Sikhs. They drew maps and created boundaries and forced people to be enemies. Riots, which were once confined to the cities, now came into the smallest of villages; people threw stones, fought in the streets and set fire to buildings. Evil forces were trying to set Hindu against Muslim and Muslim against Sikh; neighbour against neighbour. There was death in the wind.

One night Nazakhat's whole family had come running

to Uncle Pavan's workshop begging to be hidden because troublemakers had started setting fire to all Muslim houses. It was then that Jaspal began having nightmares. He would never forget Nazakhat's terrified face. The only good thing was that people trusted their friends. They hid each other and tried to protect them.

'We want India to be a country where everybody respects everyone, no matter what their race, caste or creed,' said their teacher. 'What matters is that we are all Indians and that our destiny is in our own hands.' He spoke to his children as if he were desperately pleading with the whole nation.

They looked up at him with wide but uncomprehending eyes.

'Come,' he said, shaking himself out of his despair; 'let us consider Geometry.' He went to the easel on which stood an old, faded blackboard and began to draw shapes. 'Copy!' he ordered.

The sun had lifted higher into the sky and the children hugged the ever-diminishing shade of the mango tree. They sat cross-legged with their slates across their knees and copied.

Jaspal tried to stop his mind from wandering. Tried not to wonder why his mother looked nervous and worried; why his uncle had become even more short-tempered. He noticed that people clustered round Harjit Singh's cloth shop to listen to his radio.

The teacher passed among them checking their work and cuffing their heads if they hadn't taken enough care. Jaspal was glad when at last school was over. He wouldn't dawdle home today. He had an overwhelming desire to rush home as quickly as possible and be near his mother and sister.

There was quite a group of them straggling back across the fields that day. Jaspal was running ahead of them with Nazakhat puffing to keep up. 'Hey, Jaspal! What's the hurry to get back? Are you so keen to work again?'

Jaspal suddenly pulled up so short that Nazakhat almost

bumped into him. 'Look! What's that?'

The sky was filled with stabbing spikes of yellow, like the sharp-tipped petals of giant sunflowers. How beautiful it looked but then they saw the black, billowing smoke rising upwards, blotting out the sun; turning day into night.

The children cried out with alarm and began running. Leaving the path, they plunged into the fields, which stretched between them and their village, and like an extended moving ripple ran and ran, each wanting to be the first to arrive.

Their cries became gasps of horror as they realised that the bright yellow flowers were flames.

'Fire, fire!' they screamed.

A wave of people came pouring out of the village towards them. The air was filled with desperate shouts of fear and agony.

'Ma, Ma, Ma!' sobbed Jaspal as he ran.

'Wait for me!' begged Nazakhat, his voice shrill with terror.

Then they saw the striding legs, the clenched fists and the black war-like banners thrust high into the sky. They saw firebrands and swords and knives dripping with blood.

'Quick, hide!' hissed Nazakhat pulling Jaspal down into the barley. When the men had passed, the boys were up again and running. 'Have you seen my mother, father, sister, brother, husband, wife . . .' voices cried out from every direction. Some people stumbled about as if blind and deaf with panic, and others lay dead and dying in the rubble of burned and destroyed houses.

Nazakhat's house was the nearest, so they went there first. It was not on fire. Today the property of Hindus and Sikhs was the target.

Jaspal would have carried on running until he reached his uncle's house but, suddenly, there were familiar voices calling out to him urgently. 'Jaspal! Stay here! Everyone is here, safe with us!'

'Everyone?' Jaspal rushed inside to be clasped joyfully by his mother, sister and grandmother.

Nazakhat's family, who were Muslim, had never forgotten how Uncle Pavan had protected them under his roof when they had been attacked some weeks earlier. 'Friends are friends,' they said to each other, 'and we believe in God's law, not the law of evil men.'

'Where is Uncle Pavan?' asked Jaspal suddenly noticing his absence.

Nazakhat's father shook his head fearfully. 'He wouldn't leave his carpenter's shop and all his precious furniture. We tried to persuade him, but he was so stubborn.'

They hid there for the rest of the day and night in the darkness of the food store, crouching behind sacks of grain and rice, fearful in case anyone searched the houses. They waited till the sounds of terror had died away. By dawn, all they could hear was the cackle of dying flames and the pathetic howlings of bewildered dogs.

At last Nazakhat came to tell them they were safe to come out, but he was shaking all over and tears kept rolling down his face.

'What is it, Nazakhat? What has happened?'

There were no words to describe what had happened. Whatever it was that people had fought for, hoped for or dreamed of, it hardly mattered here. The only winners from such a place were the creatures of prey, the rats and vultures and crows; the starved dogs and mangey cats; the ants, the beetles, the cockroaches, how they all came swarming out of their nests to take, to loot and consume. How confident they were as they invaded the bodies of the dead. No proper funerals here; no Hindu or Sikh cremations with the scent of sandalwood to accompany the soul to heaven; no Muslim burials with exalting angels and the promises of salvation; not the clean wholesome holy committal of the body to God, dust to dust or ashes to ashes; this was the ultimate failure of man. He had sunk so low that all he was fit for was to be consumed by the vermin of the earth, or so humans had always described such creatures.

What victories they could celebrate as they swarmed into rotting corpses, and enough grain stores and food cupboards to feed them to kingdom come. What a triumph for them. What history books, what tales, what myths and legends could be written about this conquest if only such creatures had the skills and appreciation of events that man had been endowed with.

But they had no such conceptions. They just scuttled and nibbled and gnawed and pecked, while the few dazed human survivors crept by as though they had been damned to hell.

Grandmother, Jhoti, Jaspal and Marvinder went back to what remained of Uncle Pavan's house and workshop. The charred skeletons of his furniture lay kicked about, smouldering into strange sculptures. It was a while before they found Uncle Pavan's body. He was lying among the scattered chairs he had been making. His arms were outstretched as if he had tried to protect them from destruction.

No one spoke, or wept. There was no one but them to prepare the body for cremation.

While Jaspal, Nazakhat and his father went to build a low funeral pyre, Jhoti, Marvinder and old Grandmother washed the body clean. They ensured that he bore the five Ks as all good Sikhs should; *kach*, the white shorts, *kara*, his steel bracelet, *khanga*, his comb, *kirpan*, his sword and *kesh*, his long, uncut hair which they bound into a turban.

There was no priest. He was dead, and the Guru Granth Sahib was shredded in the burnt out *gurdwara*. When they lifted Uncle Pavan's body on to the funeral pyre and Jaspal lit the fire, Grandmother began to chant some verses she remembered by their beloved leader, Guru Gobind Singh:

> As sparks spring from the flame
> And then drop back,
> As dust rises from the earth

94

And then settles back,

As tides move in from the ocean
And then recede,
So it is, that all things come from God
And then return.

They could hear a great, never-diminishing sound of creaking. On and on it went by day and by night. The creaking never stopped. It was long, low, heavy and full of weariness. It sounded as though the very rotation of the earth creaked as it continued on its orbit. The long white road was filled from end to end as far as the eye could see, with slow, plodding, creaking bullock carts. Each bullock cart was like a little mountain, it was so piled-up with goods and belongings and with old people, young children or wounded survivors of the latest massacre.

The wooden wheels of the carts turned ceaselessly and ground their weight into the ruts in the road. Where was Surya's chariot of the sun now? Where now the great symbolic wheel which fluttered on the new flag of independent India? For many weeks to come, these creaking, grinding wheels would turn and turn as they transported refugees out of one homeland into another.

Jaspal, sifting through the burnt-out rubble of his uncle's home, suddenly saw sunlight glint on glass. He had to kick aside a smouldering table and plunge his hand into the rubble to extricate the photograph of his father.

The glass was smashed and the frame broken, but the picture was unmarked. His father's face stared out at him full of solemn importance; so smart, so clean, so full of promise for the future, as if to say, 'This is what life can be.'

Jaspal was overwhelmed with pride and love. He wiped the dust from its surface with his sleeve and carried it over to his mother and sister.

Jhoti held it in her hands and gazed at it silently for a long time, then carefully rolling it into a scroll, she slotted it into the front of her tunic.

TEN

Flight

'We are going to England.'

Jhoti made her announcement to Nazakhat's family as they all crouched nervously before a low, flickering brazier. The previous days had been a nightmare of searching. She found Govind's family had fled and the family house a burnt-out rubble. She walked all day to get to her own home village only to find scenes of death and devastation. Of her family, there was no sign. They too could be dead, or perhaps somewhere on the long white road among the thousand upon thousand refugees who moved like a slow, sad river.

She was on her own now and she knew it. Every day that they stayed with Nazakhat's family put them all in jeopardy. They had to go.

'How will you manage?' asked Iqbal Khan, Nazakhat's father. 'How will you travel? And what about money? Alas, I have nothing to give you, nothing to spare.'

'I have money. Govind sent money, sometimes large amounts and I made sure that I saved some each time. Look!' She held up a biscuit tin. 'All my savings and wedding jewellery are in here. This will get us to England, and we must go immediately.'

'And what about old Grandmother?' they asked.

'We will take her too, if she will come. Will you, Grandmother?' Jhoti turned to the silent old woman who squatted with bowed head. 'Will you? There is no future for you here. All our relatives have gone or are dead. We should stick together, come what may.'

Grandmother gave a deep sigh. 'I will do whatever you tell me is right to do,' she replied in a resigned voice, 'though it would have been better if I had died alongside my son, Pavan. What use is an old woman to anyone.'

Jhoti went and put her arms around the little, sad, hunched creature. 'Grandmother,' she said gently, 'we will need your wisdom, and we need you because you are our family. We only have each other now. That is why I want you to come with us.'

'Then so be it,' murmured Grandmother.

Jaspal found a wandering buffalo and harnessed it to a broken old cart with a missing wheel. It had turned over into a ditch and been abandoned. Everyone hunted through the rubble of the village and surrounding fields until at last, they found another wheel. It took a day to attach it and it was as much by improvisation and imagination, as skill and the right tools that they finally succeeded.

Then one morning, a few hours before dawn, Jhoti, Grandmother, Jaspal and Marvinder heaved four bundles on to the back of the cart.

'You must only take what you can carry,' Iqbal Khan warned them.

Jaspal sat on the yoke behind the buffalo, looking very cold and bleary-eyed as he huddled into his blanket. An oil lamp on the verandah threw out a dim glow, just sufficient to enable Jhoti and her family to prepare for the journey. Then Iqbal took the lamp and hung it from the crossbar of the cart so that its dangling light would illumine the road.

'Here is food for you.' Nazakhat's mother came forward with a bundle wrapped in a napkin, and the whole family came out into the shivering darkness to say 'goodbye'.

'May God protect you,' they whispered to each other, for they knew that there was danger for those who were leaving as well as those who were left behind.

Nazakhat came and sat next to Jaspal on the yoke. 'I'll travel with you for a bit,' he said, climbing up and squeezing next to his friend.

Jaspal prodded the buffalo with a stick: the cart groaned and moved forward, and slowly, slowly, as if in a dream, took them away, further and further until they were swallowed up by the darkness. Only the dim, bobbing light of the lamp marked their passage, till it too faded like a morning star as daybreak cracked open the sky.

When the cart finally reached the road and joined the great procession of refugees, Nazakhat suddenly flung his arms around Jaspal. With a great sob he cried, 'Goodbye,' and almost threw himself off the cart, and was gone.

For the first time Jaspal wept.

Jhoti said they had to get a train. The trouble was that many hundreds of people were trying to board trains to get them away from danger. They would have to take their chances. Jhoti told Jaspal that he must take out his topknot and loosen his hair.

'I want you to dress like a girl,' she told him. 'There are Hindus and Muslims out on revenge attacks against those Sikhs who have killed, trying to keep the Punjab out of Pakistan and to retain it as our homeland. You will be too noticeable with your hair up.'

Marvinder gave him a set of tunic and pyjamas, and Grandmother combed and divided his hair into two plaits.

'Oh what a sweet, sweet girl you are,' teased Marvinder, and everyone was glad to have an excuse to laugh.

'How do we get to England?' asked Jaspal. It seemed to him to be an impossible destination.

'We must get a train to Bombay. The sea is at Bombay, and from there we'll get a ship just as your father did,' answered Jhoti as confidently as she could.

They arrived at a small, rural station where they decided to wait. Although the platforms were already packed with hundreds of families, there was a strange silence, broken only by the persistent howling of infants.

Whenever a train came, there would be a huge surge forward. Like a giant wave, men, women and children swamped the carriages, thrusting infants through windows, climbing up on to the roof, or simply hanging on for dear life by the handrails, as the train then moved off again.

For two days, Jhoti and her family failed to get within reach of any train; but with each train that came and went, they shuffled nearer and nearer to the edge of the platform.

Getting to Bombay wouldn't be simple. They would have first to get on a train, then change and get another one. But even the trains weren't safe from attack. They waited with growing anxiety, sometimes straining their eyes down the shimmering track for some sign of the train. They were all huddled perilously close to the edge of the platform now, when yet again, a ripple of anticipation ran through the crowd as a distant whistle pierced the air. They all rose, with a confusion of bundles and babies being lifted and raised on to heads or tucked under arms.

The people swayed and surged as the great, blackened engine wheezed its way into the station. They could see the exhausted, soot-streaked faces of the engine driver and his mate, staring with red eyes at the seething mass of humanity.

Jaspal and Marvinder had to force their bodies backwards to avoid being pushed on to the track and under the wheels. With the cruel selfishness of desperate people, there was lunging and fighting to get some kind of foothold.

Jaspal and Marvinder found themselves swept away and shoved on to the train, but with such ferocity, that they couldn't look back to see what had happened to their mother and grandmother.

'Ma, Ma!' Marvinder began to scream with panic.

Jaspal struggled to a window. The train began to move again, very, very slowly, as if overburdened with the weight of humanity.

'Ma! Oh, Ma! Quick! Get on, get on!' Jaspal was shouting with terror. Now he could see. Grandmother had fallen beneath a forest of trampling feet. Jhoti had stopped to help her. He saw his mother look up and see him. She grabbed a bundle and began to run after the train.

Faster, faster. The train was gathering speed. Jhoti ran with her arm outstretched with the bundle.

'Jaspal!' she was screaming. 'Take, take!'

Jaspal thrust his arm through the bars of the window, as far as it would go, his fingers clawing the air.

Jhoti ran and with one great effort thrust the bundle into her son's fingers.

'Take this and keep going. You must go. I'll follow and find you and . . .' Her words were suddenly annihilated by another piercing shriek of the train's whistle. The platform ended and the train galloped away leaving his mother a helpless figure waving and weeping as her children were carried from her.

Jaspal couldn't drag the bundle through the bars of the window, and had to stay like that for a long time with his arm stretched out clutching the bundle on the other side. Marvinder struggled to his side and managed to push her arm through the bars so that she could help. Crammed in on all sides, they stayed like that hour after hour, till their arms became numb and they wondered how much longer they could hang on.

The precious bundle. Marvinder knew what it contained and that they mustn't lose it. This had all her mother's jewellery and money to get them to England. When the train suddenly stopped in the middle of the night, out in the countryside, she pushed her way ruthlessly to the door, climbing over people's backs and legs and bodies. No one complained. It was each one for himself, they all knew that. The door was open as always, crowded with people clinging on for their lives.

Jaspal's arm stuck out through the window like a small thin branch, still clutching the bundle. Marvinder jumped down beside the track and ran under the window.

'Drop it now, Jaspal!' she called.

Jaspal let go. Marvinder caught it with a sense of relief. Without her mother's savings she knew they would all be destitute.

She gazed up the moonlit track wondering why the train

had stopped like that. Then she saw many swiftly-moving shadows; figures with the glint of steel in hand. A long low moan emanated from the back carriages; a moan which turned into a screaming which seemed to go on and on.

'Jaspal!' Marvinder cried. 'For God's sake, get off the train. Now!'

Jaspal hurled himself bodily over the other passengers and clawed his way to the door. Marvinder stood with arms outstretched.

'Down, down! Jump down!' she begged.

The sounds were beginning to reach the ears of other passengers. Weary heads were turning; arms began gathering in children and possessions, but all with a fatigue and a fatalism too great for panic.

Jaspal jumped and rolled on to the embankment. Marvinder didn't let him get to his feet, but dragged him all the way down a steep incline into the ditch below.

Above their heads, the screaming continued. It was the same kind of terror they had heard in their village. Marvinder clasped her hands over Jaspal's ears and drew his head into her lap to protect him from any more fear, then leaning on his bent body, she closed her eyes and rocked him through the night.

'Hey! Over here! I've found two girls. They seem to be alive!'

Marvinder awoke, immediately cowering with terror as a uniformed man leaned over her.

'Take it easy, child,' the voice softened. 'I won't hurt you.'

Jaspal awoke and huddled into his sister. It was dawn, and pale-as-death egrets stood mirrored in the pink-streaked ditch water. Blood and sunrise mixed as vultures circled overhead. Two more soldiers slithered down the embankment to view the children with amazement.

'How did they survive?' they asked.

'They're to be brought up to the truck,' said one. The

101

soldiers stretched out to pick up each child, but Jaspal and Marvinder clung together, unwilling to be separated even for an instant. Marvinder clutched her mother's precious bundle in one hand, and held on to Jaspal with the other, deciding that it was better to keep up the pretence that he was a girl.

They herded the children up the slope as gently as possible. They saw the bodies laid out in a long, long line all the way down the track.

'Mother? Father?' A soldier indicated the dead with a toss of his head. 'Anyone there who you were with on the train?'

Marvinder shook her head. 'No, we are alone. My mother and grandmother were left behind at Barodpur.'

'Will they be alive? Will we find them again?' asked Jaspal desperately.

The soldier shrugged. 'Well . . .' he hesitated. 'If they weren't on the train, then they escaped the massacre . . . but . . .' he didn't add that there had been many massacres at the stations along the way too.

'You may be lucky. You may find them again. When you get to the camp they will take down your names and details.'

'Camp?' asked Marvinder warily. 'We must go to Bombay. That is where my mother and grandmother are going. That is where we will find them. We don't want to go to any camp.' Her voice rose shrilly.

'You'll just do as you are told, my girl,' said one of the soldiers, roughly.

'Hey, *bhai*! Take it easy on them,' urged another.

The children were lifted into the back of an army truck and after a while found themselves speeding down a road, filled as all the roads of India seemed to be filled, with the long desolate plod of refugees.

ELEVEN

Into the Midnight Hour

'Jaspal, Jaspal!' Marvinder knelt over her sleeping brother and whispered urgently into his ear. 'Wake up, *bhai!*'

They were in a huge tent in which were crammed a hundred or more refugees. Ever since they had arrived at the camp, they had spent hours in queues; one queue to have their details listed: their names, ages, religion, village and hoped-for destination: another queue for injections against disease, another to have their hair inspected for lice, another for food, another for water. They no sooner dispensed with one queue than they had to join another one. At last they were allocated a tent into which they crawled, exhausted.

Marvinder still clutched her mother's bundle. Even the officials hadn't been able to prise it from her. But here, surrounded by strangers she felt vulnerable. Her mind raced over their predicament. When the camp officials asked what her destination was, she had replied, 'England.' Everybody laughed and said, 'Silly girl! She must be deranged by all the horrors she's seen. We'll send the two of them to an orphanage.'

That decided it. Marvinder knew they must run away and try and get to Bombay. If they stayed here much longer, the precious bundle would either be stolen or removed from her by the officials. Then they would never get to England. It would be best to leave quickly while there was still so much confusion as new and distressed refugees arrived by the hundreds each day.

'Jaspal, wake up!' she begged him.

Jaspal opened one reluctant eye. 'I'm tired. Can't we sleep?' he moaned.

'No, little brother. We must run away from here. They are going to put us in an orphanage and once they discover that you are a boy, they will put you into an orphanage for boys and me in one for girls, so we will be separated.'

That woke up Jaspal. He got to his knees, wide-eyed. 'They can't take me away from you. I won't go. Where shall we escape to?'

'We'll get to Bombay, somehow. We'll follow the railway track. Perhaps we'll be lucky, and get a train.'

'Huh! And get killed!' exclaimed Jaspal.

'Then we'll walk. We have no choice. If we don't get to Bombay, we'll never find Mother and Grandmother. We can't go back. I heard the soldiers talking. People were either killed or they fled. If Mother is alive, she will go to Bombay. If we can get to the station, we'll stay there and watch the trains come in.'

'If Mother is alive? What do you mean, if? Do you think our ma is dead?' Jaspal cried with anguish.

'No, no, *bhai*,' Marvinder tried desperately to reassure him. 'We don't know where she is. She's sure to be alive, and if she is she'll be trying to get to Bombay.'

'And what if she isn't on any train?' asked Jaspal. 'What then?'

'Then we'll go to England and find Pa,' said Marvinder.

'You sound like our mother,' murmured Jaspal, and his eyes filled with tears. 'Let's get going then,' he said firmly.

They waited till dead of night, when most people in the tent had finally stopped their wretched tossing and turning. Those who still lay awake, their eyes staring sleeplessly into the darkness, didn't care that two young children gathered together their belongings, and picked their way out over the prone bodies.

They made their way carefully over to the checkpoint, where soldiers guarded the barrier. The soldiers were smoking and playing cards. No one saw them slip under the barrier and walk away into the shadows.

★

'I want to open the bundle and see exactly what we have,' said Marvinder.

Brother and sister had found a place to sleep in an abandoned farmer's hut. They found a distressed buffalo in agony at not being milked, so they milked her and immediately drank the warm, sweet liquid and filled their hungry stomachs.

Feeling stronger, Marvinder untied the knots and spread out the cloth. A mixture of money, jewels, documents and letters lay before them, including the rolled-up photograph of their father.

At the sight of it, Marvinder's memory was triggered. She remembered her mother and father; she remembered the day Jaspal was born; how she thought that Basant, the blind, old midwife, was a witch, and how her father had come and carried her back to the village on his bicycle. She saw his young face looking earnestly into hers; his almond eyes and smooth cheeks; his beard neatly brushed and his hair tied up in a smart sleek turban.

'Must I still stay dressed as a girl?' asked Jaspal. He longed to look like his father.

'Yes, brother,' replied Marvinder. 'Until we know we are safe. One day, your beard will grow and then you'll never be able to pretend you're a girl!' and Marvinder affectionately pinched his cheek.

She took some loose coins and tied them into a knot in her veil, then she put the rest together and re-assembled the bundle.

Jaspal named the buffalo 'Rani' to remind him of his old charge. He rode on her broad shoulders while Marvinder guided them towards the Grand Trunk Road heading east.

Their lives could have ended then and there, and who would have known or cared? Jaspal and Marvinder were two infinitesimal drops in a deluge of humanity fleeing this way and that across the country, looking for a homeland, while politicians in Delhi poured over ancient grubby maps and drew lines which would decide the life and death of millions. Even the gods seemed to be engaged in their own petty power struggles. First there had been drought, building up through the intense heat of March, April, May and June; crops failed and rivers ran dry. Disease, starvation and thirst were everywhere.

When the first drops of rain fell with a heavy thud on the Grand Trunk Road, Jaspal and Marvinder, like everyone else, threw up their arms and lifted their faces to the dark, thunderous sky. They laughed and cheered, leaving their mouths open wide so that they could drink and drink without effort. At least for three months during the monsoon, they wouldn't have to trek to rivers or beg local villagers for the use of their wells.

Water fell from the heavens like a mighty cataract. It hurtled on to their bodies, flattening their clothes, streaming through their hair and most of all, bringing with it some coolness and relief from the burning heat of summer.

But the rain didn't stop; it didn't even pause to take breath. Day after day, week after week and for the next three months, it plunged out of the sky like an undammed river. It ripped into the flimsy shelters of the poor, it churned up the dirt roads and turned them into quagmires, it transformed ditches into lakes and streams into torrents; it turned rivers into oceans, which broke their banks and flooded across the face of the earth, drowning livestock, destroying fields and crops and people's hopes of any harvest.

The gods after all, hadn't taken pity, but sent another plague.

'This must be what it was like when Lord Brahma allowed the River Ganga to come to earth,' people said to each other, remembering the old story. 'But where is Lord Shiva? Why does he not stand underneath and break the fall of water so that we are not all drowned?'

Others said it was Lord Brahma sending another flood to wash away an evil world; but the killing went on, and no amount of monsoon rain could wash away the blood and tears, or wash away the dreadful sorrow. Once, Gandhi had said he wanted to live for one hundred and twenty-five years so that he might see a proud and independent India fulfil all her hopes and dreams; now, as the slaughter went on and not even he could stop it, he no longer wanted to live.

One night in August, those who knew or cared what date it was, those who were close to radios or lived in the cities, all waited to hear the clock strike the midnight hour. For on the last stroke of midnight when a new day began, on 15 August 1947 two new countries would be born; India and Pakistan.

But the creaking wheels never stopped. They didn't hear President Nehru's voice crackling over the radio telling them that they had redeemed their tryst with destiny. No one told them that they had suddenly been woken up into a land of life and freedom, and the gods made no sign that they understood the significance of the hour, for the rain went on raining as if it would never end.

'We have to get on a train,' said Marvinder. 'Bombay is two thousand miles away. It would be impossible for us to walk all the way there.'

'We can't take Rani on a train though, can we?' reflected Jaspal.

'No, we will have to give Rani away. There'll be plenty of people who'll want her. She is so strong, and gives plenty of milk.'

Jaspal put his arms round the buffalo's neck and wept silently. Her great, large, strong body had carried them mile after mile and day after day. She had become part of them. They both loved her; they leaned against her at night to sleep; led her along the roadside verges by day, trying to find her enough grass to nibble. But first the drought had burned away practically everything, and now the rain washed away the soil with whatever vegetation was left. Rani had become thin, though they hardly noticed, because everyone and every creature was thin to the bone. You could count her ribs and her shoulder blades stuck out like hard, grey rocks.

Jaspal and Marvinder had left the Grand Trunk Road which runs east to west, and had now turned south, heading for Bombay.

One day, as they rested, Marvinder heard, through the long continuous roar of rain, the piercing shriek of a train whistle.

Other people raised their heads too. A huge locomotive with carriages stretching down the track as far as the eye could see, had stopped at a signal.

'Now, Jaspal! Now. Come!' She grabbed his arm and pulled him to his feet. Her mother's bundle was already in her hand, for she never let it go from her person for a single moment.

'Run!' She pushed him towards the track.

'Rani! Rani! What about Rani?' screamed Jaspal.

'Rani will be all right. Someone will want her and take care of her,' shouted Marvinder as she forced him onwards. Others had got to their feet now and were running too. Marvinder urged him forwards, pushing him, tugging him, forcing him up the embankment towards the train.

The train stood puffing steam from its belly, snorting and hissing like a massive serpent. The rain slanted down into their eyes as they desperately searched up and down for a foothold and a means of getting on board. They saw an open door. Others did too, and there was a murderous scramble to get to it. People kicked and shoved and thrust each other aside; turbans, sandals and belongings tumbled to the ground.

Marvinder and Jaspal tried to grab the rail, but people from behind hurled them away.

As they lay, sprawled in the grey mud among the hard chippings, they suddenly heard a voice further down the train.

'Hey, you two! Over here. Come on, I'll help you.'

An elderly man, sitting on the step of the train doorway,

108

stretched out his hand to them.

The train was already beginning to move. The huge iron wheels ground and squealed along the wet rails. Marvinder and Jaspal struggled to their feet and stumbled towards him.

'The little one first,' said the man, grabbing Jaspal and hauling him aboard.

Marvinder was running now to keep up with the accelerating train. She could see Jaspal's distraught face in case she too, like their mother, should be left behind. But the man had his arm outstretched again, and she felt a strong grip haul her bodily on to the train.

Thin silver-framed glasses balanced on his pointed nose and hooked on either side of each ear; he was clean-shaven and wore a white cotton cap on his head. His dhoti was filthy with train soot, mud and the effects of days of travel.

His rescue of them seemed to have exhausted him, for when he was sure they were safe, he leaned back with a deep sigh and closed his eyes.

'*Babu*,' said Marvinder shyly. '*Babuji*, we thank you.'

'Hey, hey!' The old man tipped his head as he accepted her thanks, but without opening his eyes. 'It was my duty.'

They were crammed in by hundreds of other passengers, yet as the three of them crouched in the doorway, they seemed to create a little pool of tranquillity. The old man looked so serene, so calm that the children, too, were calmed by him, and leaning up against him, fell peacefully asleep.

Lucknow, Allahabad, Jabalpur, Nagpur . . . they had all just been names he had heard at school, or sprinkled into the conversations of men over their cups of tea round the neem tree; but now, as Jaspal saw the names slide by each with the new flag of India fluttering proudly from a newly-erected flagpole, he read them out loud excitedly to Marvinder. When he thought back to his village, its image shimmered in his mind like the tiniest of green beads.

Day and night the train galloped on across the Indian

plain, though they hardly saw much through the sheet of rain that continued to fall.

If they stopped at a station, Marvinder would give Jaspal a few annas, and he would run to the food sellers and buy purees and tea. They always gave the old man food and drink first, and then got for themselves.

He didn't ask them many questions. People were afraid to talk, to discover too much about each other but Jaspal and Marvinder instinctively trusted him and clung to his side as if he were their grandfather.

'*Babuji*?' Marvinder asked him warily. 'Are you going to Bombay by any chance?'

'Yes, my child, I am. I have a nephew who lives there.'

'*Babuji*,' said Marvinder. 'Is the ocean at Bombay?'

'Yes, my daughter, the ocean is there. You will see it for sure.'

'And big ships, too?'

'Big, big ships. Bigger than you can imagine,' smiled the old man. 'They sail across the world from Australia to Europe and all the way around Africa.'

'Do they sail to England too?' she asked in a small voice.

'Assuredly, they do,' replied the old man.

'*Babuji*,' said Marvinder tentatively. 'When we find our mother, we will be going to England on one of those ships.' She looked anxiously up into his face expecting to see him laugh.

But the old man only said, 'Why would you want to do that? India is the country to live in now. You are independent Indian citizens and your country will need you.'

'Pa is there,' interjected Jaspal. 'Our pa is a scholar and a warrior. He has been fighting in the war. He has medals.'

'We want to go and ask him to come home,' said Marvinder. 'He should have been here to protect us all. Now we have lost our ma and don't know if we shall ever find her.'

'She said she would come to Bombay,' cried Jaspal despairingly. 'We're going to wait till she comes, aren't

110

we, Marvinder? We won't go without her, will we?'

Marvinder stared at the old man, and saw the grim truth in his eyes. Alive or dead, he didn't think they would ever see their mother again. She bowed her head into her veil so that he wouldn't see her grief.

'*Babu*?' Jaspal huddled into the old man's side. 'Is my mother dead?'

The old man put an arm round the child and held him close. 'If your mother is dead to this terrible earth, then she is alive in some more beautiful paradise. She will be looking down on you now, saying, "Don't grieve, my children. Life is just a bubble; it is as nothing, floating for a brief moment like a droplet of water, then extinguished into eternity".' He sighed deeply. 'I know this, because my wife and all my children and grandchildren are dead. There are some things you can do nothing about. You are in God's hands, and in his hands you must trust. So don't struggle against your fate, let destiny guide you.'

The children hardly understood what the old man said, but he spoke with such gentle sadness, that they allowed themselves to be comforted.

Days and nights on the train followed one after another as if the journey would never end. Then one day, without any ceremony, the train slid into a giant station. Jaspal and Marvinder had never seen such a big building, nor so many people, who teemed like ants beneath its great curved echoing roof. It was as though every type of humanity had come among the towering stone pillars and tiled floors searching for the answer to their problems. Beggars trailed up and down with outstretched hand droning their plea; the starving, the crippled, the destitute, the orphaned, the elderly and of course, the refugees. They spilled out on to the platforms, trainload after trainload; shocked, despairing, grief-stricken, broken; they came from villages and towns all over India, but few with any notion of the direction their feet would take once they stepped off the train.

Jaspal read out the words Victoria Terminus engraved in

large letters across the platform wall.

'Where's that?' asked Marvinder, puzzled. 'Is it near Bombay?'

'It is Bombay,' said the old man.

The eager force of the passengers in the compartments thrust all three of them off the train. They clung to each other as though each were a raft being dashed this way and that in a torrent, hanging on for dear life. Briefly, they managed to snatch some space for themselves in a small enclave between two pillars where they paused and took stock.

'Shall we wait here for Ma?' asked Jaspal tremulously.

Marvinder gazed about her, all hope dying. 'Yes,' she managed to say. 'I mean . . . what else can we do?'

The old man looked at the two children through his silver spectacles. He sighed again, and placed a hand on each head.

'Trust in God,' he said, and turned from them, joining again the rapid current of the crowd.

For a few moments, Jaspal and Marvinder watched him as he was taken further and further away from them, then Marvinder called out in a high desperate voice, '*Babuji!*'

It seemed impossible that he could have heard them over the din of yelling stallsellers and porters plying for trade, and loudspeakers blaring out train departures, but as he reached one of the big stone pillars, he turned round.

Jaspal and Marvinder fixed their eyes on him and like two swimmers plunged into the vast flow of people. When they reached him, he didn't speak, but just continued walking through the crowd and out of the station. The children followed him, never letting him go more than three or four feet ahead of them. They left the station complex and walked out into the streets of Bombay.

TWELVE

The Edge of the World

From time to time, the old man paused. Sometimes he appeared disorientated and looked about him as if trying to get his bearings. Other times he seemed fatigued and would stop and put his bundle down and squat for a while. With every pause, the children paused too or squatted too, watching and mirroring his every movement. In a state of shock, they focused their full attention on the old man, unable to look at or comprehend this alien city which seethed around them. They seemed to have stepped into a labyrinth of buildings, streets, and alleyways with towering buildings, tenements, balconies and terraces, stalls, shacks and shanty towns; dwellings made of marble, stone, concrete, brick, cardboard and rags – or nothing but a space on the bare pavement.

When the old man moved on, they did too. They lost all idea of distance and time, they just moved and stopped and moved and stopped. The shadows had lengthened when they finally reached a narrow street, so narrow, that although the sun was still fairly high, the street was in deep shadow.

The old man stood before a blackened building. Its door and window were empty holes. A thin cat with a pathetically-starved litter of kittens trailed into the pokey courtyard beyond. He took a pace or two towards the doorway then hesitated and stepped back. Again he moved forward, went through the doorway sufficiently to glance around what had once been a home, then he withdrew. He stood a long time as if his limbs had turned to stone. A woman came out from a neighbouring building. She yelled at him, her hands wildly gesticulating. He finally nodded and, shifting his bundle on his shoulders, turned away. Jaspal and Marvinder followed too.

The sun was only an hour from setting when the old man crossed a road as wide as a river bordered with palm trees. He passed through a gap in a long low wall and disappeared from view. There were no buildings before them, only a great expanse of sky.

The children hurried across the road to the wall.

The sight sprang them out of their blank, shocked state. Nothing in their wildest dreams had prepared them for this. It heaved before them, vast and shining and never ending, until it joined with the sky like one seamless stretch of silk.

The old man dropped his bundle on to the sand and kicked off his slippers. He removed his waistcoat and cap and folded them into a pile on top of the bundle. Lastly, he took off his spectacles and held them indecisively for a moment before slipping them into his waistcoat pocket. Then in his thin cotton shirt and pyjamas, he began to walk forward towards the edge of the world.

The children tossed their bundles down next to his. Jaspal stripped to his waist, tearing off his hated girl's tunic, pyjamas and veil until he was naked except for his cotton shorts, and rushed over to the old man's side.

'*Babuji*!' Jaspal called, his voice bursting with excitement. '*Babuji*, what is this?'

'This is the sea, my child,' he replied in a low voice.

'Didi, Didi!' shrieked Jaspal with delight. 'We have reached the sea!' He dashed back to his sister and dragged her down towards the shore.

'Are Africa, Australia, and Europe over there on the other side?' he cried.

'Yes, Jaspal, and England is over there too. Our father is over there,' whispered Marvinder.

When the old man reached the edge of the shore, he walked on into the waves deeper and deeper until the sea swirled around his waist billowing his dhoti. Then he

114

began to bathe, cupping the water in his hands and scrubbing one arm, then the other then his face and neck, and finally with a great cry of '*Rām, Rām*' he immersed himself completely.

With cries of ecstasy, Jaspal too plunged into the water, slapping his hand on the surface, making a spray which arched into the sunlight and fell like a shower of diamonds.

For a long time, Marvinder watched them from the shore. Beyond them, the great, burning sun sank lower and lower into the sea. She walked a little way along until she felt alone, then still fully dressed, entered the water. She watched as she walked, cupping the water in her hands and tossing it on to her arms and face. She must try to wash away the grime and filth and pain and sorrow. She walked in deeper where the wind and waves clashed against each other and she could scream as loud as she liked and no one would hear her.

'Ma! Ma! Ma!' At last all her pent-up grief and rage and anguish exploded. She punched her fists, tore at her hair, twisted and lunged and shrieked, then flung herself headlong into the water as if to extinguish her agony.

Night fell. The lights of the city burned behind them as if all the stars had fallen to earth.

The old man spread out his belongings on the beach up near the wall. Jaspal and Marvinder did the same. Then they hunted along the beach among the filth and debris which littered the shore, looking for anything – strips of cardboard, tin, cloth, anything that would serve as some kind of shelter from the monsoon showers which still fell in sudden bursts.

At last, overcome with exhaustion, they rested their heads on their bundles, stretched out their limbs and fell into the deepest sleep they had known in days and weeks of travelling.

Once in the night, a ship's siren penetrated their dreams. Jaspal sat up with a shock. A huge ocean liner, all lit up like a goddess, slid away from the shore. He felt his sister's arms round his shoulders.

'Is it going to England, Didi?' he asked.

'Perhaps,' she murmured.

They watched it sail further and further away until it was a glowing speck on the horizon.

'So, you are a young Sikh warrior!' The old man looked at the boy who stood proudly before him the next morning.

Jaspal had twisted his long hair up into a topknot, fixed it with a comb and tied it into a white handkerchief. The hilt of his dagger glinted from the top of his shorts and the steel bangle shone powerfully on his wrist.

'Do you hate Sikhs?' asked Marvinder, nervously.

'Sikhs killed my family,' replied the old man without emotion.

Marvinder bowed her head.

Silently, Jaspal gathered up their bundles and went to his sister's side. 'What must we do now, Didi?' he asked.

Marvinder didn't speak.

'Shall we go to England and find Pa?'

Marvinder shrugged and began to walk slowly away.

'Children!' The old man called after them. 'Hatred is no use. We have all killed each other; Hindus, Muslims, Sikhs; we are all to blame. The only way God will forgive us, is for us to forgive each other.'

Marvinder turned round. She studied his old, kind, sad, face. He didn't blame her. She came back.

They gathered together beneath the shade of a palm tree and Marvinder opened up her mother's bundle. She showed the old man the money, the jewellery, the letters and documents. He put on his spectacles and examined each thing closely, every now and then giving a grunt. Finally he tied everything back together again and gave a deep sigh.

'Children, your mother was mistaken. Her jewels, though precious to her, are not worth much here in

116

Bombay, and there is not enough money to buy two tickets to Madras, let alone to England.'

The children sat in a stunned silence. Finally, Marvinder whispered, 'What must we do, then?'

'You told me that the English missionaries sent your father to England, yes?'

Marvinder nodded.

'Then let us go along to Trinity Church. There are English missionaries there, and they might tell you what you should do. Come.' The old man got smartly to his feet and chivvied the two children into action, so that they should not be overcome by depression. 'Let's go, let's go!' and he began to walk along at a brisk pace.

Jaspal and Marvinder leapt to their feet and followed.

They stood before a high, wrought-iron gate. Beyond it to the left, a large, redstone building rose two storeys up among the trees. It had verandahs held up by arches and pillars beneath a great thick, pitched roof which seemed to envelop the rest of the building within its cool eaves. Opposite the house, across an open stretch of compound, built in the same red stone, was Trinity Anglican Church.

Marvinder stared at the familar shape; the long solid building with buttresses and arched windows and a tall spire which pierced the blue sky like a needle.

She could hear the sound of an organ playing.

'Listen!' she exclaimed as the familiar tones drifted up the drive. 'I know that hymn!'

A watchman came to the gate and demanded to know their business.

'We wish to speak to the missionaries,' said the old man.

'Which missionaries?' sneered the watchman. 'There are many of them.'

'Who is the chief one?' asked the old man determinedly. 'Come on, now! You cannot treat us as if we were beggars!'

'Let's face it,' retorted the watchman, 'you look like

beggars, all of you – or refugees – which is pretty much the same. Every day, we get people like you hanging around.'

A car honked behind them. The old man and the children leapt aside, and the watchman hastily opened the gate for a large, black Austin car driven by an Englishman in the clothes of an Anglican priest. He glanced at the bedraggled trio and would have driven on, but the old man put a firm hand on the window as if to restrain the car.

'Please, Sahib!' he pleaded.

The cleric looked at the watchman as if to say, 'And who are these?'

'I tried to send them away, Sahib,' whined the watchman. 'They are just refugees looking for handouts.'

'That is not so.' To the children's amazement, the old man spoke in good clear English.

'I am a retired clerk from the court in Ludhiana, in the Punjab. I have been in the service of you English for nearly forty years. My family has been killed in the disturbances. It's true that I came to Bombay in search of a home only to find that my last, living relative has fled and his home burnt down. But that is not why I am here. I come on behalf of these two children. Their mother and their whole family have been killed or are missing. They have no one except their father, who was sent by the missionaries to England. They have come to Bombay in the belief that they can go to England to find him. Their mother gave them all the money she had. I have ascertained that it is not sufficient, so I have brought them here to see what advice you could give them. Please, sir.' The old man finished by letting go of the car and bowing his head over his hands as he pressed them together in a *namaste*.

'I see,' said the Englishman. He frowned. 'Well, you'd better go down to the house. Tell my secretary, the *chaprassi*, I gave you permission, and wait on the verandah till I come.' He gave the watchman a curt nod, and drove on leaving them enveloped in a great cloud of dust.

'You'd better go through then,' said the watchman with a sulky wave of his hand.

The old man and the children set off down the drive through the settling dust. They could hear the watchman muttering behind them as he shut the gate with noisy indignation.

Marvinder gazed at the house looming before them and murmured, 'It's just like the maharajah's palace back home, where Edith and I used to play.'

Jaspal turned and looked sharply at his sister. He saw that her eyes were full of tears, so he turned away without saying anything.

They found a shady spot and squatted down near the large sweep of front steps, which led up into the grand house. It could be a long wait. There was a smell of freshly-watered plants, which still dripped all along the length of the verandah, and in the distance, they could hear the clip, clip, clip of a gardener trimming the grass verges.

The organ music, which had stopped for a while, suddenly started again. Marvinder got to her feet and began to wander slowly towards the flagstoned area around the base of the church.

The large, wooden door was partly ajar, revealing only an impenetrable darkness. She stepped inside and was instantly overwhelmed by the coolness of stone floors beneath her bare feet, high beams, stained glass, the faint smell of incense and candle wax and the notes of the organ so rich, that her whole body resonated like a sounding board. She walked a little way down the aisle and softly sang the words of the hymn which was being played.

When the music stopped, a voice from nowhere called out in Hindi, 'Where did you learn that hymn, girl?'

Marvinder looked around with alarm and was about to flee the church, when she suddenly saw a small white woman leaning over the pulpit with an armful of flowers. Her old face peered down with kindly curiosity.

'You're not one of us, are you? I haven't seen you before.'

119

Marvinder shook her head and backed away in the direction of the door.

'So, tell me, where did you learn this hymn? Who taught you?'

'I learnt it at home, Memsahib,' Marvinder finally answered her. 'At All Souls' near my village. I learnt it from the Chadwicks.'

'Wait there,' commanded the old woman. She disappeared from the rail and reappeared a moment later below the pulpit.

She looked closely at Marvinder, and said, 'Which Chadwicks? Which village?'

'Deri, Memsahib. Mr and Mrs Chadwick . . . Edith . . . Ralph . . . Grace.' Marvinder's voice trailed away.

'Good heavens!' the old woman exclaimed.

'What's going on down there? Oh, hello, Mrs Russell. It's you!'

A young man's face peered over the guard rail in the organ loft.

'Amazing thing, Tom! I've just caught this child wandering in the church singing the words of "Lead Kindly Light", and when I asked her where she had learned it, she said in Deri, from the Chadwicks.'

'The Chadwicks? Dora and Harold Chadwick?' echoed the young man.

'Well . . . it seems so. Come down and ask her yourself.'

There was a clatter of feet and a tall almost gangly young man, with light brown hair which he kept tossing from his eyes, Tom Fletcher, descended from the organ loft.

'Tell me, girl,' he asked, looking at her with kind brown eyes. 'Which village and province are you from?'

'Deri, in the Punjab province, Sahib,' repeated Marvinder.

'Well, it's certainly where Harold Chadwick was running that rural school!' cried Tom. 'Good gracious!

What an extraordinary coincidence! And you knew the Chadwicks, you say?' he questioned further.

Marvinder fingered the locket around her neck. She hadn't taken it off or looked at it since the day of Edith's departure. She took it off now and pressed open the locket to reveal Edith's soft, round, English face.

'Edith!' declared Marvinder with pride.

The old woman and Tom held the locket in turn and looked at each other with amazement.

'That's certainly Edith Chadwick. The family stayed here for a few days before boarding their ship for England.'

'What an extraordinary coincidence!' repeated Tom.

Suddenly, a thin, black shadow fell across the doorway.

'Didi! Come! *Babuji* says come. The sahib is going to talk to us now.'

Marvinder looked at them apologetically. 'I must go,' she said. She held out her hand for the locket, and when it was returned to her, ran out to join her brother.

At tea-time, sitting on the verandah of the Church House, were the vicar of Trinity, Andrew Petworth, his wife, the round English lady of the flowers, Mrs Russell, Tom Fletcher, the organist and a young curate and his wife, Giles and Renée Morton-Smythe.

Before them was a table spread with a stiff, dazzling white table-cloth, and laid out with scones, butter, jam and a large pot of tea which the vicar's wife poured into dainty, blue and white cups.

'What have you decided to do about those two children, Andrew?' she asked. 'We are all intrigued to know.'

The vicar looked at his companions and shrugged with indecision. 'What can I do? It would be best if their father came back here. They had a few letters from him with an address. So I've taken it down and written to him, telling him that his children are looking for him. I've also written to the Chadwicks. I know they'd be interested to know that these children have turned up here, and I've suggested

121

that Harold goes and looks up his old pupil, this Govind Singh, and finds out what the situation is.'

'What will the children do in the meantime?' asked Tom.

'I didn't enquire,' said the vicar. 'I told them to come back in three weeks, by which time I may have heard something.'

'Do they have somewhere to live?' asked Mrs Petworth.

'I don't know and I didn't ask,' replied the vicar.

'Quite right,' agreed the curate. 'There are so many destitutes around at the moment, that those who can cope must be encouraged to continue doing so.'

'Except that we don't know if they're coping,' retorted Tom.

'They didn't look as if they were starving,' murmured the vicar, 'and I dare say the old man is caring for them. He seemed an educated and respectable old fellow.'

'Well, as you know, I'm returning to England on the next ship, so I can follow up any communications you've made. I'll get Harold Chadwick's address from you, Vicar, before I go.'

'Thanks, old man,' muttered the vicar. 'That's very decent of you.'

Jaspal, Marvinder and the old man went back to the shore, to the spot beneath the palm tree which they regarded as 'home' for the time being.

The only money they had between them was the money Jhoti had saved. Each day now, they spread it out on the cloth and counted it realising with dismay that the amount grew less and less.

'We must earn money,' said Marvinder.

After a moment's pause, while each wondered how money could be earned, the old man got to his feet and said:

'My children, I am an old man. It will be hard for me to find any work. It is time I left you. You are both young and sure to find something which will enable you to survive until the missionaries hear from your father. You still have some money of your mother's, and you should not allow me to drain any more of it away from you.'

He gathered up his bundle and adjusted his spectacles.

As one, Jaspal and Marvinder leapt to their feet and grasped his arms. '*Babuji*! Don't go! Don't leave us! Please!' Marvinder pleaded.

'Please stay, *Babuji*!' cried Jaspal. 'You are no drain on us. You eat less than I do. Anyway, I will go and look for work and we will make enough money to feed us all.'

The old man hesitated. Then he dropped his bundle and said, 'Very well! I will stay while I can be of some help to you. I will sit here on the shore and guard your belongings while you seek work and we will see how each day goes. My advice is that you, Jaspal, go to the docks over there.' He pointed over to where the shore curved round and the skyline was a zigzag of cranes and funnels and buildings. 'There are many workshops for servicing the ships. Look for jobs there.'

Then he turned to Marvinder. 'You, my child, you should go into the city and seek work, running errands or cleaning, or helping in a household.'

They knew it wouldn't be easy. Bombay was brimming with people all seeking work and food to survive.

Every day, the routine was the same. The old man settled himself beneath the palm tree with their belongings and a pile of newspapers which he had scavenged the evening before. Then with his spectacles perched on his nose, he would lean up against the trunk and read, while Jaspal and Marvinder set off in different directions to look for work.

What the old man had said was true. When Jaspal reached the docks he found a world of sea and ships. There were builders' yards and packing sheds and repair workshops and warehouses and trades of every kind teeming up and down the dockland area. He slunk in and out of them like a stray dog, sometimes getting a kick and told to 'clear off', and other times being thrown a scrap of food such as left-over *paratha*, which he would stuff into his mouth with the greed of the very hungry. But it was the odd jobs he was given, earning him a few piase, which brought him back over and over again.

Each day, he managed to take back a handful of annas for running little errands such as fetching tea or delivering notes.

Marvinder was less lucky. She often came back empty-handed and in tears. No one seemed to need household help, or office cleaning. There were always women older than her who were stronger and more experienced and she was easily pushed aside.

One day, they returned at dusk to find the old man jubilantly cooking a real feast of dahl, chapattis and some radish leaves. He had got himself a job without even moving from his spot. A passerby noticed him reading the paper and asked if he could write a letter for him as he was illiterate. For one rupee, the old man had written the letter. Perhaps more such work would come his way.

But after that success, there was nothing for a few days, and their money dwindled down and down. Once again they were gripped with anxiety as it seemed they might soon be reduced to begging.

Marvinder went down to the edge of the ocean and waded into the water. Somehow, the soft lapping of the waves soothed the anguish and fear inside her. She gazed in despair at the vast sea stretching before her. It all looked impossible. How could they ever get across to England? As she felt the pull and tug of the sea around her, she wished that its strength could just carry them away and drop them on to those far-distant, English shores.

'Didi?' Jaspal had come anxiously after her. He looked up at her face. 'Are you afraid, Didi?' he asked.

She put her arm round him and didn't speak immediately because her throat was so choked with anxiety. Then she whispered, 'I suppose we'll manage somehow. Each day is a new day. You or I might get a job. Another person might ask *Babuji* to write a letter.'

The next day, Jaspal went back to the docks with added urgency. He was bolder now, and wouldn't be driven away so easily. He hung around the workshops; just being there, ready to fetch or carry as the need arose, no matter how trivial the task.

Then unexpectedly, having decided to investigate another area of the docks, he came across the huge carpentry workshops. He had never thought he would see anything like this in all his wildest imaginings. Great heaps of wood, some raw, straight from the forests, others cut into all shapes and sizes, were piled up from vast expanses of dusty floor, up and up into ceilings as high as palaces. There was wood for the ships' decks, for stairways, balustrades, panelling, bunks, furniture; there was wood for the thousand and one things that a huge ocean-going liner needs – a liner like a floating city.

Jaspal raced round excitedly, examining everything. If only Uncle Pavan could have seen this. Even he would have been amazed.

At first the carpenters tried to shoo him away. They even picked him up and tossed him out and told him never to come back. But Jaspal came back. Carpentry was something he knew and he was determined to show that he could be of use.

He came back again and again until they got tired of kicking him out and just ignored him. Gradually, he wheedled his way into doing petty tasks. If a tool was out of reach, he noticed and handed it to the carpenter; if the floor needed sweeping, he swept it and collected up any loose nails to store systematically in a tin. He showed that he could sandpaper; use a plane and a lathe; that he understood their trade and could do a little job properly, and soon they found that he had his uses after all.

In this way, Jaspal, Marvinder and the old man managed to survive, using what little money they earned to buy food in the bazaar; scavenging along the shore for firewood after each high tide; sleeping up against the sea wall each night and waiting for the end of the month when they could go back to the missionaries and find out if there was any news from England.

One day, the carpenters told Jaspal that they were going on board a big ocean liner to carry out repairs in the cabins and on the decks. They said the ship would be sailing for England in a week and that there was a lot of work to be done; they could do with a small chap like him to sort out the tools and be on hand to pick out the right nails and screws and nuts and bolts.

'Will you do this job?' they asked him.

'I will, I will!' shouted Jaspal joyfully, and as he set off running back to Marvinder and the old man, he kept shouting at the top of his voice. 'I will, I will! I will work on a ship which is going to England.' His voice rose and mingled with the screeching gulls and the hooting of ships' sirens. He ran all the way through the docks, leaping chains and ropes as thick as tree trunks; he dodged crates and packing cases, carts and lorries, and cranes which edged their way back and forth between the liners and the warehouses, with vast bundles of cargo swinging from the ends of giant hooks, which they dumped into the deep holds of the ship.

He had got to recognise some of their names now. There were the ships going to East Africa, like *S.S. Mombassa, S.S. Amara* and *S.S. Karanja*; there were the Italian ships with names like *S.S. Napoli* or *S.S. Primavera* and best of all for Jaspal, there were the English ships belonging to P&O such as *S.S. Strathnaver, Strathaird* and *Strathmore*. They were ships as tall as mountains, with long rows upon rows of round windows like staring eyes, rising up and up and up, four or five storeys high; and huge smoking funnels as fat as giant cigars.

Jaspal ran, with darkness falling all around him. He left the docks with their blazing lights and pulsating energy, and rushed out into the stumbling fearful night of the poor, the homeless and the hopeless.

Marvinder and the old man were dim shadows on the shore. They crouched over their flickering fire of driftwood cooking a supper of thin soup and vegetables in a tin can which they used for a saucepan.

When Jaspal raced up and stood before them with his shadow stretching behind him down the shore, he looked like a giant.

'Tomorrow, I'm going to work on a ship,' he told Marvinder and the old man, his eyes burning with excitement. 'It is a ship which will be going to England in a week.'

THIRTEEN

The Ship

'Did those two children and the old man ever come back again?' enquired the Reverend Andrew Petworth of the gatekeeper.

The *chowkidar* looked vague as if trying to recall.

'Oh,' he said finally, as if a cloud had cleared in his mind. 'You mean the two Sikh children with the old Hindu.'

'Yes, that's right. I asked them to come back in a month, but it is now October and they haven't returned.'

Reverend Petworth frowned. He felt guilty because he knew he shouldn't have let them go so easily without discovering where they were living. Now he had received a letter from Harold Chadwick asking that every possible assistance be given to the children until he could find out more about Govind Singh's circumstances.

'No, Sahib, those two children never came back. Nor the old man,' said the *chowkidar* firmly. He was lying. Several times last month, one or other of the children or the old man had appeared at his gate asking to see the vicar. Each time, he had put them off. He told them the vicar was busy or away or didn't have the time, or had left instructions not to be disturbed. As to the arrival of any letter from England; 'No,' he said, 'there was no letter from England.'

The children accepted the gatekeeper's word. They had no choice. They couldn't know that the gatekeeper was ignorant and illiterate and in any case, had a grudge against Sikhs. They believed him when he sneered, 'What makes you think there would be any letter from England for you?'

After that, they never called again.

'I wonder where they are!' The vicar sighed with irritation. He didn't like feeling guilty. Now he would have to write back to Harold Chadwick and explain somehow that they had lost contact with the children and had no idea of their whereabouts. It would not look good.

'Typical of Chadwick to involve himself with natives like this. He should never have meddled in the first place; sending some peasant to England! It's ridiculous!' thought Andrew Petworth angrily to himself, trying to shift the blame elsewhere.

'Jaspal?' Marvinder hissed his name quietly into the pitch blackness of the luggage hold. Down in the belly of the liner, she could hardly hear anything above the roar of the ship's engines. There was no escaping it; no blocking of the ears could ease the battering on her ear drums or prevent it from invading every cavity of her brain.

She had curled up her body and tucked her head into her knees, like a foetus in the womb of some huge, fire-eating monster, while its relentless heartbeat assaulted the very fibre of her being, rolling over her, flattening her into a black, hot void.

A sudden rush of fresh air had made her raise her head with desperate expectation. 'Jaspal?'

Yes, he had come. A vivid square of silver light briefly revealed his thin figure clinging to the top of the ladder, then he pulled down the trap door and vanished. There was no calling out to him against the continuous throb of the engines. She would have to wait while he blindly clawed his way through the trunks, boxes, crates and suitcases to find her.

Then his strong, bony fingers scrabbled over her face. They hugged each other. He thrust a bottle into her hands. It contained water. She drank and drank then pushed it back to him. After a pause he returned it to her, and she drank again until the bottle was drained.

He put his mouth to her ear and shouted, 'It will soon be

night up there. We can go out in about an hour.'

Marvinder nodded thankfully, and leaning against her brother drifted into a half-sleeping state of dream and memory.

'*Babuji*, we want to go on this ship to England. We don't want to wait any longer.' She could hear her voice tentatively informing the old man about their plan to hide on board the *Strathmore* which was leaving in a few days.

'*Babuji!*' cried Jaspal, bursting with excitement. 'Every day, I have been going on to this ship with the carpenters. We have been doing jobs all over the ship; on the decks, in the cabins, the kitchens and store rooms and down in the cargo holds. Sometimes I had time on my hands and I used it to explore. I went along passages, you can't imagine how many corridors and passages; once I got so lost, I thought I would never find my way back to the carpenters; I went up and down ladders and stairs: grand staircases and corridors all richly carpeted fit for a king, and bare wooden stairways for the poorer classes, but they took you from one deck up to the next and up to the next so that I went from the very bottom of the ship right up to the top where the captain's cabin is. I explored every single space I could. I went in and out of cupboards and closet rooms; into ballrooms and eating-places; I found where they keep the water tanks and the food; great holds filled with ice to keep meat and fish fresh; cool pantries for butter and bread, fruit and vegetables. This ship is like a palace. I found dozens of hiding places, *Babuji*. We could all hide and go secretly to England.' Jaspal quivered with enthusiasm.

'Shall we go, *Babuji*?' asked Marvinder cautiously.

The old man closed his eyes and thought for a very long time, then he opened them, and said:

'Sometimes you have to ask yourself, "what is the best that can happen and what is the worst?" Your mother must have asked herself these questions over and over again when the disturbances broke out. She must have thought, if I stay, will worse things happen than if I go?

130

Sometimes, the risks are so great that no matter which path you take you put yourself into the hands of destiny. It is for you to think about it, and for you to make the decision.'

Then the old man took off his sandals and spectacles, arranged his bundle beneath his head and went into a deep sleep.

Long into the night, Jaspal whispered in his sister's ear, telling her how easy it would be to hide away; how they wouldn't starve; that the main thing would be to remain hidden until they were way out to sea so that they couldn't be sent back.

Marvinder wasn't sure. Once again, thoughts of her mother, Jhoti, overwhelmed her. What if she weren't dead? What if she were looking for them? She could be in Bombay right now, searching the streets and alleyways. When Marvinder's efforts to get employment had come to nothing, except for a few errands, she had taken to combing the crowded thoroughfares day by day, often going back to the station, picking her way over sleeping bodies, peering into faces, sometimes racing up to a woman, who from the back looked just like Jhoti, only to find herself confronting a stranger. She checked all the trains which came in from the north, and asked any likely person, whether they had seen or heard of Jhoti, but the word 'no' rang like a death knell.

Now she was faced with a choice; go to England and find her father, or stay behind and look for her mother, who, if she wasn't dead, could be anywhere, lost for years or forever among the millions of displaced and dispossessed.

They talked until they were exhausted, and fell asleep just before the first streaks of dawn broke through the night sky.

Marvinder woke first to discover the old man gone.

There wasn't much of him to go; just his bundle, his sandals and spectacles and a bundle of rolled-up newspapers. But Marvinder realised his loss with a wrenching cry which woke Jaspal.

'*Babuji*!'

Jaspal raced frantically up and down the shore, yelling and yelling, '*Babuji*! Hey, *Babuji*!' But the old man had been gone some hours now, and there was no sign of him.

When Jaspal returned, Marvinder held out a scrap of paper with words written on it. She had found it tucked into Jhoti's bundle.

'Can you remember how to read, Jaspal?' she asked.

The words were simple, and Jaspal read them haltingly but correctly.

'It is time for us to part. I said "goodbye" while you slept. I will say prayers for you every day. May God go with you always.'

Jaspal wept. 'Why could he not have come with us?' he cried.

'Nay, *bhai*! What could an old man do in a cold foreign country?' murmured Marvinder with a heavy heart.

'We would have looked after him, wouldn't we, Didi?'

'Yes, we would. But he has done what he thought best, now we must do the same.'

Down in the pulsating darkness, Jaspal and Marvinder groped and writhed like babies waiting to be born. They hadn't been out on deck since the ship released its moorings four days ago. So they hadn't seen the ladders and gangplanks hauled on board, the huge thick ropes tossed away, the long grinding roll of the anchor being sucked up into its body; nor had they watched the slow slide of the great ocean liner pulling away from the docks, gradually reducing everything to a miniature so that the giant cranes and buildings looked like toys and the waving people nothing more than a swarm of ants. They only heard a bellowing cry, as the ship's siren blasted its farewell and they felt the huge shudder as the engines started up.

At first they stayed put, terrified to go out in case they were discovered. They survived on the provisions they

132

had brought with them in their bundles. But after a couple of days, hunger spurred them into action. Jaspal began to sneak out at night. He found his way to the galley where the kitchens were and stuffed a bundle with as much food as he could carry. As he got bolder and more confident, he persuaded Marvinder to come too. She hardly needed urging. The impenetrable blackness of the hold and the stifling heat had become more than she could bear.

They became creatures of the night, scurrying down long, dim passageways, searching for food and drink and creeping up on deck to suck in the fresh, salty air and gaze at the incredible vast canopy of stars. They became children again; they played among the deck chairs and the lifeboats; they chased round the decks, up and down the iron stairways; they slid down the wooden banisters and rolled about on the plush sofas and easy chairs in the lounges.

At first, the sight of another person, especially the dark uniform and gold epaulettes of a ship's officer, filled them with dread and they dived for cover. But gradually, they got bolder. They turned their existence into a long game of hide and seek exploring the ship from one end to the other by night, and returning to their embryonic existence down in the ship's hold by day.

The sea was as smooth as glass when, ten days on, they had crossed the Indian Ocean, up into the Red Sea and like a thin thread passed through the Suez Canal, that man-made slit in the desert which linked them to the Mediterranean and Europe. Then one day, down in the dark hold, they became aware of a tipping and a pitching, a sliding and a bumping, as the ship entered the rough waters of the Bay of Biscay off the coast of Gibraltar. All around them, the ropes which held huge crates, containers, trunks and suitcases creaked and groaned as their strength was tested and tried to the limit.

The children clung to each other in horror as they were flung this way and that, blinded, confused, and terrified that they would be crushed to death and plunged into oblivion. At last, retching and vomiting, they struggled up the ladder on to the deck and, even though it was broad daylight, flopped exhausted like dying fish, gasping frantically for oxygen.

A high child's voice exclaimed, 'Mummy, look! Indian children!' Heads turned curiously.

'What are they doing here?' complained a woman petulantly. 'This is the first-class area. They have no business being here, that's for sure. Keep away from them, Edward.'

'I've never seen them before,' said another. 'I'll call the steward to sort them out. They must have wandered in from the third class. Someone returning home with their servants, I suppose.'

A steward came and looked distastefully at the filthy, bedraggled children. Hardly liking to get his fingers dirty, he plucked them by their collars and pulled them to their feet. Jaspal immediately vomited again, and Marvinder fell weakly to her knees, her strength drained away by dehydration.

The steward summoned a more junior deck-hand. 'For God's sake, get these beggars out of here and into the third-class area. Then find someone there to sort them out. See who they belong to.'

Half-carrying and half-dragging them, the deck-hand roughly removed them.

Tom Fletcher, the one-time organist of Trinity Church, Bombay, was playing a reluctant game of quoits on deck with the dreadful Morton-Smythes, Giles and Renée, who were also on their way back to England. As the deck-hand edged past, almost unnoticed with the two children, it was the locket dangling free round Marvinder's neck which caught his attention. He looked again more closely, and then gave an astounded cry.

'Good gracious! Stop!' He raced up to the steward. 'Who are these children?' he demanded.

'Haven't a dicky-bird,' replied the deck-hand. 'We've just found the bleeders up in the first-class area, stinking to

134

high heaven,' he informed him. 'I'm taking them along to the third–class area to get them out of the way, then I'll get hold of the purser.'

'I think I know them!' exclaimed Tom.

'You do?' The deck–hand stopped and held the children up higher for inspection. 'Taking your servants and their families back home, are you, sir?' he asked.

'Of course not,' retorted Tom impatiently, 'but I think they're the children we met in Bombay who have a father in England.'

Tom addressed Marvinder in Hindi. 'Hey, *lurkee*! You girl! Didn't I meet you in Trinity in Bombay? Aren't you the one who knew the Chadwicks from Deri?'

Marvinder nodded her head feebly. She wanted to look up at his face and tell him, 'Yes, yes, you're right! That's me! We have met, and we did know the Chadwicks,' but she was too weak, and all she could do was nod her head, while tears rolled down her cheeks.

'Please don't let them throw us over into the sea,' begged Jaspal.

'I'm going to come along with you to find the purser,' said Tom, determinedly. 'These children are obviously in trouble.'

'Oh, Tom! Won't you finish the game first?' wailed Renée.

'Sorry, you two! You'll have to get along without me. See you at supper!' cried Tom, walking away.

'So,' said the purser. 'You think you know these two girls, do you?' he asked stiffly, as though somehow Tom was responsible for their presence.

Tom Fletcher sat in a leatherbound chair in the purser's office.

'They're not both girls,' corrected Tom coldly. 'The younger one's a boy. Sikh. They don't cut their hair.'

'Humm!' The purser snorted. 'Makes no difference. Looks to me like they're stowaways. That's a serious offence.'

135

'They're both in a frightful state. May I make a suggestion?' asked Tom reasonably. 'Give them a good bath, put them in a couple of bunks and let them sleep. Tomorrow we'll get a lot more out of them and we can decide how to proceed. Doesn't that make sense? I mean, look at them! They're practically dead on their feet. I'd like to take responsibility for them until this is sorted out.'

'Very well.' The purser sighed heavily. 'I'll make arrangements for them. Perhaps you can report to me here tomorrow morning after breakfast – say at ten o'clock?'

'Fine. I'll be there!' Tom patted each child reassuringly. 'Don't worry about anything,' he told them gently. 'Everything will get straightened out tomorrow.'

FOURTEEN
Changing

'Wake up! Wake up!' Marvinder could hear voices in her head, urging her to open her eyes. But she couldn't wake up from the deepest sleep she had ever known in her life.

They had been put in the charge of the matron on the ship. She was a large, round, practical woman, with big red hands and strong arms, but everything about her was stiff and shiny. She was stiff as the stiff black skirt which fell almost to her ankles beneath a dazzling white apron, starched into solidity. Her light brown hair was almost hidden from view beneath a white nun-like headdress which imprisoned her head in its grip. And she shone with cleanliness from her taut, unsmiling, rosy-cheeked face, down to her glittering patent leather lace-up shoes.

She had picked them up bodily and put them into a large white iron bath of deep warm water and scrubbed them both so hard, Marvinder thought she would have no skin left. Neither she nor Jaspal protested as their bodies were fiercely soaped, and their scalps were rubbed and hair tugged; and they hardly squirmed when the matron's toughened fingers probed round their faces: their eyes and ears and round their necks and backs and tummies and all the way down to their feet; or when she lifted each foot up into the air and scrubbed every toe as if she thought a dung heap existed between each one.

They were scooped out into huge, white fleecy towels and rubbed again very, very hard.

'That's better,' muttered the matron without smiling, and put them both into prickly, overwashed pyjamas which were too big for them, then herded them down a corridor to a two-berthed cabin in the staff quarters. It was

137

a room no bigger than a cupboard with just two bunks, one on top of the other and a round porthole barely above sea-level.

'You stay there, now, you varmints!' said the matron as she plonked Jaspal into the upper bunk and Marvinder into the lower, then after tucking them in tightly, without even a stroke of the head or a 'sleep well', she marched out and locked the door behind her.

Each child lay silently for a few moments, absorbing the alien sensation of the stiff whiteness of starched sheets and pillows. Tightly swaddled as they were, the rocking and tipping of the ship no longer felt frightening, but as comforting as the arms of their mother when she used to rock them across her lap.

'Marvi?' Jaspal forced his arms out of the bedclothes and rolled over on his stomach. He reached a hand down over the side of his bunk to touch his sister.

Their fingers clasped and held for several minutes, until they slid apart as each child fell into a deep sleep.

'Wake up, wake up!' In her dream, Marvinder was lying on her mattress in Uncle Pavan's workshop. She knew that if she didn't wake up, Jaspal would be late for work, and if he was late for work, he would be late for school. So she was trying desperately to open her eyes, but couldn't.

'Wake up, wake up!' Voices came again. This time, they seemed to be the high-pitched voices of Grace and Ralph. They were calling to her over and over again.

'Wake up, Marvi! Wake up and save us!'

Marvinder struggled and tried, but it was as if her eyes were glued down. She couldn't open them, yet she felt the tears somehow breaking through from under her lashes and trickling down her cheeks.

'It's all my fault,' she was crying. 'I shouldn't have left you.'

She felt hands shaking her. 'Didi! Wake up, Didi!' and at last she opened her eyes.

Jaspal knelt by her pillow. 'You were dreaming,' he said apologetically. 'Were you having a nightmare, Didi?'

Marvinder pulled the sheet over her head and didn't speak.

Jaspal went over to the one round porthole and looked out. He couldn't tell if they were below the surface of the sea or above it; everything was so watery and misty.

Suddenly, there was the sound of the door being unlocked. The matron strode in grim-faced, followed by Tom Fletcher who immediately greeted them warmly, by lifting Jaspal into one arm and hugging Marvinder with the other.

'And how are you two scamps?' he asked jovially.

'Really, Mr Fletcher, I don't think you should give the children the impression that they have done anything to be proud of. They should be treated with the utmost severity, in my view. Stowing away is an extremely serious offence,' lectured the matron primly.

'Of course it is, Matron, under normal circumstances,' agreed Tom in a conciliatory voice. 'But I don't think you realise what these children may have suffered. We have not yet heard the full story. I think until then, compassion would not come amiss, wouldn't you say?'

She snorted, and plonked down a pile of garments on a table.

'I sent their clothes to the laundry, though perhaps they should have been burnt. They were quite disgusting. Here is the girl's bundle, it seems to contain some personal possessions. I have managed to rustle up an outfit each, which will have to do them till we arrive in England. Now, if you don't mind leaving, I will see the children get dressed and then I will allow them into your care for the day.'

'Right, Matron!' agreed Tom, goodhumouredly, and explained the plan to Jaspal and Marvinder.

'I'll see you upstairs in a jiffy!' he ended, pointing above his head.

The children nodded their understanding as he left. They looked with dismay at the clothes the matron now began to unfold. She handed Jaspal some underwear, a pair of grey, flannel short trousers, a plain white, long-sleeved shirt, a tie and a grey pullover. Marvinder was given underwear, as well as a navy blue pinafore dress, a blue-checked blouse and a red cardigan and they were given some pairs of shoes to try on.

When they were dressed, brother and sister looked at each other in amazement and then felt suddenly awkward and shy.

'You look just like a Britisher!' exclaimed Marvinder.

Jaspal looked upset. He ran his fingers over the thick material and pulled at his collar which felt too tight beneath the unfamiliar tie.

'Where is my *kara* and *kanga*?' he asked.

'Memsahib!' Marvinder tried to explain to the matron. 'Where is my brother's knife and comb? He must always carry them. He is a Sikh.'

'All your possessions are with the purser. You will get them when you leave,' said the matron, curtly. 'Now let me do your hair.'

She got out a hair brush and started first on Marvinder. She brushed so hard, digging the bristles into her scalp and forcing her way through the tangles, that Marvinder's eyes watered with pain though she dared not cry out. Then the matron divided her hair into two plaits and tied the ends with red ribbons.

When it was Jaspal's turn, she looked disapproving because it was as long as his sister's.

'He should cut it as English boys do,' she said bluntly.

Jaspal sprang from her grasp at the word cut. 'No cut!' he shouted. 'Not cut hair. I Sikh.'

The matron reached out with her large hand and pulled him back within reach.

'Don't you shout at me, young man, I'm not going to cut your hair. I know you are a Sikh. Your long hair may be all right in India, but in England, the boys will call you a sissy. They won't understand. However, no doubt you'll find out for yourself,' she said, and started roughly brushing Jaspal's hair.

140

'Me,' said Marvinder quietly stepping forward and taking the brush from the matron. 'Please. I do brother's hair.'

Matron relinquished the brush without comment and set about making up the bunk beds, but noting out of the corner of her eye how Marvinder deftly brushed and twisted her brother's hair into a neat topknot.

When they were ready, the children followed the matron to an upper deck where Tom Fletcher was waiting for them.

They moved awkwardly in the unfamiliar shoes, and in their English clothes their arms and legs were revealed as nothing but skin and bone. Jaspal's elastic garters were not tight enough to hold up his long grey woollen socks, which were already beginning to wrinkle as they slipped down his thin legs.

'What you need is some good food,' murmured Tom, looking them over. 'I wonder if you can hold down some porridge. I don't think the sea's quite so rough today.'

He led them into the dining room.

Jaspal and Marvinder looked in awe and some dread. They had often crept into the dining room at night, when it was a vast empty space of tables and chairs and white tablecloths, but they had never seen it like this – crowded with people – mostly English people, sitting before steaming bowls of porridge, or thick white plates of eggs and sausages and bacon and tomatoes, and great pots of tea; while whisking to and fro in and out of the kitchens, came waiters, dressed in black and white, carrying large silver trays containing orders of food.

They hung back timidly. A number of heads turned and stared at them; comments were exchanged. Tom had to clasp each child by the hand and almost drag them in. Weaving in and out of the tables, sometimes acknowledging acquaintances with a nod of the head, he led them to a table at the far end which he shared with the Morton-Smythes.

'Good morning, Renée! Good morning, Giles!' Tom

141

cried cheerily, pulling out a chair each for the children.

The Morton-Smythes looked up with bemused expressions. Jaspal and Marvinder stood as if frozen.

'Sit down, sit down,' Tom urged them.

'Shouldn't think they've ever sat on chairs at a table before,' observed Renée sharply. 'Do you think it's fair of you to bring them up here with everybody? They'd be much happier squatting in some corner with a bowl, eating with their fingers, wouldn't they?'

'They've got to learn, Renée dear,' said Giles, 'and the sooner the better, I should think.'

Marvinder felt a sudden surge of pride. She understood what they were saying. Well, they hadn't been part of the Chadwick household for nothing. Did this English woman think they were some kind of jungle animals who didn't know the difference between a chair and a table, let alone a knife and a fork? It's true they weren't used to using such tools, that they did indeed use to squat in the kitchen and eat with their fingers, and what was wrong with that? That was their custom, and at least they knew that their fingers were clean because they always made sure their hands were washed before and after eating. How could they tell that the knives and forks were clean? But she saw a flicker of doubt pass over Tom's face, and he hesitated as if wondering, after all, about the wisdom of having brought them both into the dining room; so Marvinder took Jaspal's arm and signalled to him to sit down, then just as she used to with Ralph and Grace, she heaved the chair closer to the table and tucked the napkin under his chin.

Tom laughed with relief, and when Marvinder then sat down, too, he helped her to push her chair in.

'That's the ticket!' he exclaimed. 'Now what are we going to order, eh?' he asked cheerfully sitting down himself.

A waiter came over with notebook at the ready. He eyed-up the two newcomers.

'Am I to assume that there will now be five people at

142

this table until the end of the voyage?' he queried.

'Yes, you are,' answered Tom. 'Now let's see. We'd like porridge, eggs, toast – plenty of it, mind – two glasses of milk and a large pot of tea, thank you.'

'Well, what is to become of them, Tom? That's what I'd like to know,' demanded Renée.

'I hope you haven't landed yourself with being responsible for them once we arrive,' frowned Giles.

'I'm hoping I can get in touch with Harold Chadwick pretty quickly, and through him, track down the children's father,' Tom told them. 'I've looked through some of the letters and documents, which the girl had rolled up in a bundle, and there seems to be an address in Whitechapel. I think, now that I have taken responsibility for them on the ship, I'll have to see it through until I can hand them over to a proper guardian. I will take them with me to my aunt's house in Hampstead, and sort things out from there.'

'Well, I hope you know what you are doing,' asserted Giles, grimly. 'My advice to you would be to leave the whole thing in the hands of the ship's authorities. They would probably send the children back to India, and in my view that is the best thing that could happen.'

'Yes, I agree,' nodded Renée. 'I mean, even if you do find their father, how can he look after them? Look at them, Tom, they're like fish out of water. They'll be miserable in England.'

Their eyes regarded the two children, who were engrossed with what they were eating.

When the porridge had been put before them, Jaspal had begun to dip his fingers in, but Marvinder kicked him under the table and hissed, 'No, *bhai*, like this. Watch me!' and she picked up the big, silver spoon and ladled some into her mouth. Jaspal copied.

'Yes, but now they've come this far, it's ridiculous for them not to find their father if it's at all possible. He should be encouraged to take responsibility for them,' argued Tom. 'If these children are simply returned to India, they

143

may lose the chance to make contact with their only living relative, and after all, what do they go back to? An orphanage? It's a grim prospect.'

'I wouldn't say that,' shrugged Renée. 'I've seen some of these orphanages. At least the children get fed and educated, and they might even make Christians of them.'

'Hmm,' grunted Tom, who didn't give the impression that he saw that as a major priority.

'I sometimes wonder, Tom, what possessed you to leave a prosperous job in the City and become a missionary,' commented Giles. 'I often feel that as far as you're concerned heathens and Christians are all the same.'

'Yes, well I think they are in so far as they are all human,' answered Tom firmly. Then rapidly changing the subject, he turned his attention to Jaspal and Marvinder.

'How are you doing?' he asked.

Marvinder sat curled up in a corner of the deck, her face pressed to the bars of the railing overlooking the sea. She could sit there hour after hour, never tiring of watching the waves heaving and slanting, forming endless patterns and rhythms as the great ship ploughed a path across its surface. Sometimes the water looked very green, other times black; always powerful.

Tom had told them that they would soon see England, and for the last two days, they had had an escort of gulls, who kept pace with the ship with fixed outstretched wings and legs tucked back. Only their inquisitive heads, with glittering eye and curved beak, twisted round from time to time.

Jaspal had taken toast out with him after breakfast and shrieked with delight when he tossed a piece into the wind and it was snatched up in mid-air by a watchful gull.

But it had become colder. Much, much colder. The brilliant hot blue of the Indian Ocean and the Mediterranean had given way day by day to a sea and sky which became increasingly grey, and merged together in a shivery mist of rain and spray. Tom called them in.

144

'Look at you! Your lips are purple. Sorry, you two, this is England now, not India. You're not used to this weather yet and I don't want you arriving with colds. You'll have to make do with looking out of the lounge windows.'

So they went inside. But inside or out, watching the sea or observing the way people amused themselves in the lounge by reading, smoking or playing cards, Jaspal and Marvinder only had one image in their minds, which was superimposed on everything else; it was the image of their father, Govind. It was the one and only image they had, the photograph of him with his degree. Govind the scholar, Govind the soldier and warrior, Govind, whose photograph had been garlanded alongside that of Guru Nanak, so that they were sure of his saintliness and goodness.

Neither of them spoke about him to each other, but they both knew he was out there somewhere on that thin grey strip of land, which was now slowly materialising through the mist. England crept closer and closer, and with it a hope. Each began to imagine what their father was like. They imagined and rehearsed in their minds how they would meet him; how his face would light up with joy and love at the sight of his children. How he would clasp them in his arms. Then they would tell him all about the misfortunes which had struck the family; how they had lost their mother; and they knew that his face would furrow with concern and grief, and he would be determined to go back to India and look for her. They were sure this is how it would be.

'Look! England!' People were now crowding up to the lounge windows to peer out at the misty horizon. Others, more hardy and indifferent to the cold, wet wind, huddled on deck waiting with fixed eye as the gap between ship and shore narrowed.

'We might as well relax,' said Tom. 'They're not going to let us off until last. No tickets, no passports! It's a wonder they don't throw you into prison!' he exclaimed.

The children looked alarmed. But he grinned, and said,

'Don't worry. You'd be more trouble in prison, I dare say. So they'll hand you over to me until we can find your father.'

Now they could see a long, extended shoreline trimmed with white, where the waves broke on to the beach; and as the eye travelled along, they saw buildings. At first they were low and small like houses and cottages, but gradually they built up until, as the ship eased closer and closer to the land, the sky was a jungle of tall cranes and funnels and masts, and long high buildings with sloping roofs and forests of chimneys.

The decks became crowded with excited passengers, their eyes greedy for home and scouring the approaching docks for signs of friends or relatives.

Small craft streaked up and down near the harbour as the giant vessel slowly eased itself in with cheerful blasts of its siren. Jaspal could hardly be restrained. He jumped up and down and ran from one window to another pointing out so many things of interest he made himself dizzy.

Huge gangways were raised at different points along the length of the ship, and people were streaming down on to the dockside. The sailors and crew lined the decks and waved goodbye.

The purser asked Tom Fletcher and the children to come to his office. There was another man there wearing a different uniform. He looked very solemn, and not too pleased at the situation.

Suddenly, Marvinder was full of fear. Had they changed their minds? Would they not be allowed to leave the ship? Would they be taken all the way back to India? She looked up desperately into Tom Fletcher's face. His face was serious, too, but when he caught her eye, he smiled reassuringly and squeezed her hand.

'It's all right. They want the ship's doctor to check you both over, and I've just got to fill in these forms which put me in charge of you for the time being. I have to promise that you are not smugglers bringing in gold, tobacco or wine!' he said with a laugh.

146

'Well, sir,' said the other man. 'I must ask you to check in every week at your local police station with the children until their father has been located and their status regularised.'

Then everyone was shaking hands and wishing everyone 'good day'. Matron came in with two coats. She looked a little less stiff as she helped Jaspal and Marvinder to put them on.

'It's cold out there,' she said, and her voice sounded kind.

'Yes,' sighed Tom. 'I'm going to miss India.'

'Goodbye, goodbye!'

The children stood at the top of the gangway. It stretched before them long and slightly swaying. If they looked over the side, they could see the black water heaving below. Marvinder shivered. It was cold. She could feel her skin tingling, and a bitter wind nipped at her cheeks. Hanging tightly on to the rail, Jaspal and Marvinder walked down and down until they reached the bottom, where a sailor was waiting with a helping hand to jump them on to the quay.

Tom followed closely behind, and as the children hesitated with the strangeness of being on solid ground, he came between them and took a hand each.

'Welcome to England.'

FIFTEEN

A House on the Heath

They found it hard to walk when they finally stepped on to dry land. Everything still heaved and swayed, as it had done on board ship for nearly three weeks, and they staggered unevenly.

A train was waiting, right there at the dockside. Its huge, black engine gleamed beneath a hissing mist of steam, smoke and drizzle. Tom called it the boat train, and said it would take them to London.

The children stared blankly. They hardly said a word and looked as if they were sleepwalking, their faces were so empty of expression. They felt desperately uncomfortable in the strange clothes they were wearing and the unfamiliar shoes on their feet. The cold had got into their bones, and they couldn't believe the grey, hard world they seemed to find themselves in.

Even getting on the train didn't shake them out of the shock of their arrival. They sat back uneasily in the soft, upholstered seats and stared without understanding.

It was raining hard now, and darkness was falling. There was nothing to be seen through the windows, except their own reflections gazing back like strangers and the constant lines of trembling raindrops, which juddered their way down the glass, as the train pounded and whistled its way to London.

They occupied a carriage, with four people on one side and four opposite. Once the seats were full, nobody tried to barge in, or climb on the luggage racks or hang on to the outside door rail, as they would have done in India. They sat as if they were in church, talking in whispers, if they talked at all, and lowering their heads on to their chests as though they were praying.

They must have dozed, and time must have passed for, suddenly, they were aware of movement, sounds, raised voices; the squealing of brakes and the huge hiss of steam being expelled. They had arrived at a great station. Porters, in navy jackets and peaked caps, were milling around on a vast platform and voices were shouting out up and down the train, 'Porter! Porter!'

Tom lowered the carriage window and stuck his head out.

'Hey! Porter! Over here, please!'

Jaspal read out the name of the station incredulously, 'Victoria Station! But that's in Bombay!'

'Yes,' said Tom, 'they named the station in Bombay after Victoria Station in London.'

London. Marvinder came awake and looked around her urgently, as if expecting to see her father. Was he there, or there, she looked this way and that, her eyes searching the crowds of people, who flowed on and off the trains, which waited side by side in the huge platforms. But the crowds were alien. Among all the white-faced men and women hurrying away in their hats and coats, with umbrellas, briefcases and handbags, she saw not one brown face; not one turbaned head; not one man who could conceivably have been her father. But still she looked, even as she was urged to follow the porter, who wheeled Tom's trunk towards a taxi rank. Jaspal whispered, 'Fancy a sahib being a porter!' A white man carrying luggage for another was something they would never have seen in India; still her eyes roamed feverishly around.

'Are we going to my father?' asked Marvinder. 'We have his address, don't we?'

She had to ask the question, even though she already knew the answer. She just wanted to be sure that Tom wouldn't forget why they had come.

'Soon, Marvinder. Soon. It is dark and late. We'll rest first for a day or two and then see if he's at the address you have. But his letter was written a very long time ago and

149

he may have moved. It may take time to find him. Do you understand?'

Marvinder sighed, and nodded slightly. She didn't really understand. If only she had the power, nothing would have come second to searching him out. Nothing. She would have gone straight there, even if she had had to walk, even if she had arrived in the middle of the night.

'I'm taking you to my Aunt Gertie,' Tom went on. 'I know you'll like her. She's a brick.'

The porter left them standing in a queue, all waiting patiently, as one by one, the large, black, square-looking vehicles edged forward to pick up their passengers and whisk them away.

'This is the famous London taxi cab,' said Tom, as their turn came. The cab driver jumped out, and he and Tom lifted the huge trunk on to the luggage space where it was strapped firm. Then he and the children climbed into the spacious interior of the cab and settled back in the comfortable leathery seats.

A dividing window was pushed back. 'Where to, guv?' asked the taxi man cheerfully.

'Hampstead,' replied Tom. '26 Heath Drive.'

Jaspal and Marvinder had already taken in too much. Their brains could absorb no more. They looked blankly out of the window, not sharing their thoughts; seeing, but not comprehending the crowded London pavements; the trams, buses and cars moving up and down the yellow lamplit streets; the tall buildings and the great advertisement hoardings. In the chill autumn night, people hurried through a murky haze; they seemed self-absorbed, depressed even, as with heads down they moved rapidly, yet surreptitiously, as if fleeing from some hidden danger.

But gradually the busyness of the streets gave way to quiet almost deserted suburbs; row upon row of houses and streets led into more houses and streets until at last, the taxi cab pulled up in front of a tall house with windows that went up three storeys. On the other side of the road was nothing, except the black night.

150

'Have we left London?' whispered Jaspal fearfully.

'We're in Hampstead,' said Tom, 'and tomorrow you can go on the Heath, which is just across the road.'

Tom and the taxi man heaved the trunk up to a large front door, and as Tom was paying him off, the door opened wide with welcome, and a tall, grey-haired, but not too elderly woman flung her arms open with affection.

'Tom, Tom! My DEAR boy!' she exclaimed in a rich, fruity voice. 'Oh how WONDERFUL to see you.'

Tom turned and greeted her with equal enthusiasm. 'Aunty!' He slapped a noisy kiss on each cheek and hugged her till her feet left the ground.

Jaspal and Marvinder hung back outside the circle of light thrown out by the open door. They were consumed with shyness and embarrassment, as they had never seen anyone being greeted like that before. Why did Tom not kneel down respectfully and kiss her feet and bow his head over hands pressed humbly together?

'Good heavens! Tom! Who on EARTH are these? Are these children with YOU?' she cried, gazing at them with wonderment.

'Are they INDIAN? Or what?' she demanded. 'Oh, TOM! You didn't bring them with you, did you? Not ANOTHER of your stray creatures which you are always rescuing? Stray cats, dogs, broken-winged birds, that's bad enough, but really, Tom, CHILDREN, isn't that going a bit far?'

'Hang on a minute, Aunt!' Tom broke into her theatrical tirade. He ran to the children and putting his hands on their shoulders from behind, ushered them into the porch.

'We should go inside, don't you think? We're letting all the heat out of the house.'

Marvinder wondered what heat could escape from the house, as it seemed to be even colder inside than out.

'Forgive me, Aunt, for springing this on you,' said Tom, as his aunt closed the front door and turned to confront the three of them. 'You see, they came into my charge on board ship, and I couldn't let you know ahead of my arrival to ask if I might bring them with me to stay here for two or three days.'

'Came into your charge ON BOARD SHIP? Stay here for two or three DAYS? Oh, for goodness sake. Before we hear any more of this, take off your coats and come into the living room. Annie? Come here, girl!' She called out.

They heard a door open at the end of a long corridor which led into the hall, and a girl appeared, dressed in maid's clothes. She was a thin, very white-faced girl of about fifteen years old, with yellow, lank hair smoothed back under a white head piece, and a white apron over a black skirt. She looked at them with large, brown, mournful eyes.

'Yes, miss?' She bobbed respectfully at the sight of Tom.

'We have two unexpected extra guests. Two CHILDREN. You'll need to make up the beds in the nursery and put in hot water bottles, it's pretty cold up there as it hasn't been used for years.'

'Yes, miss,' said Annie, and left quickly to do her bidding.

'Oh, and tell Cook! We have two more for supper!' Aunt called out after her.

The living room was warm in parts. They felt the chill of the room on their backs, though a cheery coal fire blazed in the grate and warmed their fronts. But the room looked welcoming and comfortable, and reminded Marvinder of the Chadwicks' living room in India. There were a lot of things from India; Indian carpets were strewn on the floor, intricately carved mahogany coffee tables stood in strategic positions; there were two large cushioned sofas piled with Indian cushions, and two or three easy armchairs, all somehow turned towards the focal point which was the fireplace, where there were lots of Indian brass animals decorating the hearth.

But there were also live creatures, which somehow gave

the whole room a sense of animation. There were cats everywhere, it seemed to the children. Two spread out like hearth rugs in front of the fire; one sprawled among the cushions on one of the sofas, and another two walked over to Aunt Gertrude and entwined themselves around her legs demanding attention.

Marvinder counted five cats, then immediately saw another sitting in the window.

Tom said, 'Aunt Gertrude, let me introduce you properly, before I tell you their extraordinary story. This is Jaspal Singh and his sister Marvinder. Jaspal; Marvinder; let me introduce you to my Aunt Gertrude.'

Aunt Gertrude looked each child in the eye and they looked at her. She was a tall woman. In fact, Marvinder didn't think she had ever seen a woman as tall as Aunt Gertrude. She was slim, too, gaunt even; her shoulder blades stuck out through her hand-knitted cardigan, and her legs were thin beneath her faded tartan skirt. Her long grey hair was swirled back into a bun and held together with combs and hairpins. They could have felt afraid of her, but her face was kind; her large pale blue eyes studied them intently and she held out her right hand, first to Jaspal and then to Marvinder. Each child awkwardly took her hand, as they had observed was the custom among the English, and shook it limply.

'HOW do you DO?' asked Aunt Gertrude with great seriousness.

Marvinder suddenly wanted to cry. She lowered her head and let her hand drop.

What were they supposed to say? At this moment, with all her energy drained, she could have found it in herself to wish with all her heart that they had never left Bombay; never set out to search for her father. They could have stayed on the beach forever; living under the palm tree, with the old man to guard their belongings each day when they went off to look for work. 'Old man, old man!' her heart cried out. 'I wish we were with you now.'

153

'Aunt, you know, I think these children should be excused. They are exhausted and utterly disorientated. May I see them to bed?'

'My DEAR boy, I'll see to it, of course I will. Leave it to ME. Help yourself to a gin and tonic, dear boy, or a whisky, you know where the drinks cabinet is. I'll get Cook to give the children some milk and toast and we'll get them to bed in a jiffy. Come, COME, my dears,' she cooed, and herded them away.

The gas fire, skilfully inserted into the Victorian grate in the dining room, burned a bright steady orange, and cast a cosy glow across the large, oak dining table and the remnants of supper, which Tom and his aunt had just eaten.

Tom had turned his chair slightly, so that he could feel the warmth on his back, and stretched out his long legs while he sipped the ruby-red port his aunt had thoughtfully provided for him.

'I think you're looking marginally better than when you arrived, dear boy,' remarked his aunt gently as she studied his thin, fine-boned features. The light from the fire made his skin look almost transparent, and it was with concern that she enquired, 'Are you completely free of that wretched tuberculosis? No recurrence?'

'Completely free, Aunt, though they still wouldn't have me in the army. Glad I was in India throughout the war, though. Saved me having to answer quite so often, why an apparently able-bodied chap like me wasn't out there fighting Mr Hitler.'

'Your parents must be longing to see you, Tom. You can't let these children hold you up. What are you going to do? I'm not quite sure why YOU got involved. I didn't know you liked children specially.'

'It's not that, Aunt. I think it was such a strange coincidence. I mean, I didn't set out to get involved, but I was there – not just once, but twice.'

Tom took the bottle of port and filled up his glass again,

before pushing himself a little closer to the gas fire, so that the crystal of his glass burst into a thousand miniscule reflections.

'You see, I was at the Mission House in Bombay when the Chadwick family arrived from the Punjab. They were staying for two or three days at the Mission House, prior to embarking for England. We'd heard in advance about the tragedy.'

'What tragedy, dear?' Aunt Gertie leaned forward with interest.

'The Chadwicks had six-year-old twins, a girl and a boy called Grace and Ralph, I think. They were drowned in a boating accident in a lake near their home. Terrible thing to happen, and of course, everyone was very cut up about it. Apparently, the mother, Dora Chadwick, became quite deranged; had delusions that her children were still alive, and that she would be returning to them in due course.

'In those few days, I got to know Harold Chadwick a little. Fact is, he was tremendously cut up too, but had bottled it all up. I suppose he felt he had to be the one to keep things going, especially for the sake of their older daughter, Edith.'

'Oh, so there was another child too?' murmured Aunt Gertrude. 'Well, I suppose that's something to be grateful for.'

'Strange girl,' said Tom. 'Something cold about her. Didn't seem close to either of her parents. I know Chadwick was worried about her. Said she hadn't yet begun to grieve.' Tom shrugged.

'Anyway, after supper, when Mrs Chadwick retired to her room, he would join me in the living room for port, and later, for a short evening walk around the compound before turning in. He was a very nice sort of chap, I must say. He talked a little about the tragedy; added a few details, such as the fact that there had been two Indian children around at the time. A boy, Jaspal, who had been with the twins when the boat went down and who had been brought ashore, apparently drowned.'

155

'Jaspal?' interrupted Aunt Gertrude. 'You mean the boy upstairs?'

'Precisely; and the girl, Marvinder, who had been playing with Edith at the time, and was responsible for saving her brother's life. In fact, these two children were the children of Chadwick's protégé, the young Punjabi he had sponsored since childhood – Govind Singh. This man is here in England, as far as we know. Well, you can imagine my interest, when months later, in the midst of all the chaos of partition, I am back in Bombay, this time just before coming to England, when these two childlren turn up out of the blue. I mean, the coincidence was astounding!'

'How on earth did you know who they were? How did you make the link?' asked Aunt Gertrude.

'That was the easiest part. First of all, both children spoke English. Fairly basic, but nonetheless, unusual, since they looked like a couple of beggars; secondly, I met the girl wandering round the church, actually singing the hymn that I had been practising, and then on questioning her, she told us she had learnt it all from the Chadwicks, and to prove her connection with them, showed us the locket she wore round her neck. It was a locket Edith had given her. It had Edith's photograph in it.'

'How extraordinary!' exclaimed Aunt Gertrude.

'Yes, extraordinary indeed, but the real miracle was that they should have turned up at all! They survived massacre, death, disease, famine; they crossed two thousand miles of India and arrived at the Mission House in Bombay at the same time as me. Somewhere, in the confusion they were separated from their mother. Even if she's not dead, it's still very unlikely that they'll see her again. Thousands of people have lost their families. So they went looking for their father who seems to be their only living relative. Of course, they had no idea what they were undertaking when they decided to stow away on a ship to England, but my goodness, you have to marvel at their single-mindedness and ingenuity. Well, since fate ordained that I

156

should be there at that exact moment in Bombay when they arrived; and again on board ship when they were caught stowing away, I have a duty to see to it that I find their father. Don't I?'

'Didi?' Jaspal's voice came from across the bedroom and sounded so far away in the darkness.

'Yes, *bhai*?'

'Will we see our father tomorrow?'

'I don't know. Perhaps. If the sahib will take us.'

'Didi?'

'Yes, *bhai*?'

'I don't like England. It's cold. I'd like to go back to India.'

'We'll go back, *bhai*. Our father will take us back.'

'What if he doesn't? What then?'

'Oh, Jaspal, no more questions. Sleep, brother, sleep.'

'Didi?'

'Yes, *bhai*?'

'Please, come over here. I don't like you being so far away.' They had never slept out of each other's reach since the day he was born.

Marvinder got out of bed. She shivered. The room was big and high and there seemed no escape from the cold except to get into bed. In the darkness, she could hardly see Jaspal. She hauled the eiderdown around her, and shuffled tentatively towards her brother, whom she could hear snuffling softly.

'Hey, *bhai*,' murmured Marvinder in a concerned voice. 'You're not getting ill, are you?'

'No,' sniffed Jaspal, but his voice sounded thick.

Marvinder reached his bed. 'There, little brother!' She patted him. 'Sleep now.'

She stroked his head until he was asleep, and then, too sleepy herself to cross the room again, she untucked the blankets at the foot of the bed and crawled inside.

SIXTEEN

An Address in Whitechapel

In a chill, grey November light, Annie shuffled out of her attic bedroom. She had dressed quickly because it was so cold, stiffly fumbling with the rubber buttons of her under-bodice, and pulling on a pair of black woollen stockings under her shabby, second-hand worsted dress. She was grateful for the stockings, which her mother had knitted her from random sections of black wool, resourcefully unravelled from old cardigans. Annie knew lots of girls who couldn't afford stockings, and who went around bare-legged, even on the coldest of days. Not that she would ever go out of the house wearing such stockings – to the pictures or dancing – oh no, then she, too, would go bare-legged, and maybe get her best friend to draw a black line up the backs of her legs. They all did that so that it looked like the seam of a stocking. But her mother's stockings were just the thing for working in a large cold draughty house like this one, and she didn't care what she looked like, so long as she was warm.

Her hair was still rumpled from sleeping, but she pushed it back under a grubby headscarf. She wouldn't smarten herself up until after she had gone downstairs to the kitchen and performed the first jobs of the day. She would empty all the grates of ash and cinders and reset the kindling and coal for fresh fires in the kitchen boiler and the living room. Then she must dust and brush the downstairs rooms, put a damp mop over the stone floor in the kitchen and scrub the front doorstep.

A cat stretched itself out of sleep to greet her from its basket on the landing, and another appeared from out of the shadows to follow Annie down the long staircase.

'Cor blimey!'

Annie halted halfway down and gripped the bannister with fright. Two figures stood by the front door. Their eyes shone in the gloom as they watched her descending. When she realised who it was, she laughed with relief.

'You didn't 'alf give me the fright of me life standing there like a couple of ghosts. What are you two doing up so early, eh?'

Jaspal and Marvinder were standing there in the darkness of an unlit hall. They were fully dressed but in their own Indian clothes; Jaspal was in a tunic, pyjamas and jacket and his hair was neatly combed up under a white handkerchief on top of his head. Marvinder, too, was wearing her tunic and pyjamas and her veil was drawn round her shoulders for extra warmth. They stood like sentinels at the front door. They didn't speak. Didn't move.

Annie shrugged, 'Suit yourself!' and carried on down the passage to the kitchen, breaking into a cheerful whistle as she went.

They continued standing there, as for the next hour, Annie traipsed to and fro carrying out the ash and hauling in the full coal scuttle. Her face and hands got smeared with grey and black, and her skin was shiny with perspiration. Every time she passed the children, she gave them a grin. They didn't respond but stood like prisoners waiting for a gaoler to come and release them. Even the cats, all awake now and prowling up and down the passageways and occasionally wrapping themselves round the children's legs – even they were ignored.

'Lord love us!' exclaimed Cook when she arrived. 'What the dickens are them two doing there?'

'Don't ask me,' sniffed Annie. 'Can't get a word out of 'em. They won't move. Turned into flippin' statues, they 'ave, so I just left 'em.'

Cook went into the hall to see if she could persuade them to come into the kitchen. She pointed to her open mouth, and said, 'Food. Food,' very loudly.

But the children didn't respond. They had a fixed purpose and nothing was going to divert them from it.

When Annie had done all the dirty jobs, she went outside the kitchen door where there was a tap fixed to the wall and a bar of green, carbolic soap in a saucer on the ground. She rolled her sleeves up to her elbows and opened the top buttons of her dress, then turning on the tap, she began to wash in the cold silvery water which spurted out and fell into the gutter beneath. She washed her face and neck and ears and her arms up to her elbows. Her skin turned raw red with the cold, and as quickly as possible when she had finished, she grabbed the small, hard towel to scrub herself dry.

'Right, Miss Hawkes's morning tea is ready for you to take up,' Cook told her, 'and one for Mr Fletcher.' She handed Annie a tray.

'You'd better tell 'er about the kiddies,' Cook added.

By this time, it was half-past seven. Annie climbed the stairs carrying the tray. Jaspal and Marvinder watched her, but still said nothing. They didn't seem to have moved an inch in the past two hours.

Annie knocked and entered Miss Hawkes's bedroom. As usual, she placed the tray on a bedside table, then went to the windows to draw the curtains. Before the war, she would have lit the fire in the bedroom grate, so that Miss Hawkes would have had some warmth by which to dress. But even though the war had been over for two years, everything was so strictly rationed and in such short supply that these luxuries had not yet been restored. So Gertrude Hawkes sat upright in bed, and pulled a warm woolly shawl round her shoulders and cuddled two of her cats who had followed Annie in and leapt on the bed. The tea steamed in the bitter air.

'Er . . . Madam,' said Annie, 'them two children what came with Mr Fletcher. You know, them blackies . . . well . . . they're standing by the front door, miss.'

'What DO you mean, standing by the front door?'

'What I said, Miss. They're standing by the front door, like as if they want to be let out. Should I let them out, miss?'

'Good GRACIOUS, no! Don't do that. Ask Cook to take them into the kitchen then, and give them some tea,' said Aunt Gertrude in an exasperated voice.

'They won't move, Miss. I mean . . . well . . . we've tried, Cook and me, to get them to come into the kitchen, but they just go on standing there by the front door. They must be frozen, Miss, it's right cold in the hall. Didn't 'alf give me a turn when I come down this morning first thing.'

'WHAT?' exclaimed Aunt Gertrude. 'Do you mean to say they've been standing there since before SIX o'clock?'

'Yes, Miss. They 'aven't moved a muscle, Miss. They're really queer, if you ask me.'

'Thank you, Annie. I'd better see Mr Fletcher about it. Have you given him his tea yet?'

'No, Miss. I was going to do that now.'

'Leave it, girl. I'LL give it to him,' said Gertrude, pushing back her eiderdown and tossing her cats on to the floor. 'Oh and Annie, don't call, them BLACKIES. They're INDIAN.'

'Yes, Miss,' answered Annie meekly.

'Tom?' Gertrude knocked on his bedroom door. 'I have a cup of TEA for you. Can I come in?'

'Enter, my dear Aunt!' Tom's voice called from within.

She had brushed her hair, which hung loose down her back in long grey wisps, and she looked quite regal, enveloped in her warm, checked dressing gown, which was held together by a silken cord round her waist.

'I've brought you your TEA, dear boy,' she said. Tom had shuffled up into a sitting position and was attempting to smooth back his hair.

He shivered when he saw her.

'I can see your breath in the air,' Tom grumbled. 'It must be cold. I think I'll just crawl back under the blankets!'

'TOM, dear,' said Gertrude, coming straight to the point as she handed him a cup of tea. 'I think you'd better get up quickly and see to those CHILDREN of yours. They've been standing by the front door for the last TWO hours, according to Annie, and they won't MOVE.'

'Good heavens!' Tom swung out of bed and grasped his dressing gown and hurried downstairs after his aunt. Jaspal and Marvinder were standing just as Annie had described.

'Hey! Hey! You two. What are you up to?' Tom took Marvinder's hands in his. They were like ice.

'Come!' He tried to lead her gently towards the kitchen. 'Come, Jaspal, come and get warm and have some breakfast. You'll freeze to death out here.'

But Jaspal hung back and Marvinder pulled herself rigidly away. She put her hands behind her and said with low intensity, 'Find father. Now. You have address. Whitechapel. Let's go now.'

Tom was about to reason with them; explain once again the difficulties, and the disappointment they might expect; that it would be better to be cautious and systematic, but when he saw the desperation in their faces he relented.

'Yes,' he said, 'you're right. We shouldn't waste a single second. We must go to Whitechapel immediately. I need to get dressed first though. Can you wait a little longer till I'm ready?'

Marvinder nodded. Relief flooding across her face. 'You get dressed, then we go to Whitechapel?' she cried.

'Yes, and while I dress, you and Jaspal go with Aunt Gertrude to the kitchen and have some breakfast. You're going to need a full stomach to get you through the morning. So eat plenty.'

Marvinder took her brother's hand and, almost skipping, followed Aunt Gertrude into the kitchen.

When Tom re-emerged, it was with Jhoti's bundle,

which Marvinder had guarded with her life, until it had been handed over to the purser on the ship for safe keeping.

They unfolded the grubby cloth on the kitchen table and exposed the tin box and the rolled-up photograph of Govind Singh.

Jaspal was thrilled to see it again. He carefully smoothed it out and pointed to his father holding his degree. 'Father!' he exclaimed proudly. 'Scholar. Warrior. Me too. I am scholar. I can read, and I am a warrior,' he declared drawing out his knife – the Sikh *kara*.

'Lawks!' exclaimed Cook. 'What's a kid like him doing with one o' them? Bloomin' lethal, that is.'

'It's his religion, Cook,' Tom told her. 'Don't be alarmed. All male Sikhs carry one, just as all of them grow their hair, wear a steel bracelet and a comb and wear special shorts.'

'It don't seem right to me,' muttered Cook.

'Ah! Here's a letter from Whitechapel,' said Tom, who had been fumbling through the various documents and letters. 'It's dated August 1943. He's home for some leave. Two weeks, then back to Italy, he says. He's sent your mother some money. Of course, that wasn't the last letter he sent. There were a couple of others – one, a few days after the war ended, dated 1945, when he talks about staying on because of a war wound, but there's no address. So we'll have to start in Whitechapel and see where it gets us. 58 Whitechapel Lane. Right, I think I know where that is. But remember it is five years since he wrote from there.'

'Take my car if you like, Tom, I've got some spare petrol coupons,' offered Aunt Gertrude.

'Oh thanks, Aunt! That would be grand,' said Tom. 'Come on then, you two. Let's get going.'

From time to time, as they drove down from Hampstead into the heart of London, Tom snatched glances at the faces of the two children in his rear mirror. They didn't relax and lean back in their seats, but sat forward watching the road ahead as though they were afraid that without their concentration, they wouldn't get to their destination.

As they got closer into the centre, there were more and more signs of the battering London had received from the bombs. There were crumbling walls, damaged offices, battered and peeling paintwork – and those were the buildings that were standing; but then there were the empty spaces where buildings had once stood, but which had been utterly destroyed by bombs. Sometimes, just part of a building remained, as though it had been dissected by a surgeon to reveal its insides, so that curious eyes could see what kind of wallpaper had been chosen, and what kind of fireplaces, and whether or not there was a good-sized bathroom.

Where man had failed to reclaim the site, nature took over. Weeds, grasses, saplings, all grew profusely, camouflaging the rubble, pits and scars; and reaching up through several floors were the imprints of what had once been staircases, leading up and up to the roofless attics.

They reached Whitechapel Lane. This was the East End of London, the poorest side; thin little children, who were too young for school, played hopscotch on the pavements; shabbily-dressed women clustered, gossiping round doorways, some with large, black battered prams, which were used for everything from accommodating infants, to ferrying the shopping, firewood or coal.

They stopped and stared as Tom drove the car slowly down the broad cobbled street. It wasn't often they saw a private car round these parts. He was studying the numbering. The house would be on the evens side; number 14 . . . 16 . . . 18 . . . he drove on slowly, but as he did, his heart sank. He could see ahead of him great gaps in the row of houses. The top of the street had taken a terrible battering and there were several gaping holes on both sides of the road where houses had been bombed to bits.

He stopped the car outside Number 28.

'Stay here, while I go and ask if we are in the right street,' said Tom. Somehow, he couldn't bring himself to reach Number 58 and allow the children to see nothing but a bomb site.

He walked slowly down past the houses; 30, 32, gap, 36, 38, gap, gap, gap, 46, gap. A man leaning on a crutch watched him suspiciously as he walked by. 'That your car, mate?' he asked gruffly.

'Nope. Borrowed it,' replied Tom.

'You don't live round here, though, do ya?'

'Nope. I'm looking for someone. He lived at Number 58.'

The man with the crutch burst out into a fit of laughter which turned into bronchial coughing. 'Well, mate,' he said after he had recovered his breath enough to speak. 'You'll just 'ave to look elsewhere, won't ya? Ain't no one now lives at Number 58 except the rats.' He waved his stick in the direction of a gap.

Tom walked on until he reached the spot, and stood dejectedly in front of the huge pile of rubble that had once been Number 58.

'Your someone's gorn, 'asn't he?'

The man with the crutch swung agilely alongside Tom, unwilling to lose his company. 'Who was he then? Eh?' he demanded inquisitively.

'An Indian gentleman. Perhaps you remember seeing him. He was in the army, but this is where he lived, at least till 1943. He came back on leave, but then I suppose it was bombed by the time he returned after the war. You wouldn't happen to know him, would you?' asked Tom with sudden hope.

'Indian?' The man said it with such emphasis, that Tom was sure he was going to say he knew of Govind Singh, but instead, he opened his mouth and shut it again, saying, 'Nah! Don't know of no Indian.'

'Them two nippers Indian, too?' He jerked his head, and Tom turned to find that Jaspal and Marvinder had got out of the car and followed them up the road.

165

'I'm sorry, children,' said Tom quietly. 'The house your father lived in was bombed.'

Somehow, there was something all too familiar about the scene of devastation which lay before them. Marvinder looked at it in the same way as she had looked at Uncle Pavan's house. She didn't know what it meant for a house to be bombed, but bombed or firebranded by a mob, it amounted to the same; destruction, rubble, death and desolation.

'Is my father dead?' she asked in a voice like stone.

'Oh no! It doesn't mean he's dead,' said Tom emphatically. 'It just means he's gone somewhere else, and we're going to have to look for him.'

Then bending down so that he looked both children in the eye fair and square, Tom said, 'This isn't the end of our search. This is just the beginning. Remember? I did warn you. Lots of London was bombed, and it meant people were moved about all over the place to be rehoused, so don't get disheartened.'

But Jaspal and Marvinder were stunned by the disappointment and hardly seemed to hear. They stood there staring at the brambles and weeds, and the great clumps of Michaelmas daisies, and the scattered bricks and charred beams and the deep muddy crater right in the middle of it all, glistening with rain water.

'Come on!' said the man with the crutch suddenly waving a hand. 'Come with me. We'll go and visit Mrs Salter. She knows everything about everyone round 'ere. I was in the Merchant Navy for years, so I was hardly ever around till I lost my leg during a U-boat attack. That's why I don't know nothing. She's only over at Number 41. Follow me.' He took off across the road, his good leg swinging vigorously forward to take the weight alternately with the crutch.

Mrs Salter was a round, tumbly woman with a bosom that came down to her waist, and blotchy bare legs the shape of skittles. Her arms, though, were a surprise; they were muscular and as powerful as any man's, though her hands were rough and red from all the washing and cleaning she had to do, looking after her eight children. She was carrying one of them, a great grubby lump of a boy, when she came to the door. A frightful dank smell, mixed with washing and cooked cabbage, swept up behind her and made Jaspal recoil behind his sister.

'Oh, it's you, Wilf,' she greeted the one-legged man warmly. And her round, pallid face with particularly large, hazel eyes, lit up with a friendly smile.

'Wanna cup o' tea, do ya? Eh, who've ya got there then?' She eyed up the trio behind him on the steps.

'They come to visit a friend at Number 58!' exclaimed the man with the crutch, and once again, he burst out laughing and coughing all at the same time.

'Lord love you,' she exclaimed, throwing up her eyes. 'That house took a direct hit. Don't know why he finds it so funny. Reckon he's got a screw loose since losing a leg. Mind you, they was lucky, the Warburtons, an' all their lodgers. Only old Grandma Warburton copped it, cos she wouldn't leave 'er bed. The rest went down the Underground. Who was your friend then?' she asked, looking at Tom.

'Er . . . well, he's not exactly a friend,' said Tom. 'I'm looking for him on behalf of these children. It's their father, you see. He's an Indian called Govind Singh.'

'Oh! Old Govind! You looking for him?' exclaimed Mrs Salter with a shout. 'And are them two his kids? He was a dark horse and no mistake. What a character he was. Joined up, didn't he? The rascal! Don Juan we called him! Proper lady's man, he was, and all the time he'd a wife and kids, eh?'

Then she glanced at Jaspal and Marvinder. They were staring at her with wide eyes.

''Ere. Do they understand English?' she asked, realising her indiscretion.

'Yes, they do, though perhaps not your fast talking. I hope not anyway, Mrs Salter,' said Tom anxiously. He hoped fervently, that they would not have understood

167

Mrs Salter's heavy cockney accent.

'Look, have you any idea where he's living now?'

'Blimey, I don't know. I mean his place was bombed while he was in Italy. He come back, saw the damage and went.'

'Didn't he even say goodbye to any of you? None of his . . .' Tom paused meaningfully . . . 'friends?'

'Yeh, sort of, but only quickly. He seemed keen to be off. Didn't hang about. Said he'd write once he got a place, but of course he didn't. We didn't expect him to neither. But look, try old Mrs Gardner at Number 5. He er . . . you know . . .' she glanced again at the children . . . 'fancied 'er daughter Edna. Edna might know, but watch out for 'er mum! Proper terror she is! She lives down the bottom of the road over there. Tell you what. Leave them nippers with me. Mrs Gardner hates children. You'll have more of a chance without them.'

Obediently, Jaspal and Marvinder squatted down on the crumbling steps, but their eyes never left Tom as he crossed the road and walked down to the far end of the street.

Like all the houses in that road, Number 5 was run–down, grubby, almost bordering on a slum. The frosted glass in the cracked and peeling front door was broken and held together by sticky brown paper. There was a bell and a list of several names, which were too faded to read; and instructions to ring, once for the first floor, twice for the second and so on. Tom rang once, and waited. No one came. He rang twice, and almost gave up when he heard footsteps thudding down the stairs from the first floor, and at last the door was opened – just a crack.

''Oo is it?' asked a child's voice.

'I'm looking for Mrs Gardner. Does she live here?'

'In the basement,' said the voice and slammed the door. The footsteps thudded back upstairs again.

Tom went down a narrow alleyway to the side, edging past a row of over-filled rusting dustbins. He instinctively put a hanky to his nose to block out the stench, as he made his way down the uneven steps to the basement. He found the door. There was no bell, so he tapped sharply on the dirty frosted-glass panel. Again, there was a long pause. A gloomy silence hovered over the place. He wanted to leave. Then he realised that the door was slightly ajar, and when he nudged it further open, it revealed a dark passage, crammed with boxes of newspapers. He knocked again, and called in a hoarse whisper, 'Is anyone there?'

A side door at the far end of the passage opened slightly. Enough to reveal a woman of indeterminate age. She had a long, thin face – more chin than jaw – with a narrow nose which seemed to be permanently red, either from sinuses or too much crying. She had eyes which were more used to being lowered than meeting another's. Her head was bound in a headscarf and she wore a dirty flowered overall.

'Who are you?' she whispered.

'Are you Mrs Gardner?'

'No, I'm 'er daughter. What do you want?'

'Mrs Salter said you might be able to help me. Could I have a quick word, please?' Tom replied, also in a whisper.

'What about?' asked the woman, her body still in a state of retreat behind the door. 'I don't know nothing about anything. How should I?'

'I'm looking for Govind Singh,' said Tom.

The woman looked startled, and she glanced behind her as if afraid someone might have heard. At last she emerged and hurried down the passage towards him. 'Outside!' she hissed, and almost pushed him out of the door.

He saw her more clearly now. He wouldn't have described her as a girl; more of a woman, perhaps of thirty years or more but with the look and mannerisms of a frightened little girl. She went down a broken and overgrown garden path towards a washing line and made him stand behind some damp sheets, so that they were shielded from any eyes that might look out from the house.

'Govind?' she suddenly exclaimed with passion. 'Do you know where he is?' she begged. 'Have you come with a message?'

Tom was disconcerted and embarrassed. 'No, no! I don't know him at all. That's why I've come to you. I went to find him at his old address, Number 58, but of course, it was bombed. Then someone told me that you were a good friend of his, and that you might know how I could find him.'

'Who told you that?' Her neck and face flushed a deep red, and she twisted her apron in her hands. 'Who's been gossiping about me?'

'Oh, it wasn't gossip,' Tom reassured her. 'I'm looking for Govind. It's really important that I find him.'

'Why?' she asked sulkily.

'I've just come from India,' explained Tom. 'I have news from his family. He hasn't been in touch, you see, and they were worried.'

'I don't know where he is.' Tears began to trickle down her face, though her voice was steady. 'He was a good person. Really kind and considerate. Oh, I know how they gossiped in the street, but he never laid a finger on me, I'll tell you that.' She looked up at Tom fiercely and wiped her nose with the end of her apron. 'He was lonely, see, when he first came here before the war. Only had the one little room at the Warburtons, and she was a right bitch, that Mrs Warburton.'

Tom was shocked at Edna's sudden vehemence.

'Oh, I know you shouldn't speak ill of the dead, but she treated him like dirt. She was happy to take his money – and she charged him ten bob a week more than she should 'ave – but she was always interfering; got at him about everything and wouldn't let him cook curry or anything like that. He used to go down the fish 'n' chips. That's where I met him. We got chatting. Me mum likes fish 'n' chips every Friday, see? So I told 'im that every Friday, I'll be down at the fish 'n' chips at six o'clock. Well, he was always there, and we used to talk. He could make me

170

laugh with his funny sing-songy accent. He walked me 'ome – just like a gent. Then he took to coming round most evenings after Mum had gone to bed. There was nothing untoward, so don't you go getting the wrong impression. He was lonely, see.' Then Edna hung her head. 'So was I. Me mum never allows me out. Won't let me have friends – not girls or men. There's no time really, what with her being poorly and needing so much looking after. So it had to be a secret. She'd have killed me, if she'd found out.'

'When did you last hear from him?' asked Tom gently.

'He joined up, when war broke out. He was so dead keen to fit in – you know – almost as though he would like to have been an Englishman. When he first came, he had long hair; told me it was his religion. Wore a turban an' all that. The kids didn't 'alf tease him. Rotten they were. Even at the university, I don't think he was that happy. Didn't seem to have any friends. That's why he liked me. I spoke to him civil-like. I'd listen, and he'd tell me all about India and his family.'

'Oh, did he tell you about his family?' Tom interrupted eagerly. 'Who did he talk about?'

'Oh, about his mum, dad and all his brothers and sisters, that sort of thing. He told me they were farmers, that he had some land if he wanted it, but not enough to be rich. He said the whole idea had been for him to become a lawyer or somesuch and go back to India, but he reckoned he'd like to stay on here after he'd finished at the university. Give up law and go into business. Buy a shop, maybe. Course, then the war broke out, and that put paid to his studies. He wanted to be like an Englishman, so when all his mates at university joined up, he did too. He was sent straight off to some training place, and when he came back, he'd cut off his hair.'

'The army didn't make him, did they?' asked Tom indignantly.

'No – not by rules, if you see what I mean – but by making him feel a freak – and 'im wanting so much to be accepted.'

171

The tears which had dried up while she spoke, began to fall again.

'But it changed him. I wish he'd never cut it. It changed him so much. He went off – to France first, then later to North Africa and Italy – and all sorts. He came back half a dozen times on leave, throughout the war, and each time he came back, he was different. He still came to see me, but . . . well, he was a handsome chap – and without his beard and turban and all that – well the girls didn't half fall for him. There was always a girl willing to be taken down the palais dancing, or to the pictures. I never could go to that sort of thing. Me mum you know . . .' her voice tailed off as if she couldn't explain.

'But he never saw me as a woman.' She was sobbing hard now. 'I was just someone to talk to. Then, just towards the end of the war, when them doodlebugs things were coming over, Number 58 took a direct hit. When Govind came back, after the war – he was even more different. His character, I mean. He'd become hard-like. He was dressed in his civvies – but – he looked like a spiv – you know. Sort of slick. His hair was all smoothed back with Brylcream. He wore a posh suit and smart shoes. God knows where he got the money from. That was the last time I saw him. He came round. Hadn't got anywhere to sleep. Risked my life for him, I did. Put him on the sofa when me mum had gone to bed. When I said how sorry I was about his place being bombed, an' all that, he just said, "Don't care at all. I wasn't going to live there any more anyway. I just came back to collect some things and to say goodbye." And that's exactly what he did. When I come in the next morning to get him out of the house before me mum got up, he'd gone.'

Edna sniffed hard into her apron. 'He left a note saying he'd get in touch when he'd found somewhere to live; but he never did. I never heard from him again. So, you see, mister, I can't help you at all.'

'Edna! Edna! Where are you, girl. What the blazes are you up to? Get me dinner.' A grating, cruel, old woman's voice screamed from inside.

Tom couldn't believe the look of terror and submission which overwhelmed Edna. She hastily rubbed her eyes and cheeks as if to get rid of any signs of crying, and with the look of a frightened rabbit excused herself from Tom.

'I must go, or me mum will kill me,' she gasped.

'Are you sure you've no idea where he might be?' begged Tom, as she backed down the path. 'Is there anyone else who might know?'

'Might know what, may I ask?' demanded a harsh voice.

Suddenly, the sheet was thrust aside and there was the old woman. She leaned menacingly on a stick, though she looked strong enough to do without one. She had dark grey hair pulled tightly back into a bun, emphasising her gaunt, bony face and narrow, malicious eyes.

'What are you up to behind the sheets, eh? Who the hell are you?' She swung her stick and pointed at Tom.

'My name is Tom Fletcher. I'm looking for Govind Singh. I was told you knew him. It's very important that I find him.'

'Very important, is it?' sneered old Mrs Gardner. 'Why should anyone want to find that good for nothing! My poor, pathetic daughter perhaps? What 'ave you been telling him, Edna?'

'Nothing, Mum. Nothing. I don't know nothing. I don't know where Govind is, do I?'

'That's right. You don't, so clear off, you,' she snarled at Tom. 'We don't want no one round here who has anything to do with that man.'

'If you have any information at all, please tell me,' Tom tried once more in his most concilliatory voice. 'You see, he had a wife in India and his two young children have come all the way over to look for him.'

'A wife and kids?' The old woman almost shouted in astonishment. Then she burst out cackling with laughter, rocking to and fro and repeating over and over again, 'A wife and kids, a wife and kids! Cor luvva duck! What a turn-up for the books! Oh, my lord. Did you hear that, Edna? Did you hear that, my darling daughter? That'll put a stop to your mooning around over him, won't it? Well, now you've told me that, it puts a different complexion on things. I'll tell you where he's living. It's 18 Whitworth Road, Clapham. Right? Now, go away. Come on, Edna, get inside this minute.'

Edna had turned as white as the grubby sheet hanging on the line. Tom thought she was going to faint.

'You knew,' she gasped. 'You knew where he'd gone all along.' She stared at her mother, aghast.

''Course I knew, you silly baggage. When I saw his letter addressed to you, I took it. Reckon I had a right. I wasn't having no black man getting off with my daughter.'

'Oh my God! You knew, you knew!' Edna wept. Then suddenly lifting two clenched fists, she shook them at her mother. 'I hate you! I really hate you!' and as if appalled at what she had blurted out, fled weeping into the house.

Tom and the old woman regarded each other with stony faces. He had never before sensed such malevolence. Rather than risk going anywhere within reach of her, he stepped off the path into the tangle of deep purple Michaelmas daisies, and keeping to the other side of the washing, made his way towards the front. When he turned round, she hadn't moved.

Now that he was safe, he ventured one more question. 'By the way, we heard that Govind was wounded in the war. Was it serious?'

'Wounded?' Mrs Gardner stared at him with her small, black eyes. 'He came through without a scratch. Had the luck of the devil – he said so himself. He was never wounded, more's the pity. Wouldn't 'ave bothered me if 'ed been killed.'

Then she turned and stumped back into the house.

SEVENTEEN
The Meeting

Whitworth Road must have been elegant in its time. The houses were grand and imposing. They rose all the way from the basement, which was below street level and up three floors to attics at the top. Each had front gardens flanked by tall pillars, and long stone steps which led up to a very large front door, which would have had a shiny brass knob and knocker; the sort of door which at one time, had you knocked, would have been opened by a trim, smartly-dressed maid, who would have asked for your card and seated you in the hall to wait.

The high, first-floor bay windows, which would have been hung with lace and velvet curtains, might have displayed tropical plants, which could bring a sense of wild jungle and the invasion of nature into the most civilised of drawing rooms.

But as Tom drove Jaspal and Marvinder down the road, looking for Number 18, all they saw were grimy, peeling, crumbling buildings; the pillars and porticos pitted and chipped, the mouldings disintegrating, the flights of steps broken and the front doors in need of repainting; the once beautiful bay windows were all blackened with soot and greasy condensation, and the curtains hung like rags, hardly even meeting in the middle to provide privacy.

As with most roads in London, there were the gaping spaces where bombs had fallen, obliterating or damaging houses: but it was not Hitler's bombs, which had brought despair to roads such as these, it was changes which had begun before the wars, when families moved away because it was too expensive to live in such large houses; when people who might have had jobs as maids and cooks and butlers, now worked in factories earning more money; when people, driven by poverty and despair, poured into the metropolis looking for a livelihood.

Then the developers moved in; developers, who turned one room into two, by building flimsy partitions; who split houses into flats so that instead of accommodating one rich family, as many as six poor families with children moved in, squeezed into one or two rooms, paying rents to shadowy landlords who called each week, and threw them out if they couldn't pay.

Marvinder couldn't explain the heavy feeling of depression which filled her chest. In a few minutes they could be face to face with their father at last, yet as she looked at this grey, alien road, all she could yearn for was the long white road stretching away from her village in the Punjab, and wish that she could once more see her father cycling down the road towards her.

Number 18 was as much a slum as any of the other houses in the road. No sooner had Tom pulled up, when a hoard of children surrounded them, peering in through the windows, fiddling with the mirror, jumping on the running board and smoothing their hands along the bodywork. Jaspal and Marvinder shrank back in their seats.

'Stay in the car, while I see if your father is here,' said Tom gently. 'I won't be long.'

He got out and leapt two at a time up the dusty front steps and looked at the familiar row of bells down the side. Whatever brass knobs had been on any of these doors, had long ago been ripped off or sold.

He saw the name Singh. It was the top-floor flat. So he had to press three times.

The neighbourhood children had now gathered so thickly round the car, that Jaspal and Marvinder didn't see who came to the door. All they saw were faces; cheeky, grubby, smiley. They squashed their noses and lips up against the glass; they giggled and pointed and stuck out their tongues; they nudged, jostled, poked and prodded each other, and then when Tom returned, fell away warily, anticipating the clip round the ear or being told to clear off.

But Tom just smiled at them and said pleasantly, 'Excuse me!'

He opened the back car door and indicated to Jaspal and Marvinder to get out. The children closed in on them again shouting out questions.

'Hey, Mister! Who are them kids?'

'Are you visiting or something?'

'Hey, Mister! Where do they come from? Why are they wearing funny clothes?'

Tom didn't answer. He just smiled and waved them away, as with an arm around each one, he led Jaspal and Marvinder up the steps and into Number 18.

The front door closed behind them, shutting out the light and the fresh air. The hall was cold and dark and brown and dingy. The glass in the front door had been broken and never replaced, except by a brown piece of cardboard stuck on with tape. The lino, too, was brown and old and worn into patchy holes. It ran the length of the hall and ground its way up the stairs. There was a horrible smell of stale food, which hadn't dispersed for hours and would only be reinforced by the cooking of the next meal. Marvinder instinctively pulled her veil around her nose and mouth, and Jaspal buried his face in her back.

'You'd better come upstairs!'

Marvinder looked in amazement at the person who had let them in. She was a young girl about Marvinder's age – thirteen or so, but Marvinder had never before seen another human being like her. It was the girl's hair which first astonished her; the colour of fire – red and gold, and so wild, that it hardly seemed to stay caught under the ribbon which tied round her head with a bow on top. And then there was her skin; it was white – and yet not white, for it was covered in light reddy-brown freckles – on her arms, her legs and her face, as though she had been rolled in gold dust. Finally there were her eyes, so startlingly

177

blue, that they looked as if they had been cut out of an Indian sky and placed in her head.

'My sister's upstairs. Come on up.' Her voice was softly Irish. She gripped the bannister and led them, sixteen steps up to the first landing, then eight more up to the second. All sorts of voices and sounds came from different rooms as they climbed.

If it had been dark and gloomy at the bottom, it was almost pitch dark at the top, but a door was slightly ajar, throwing a patch of dull daylight on to the narrow landing.

They stepped into the flat and suddenly it was light again. There were two rooms divided from each other by a faded flowery curtain. One with a window overlooking the street at the front, and the other at the back with a window overlooking the garden. In here, the smell wasn't so bad – a smell of carbolic soap and washed clothes, some of which were tossed over chairs to dry.

Jaspal, who had held his breath most of the way up the stairs, exploded as he let it all out and took another breath. For the first time they all grinned at each other.

'Maeve! There's a man here with two kids. Says they know Govind or something!' the girl called through the curtain.

'Won't be a tick,' came an answering Irish voice.

They looked around the front room. It seemed to serve as a bedroom and a living room. There was a sofa bed which had been made up hastily with bits of blanket and sheet hanging out; there was a saggy old armchair and a small side table. In one corner was a cheap wardrobe and in the other a wash basin with a shelf, on which stood a toothmug with three toothbrushes, a tin of toothpowder and some shaving things.

They could see, through a slight gap in the dividing curtain, that in the back room there was another bed, a wooden table, a gas cooker with a kettle and various saucepans standing on top. There was a food cupboard, and shelves with tins of beans, jars of jam and packets of tea.

The woman had been dressing a little girl of about three years old and she now emerged with the child in her arms.

She looked twenty-five and an older version of her sister. She, too, had the flaming red hair, only hers was bobbed and held back from her face with combs. Her eyes were dark blue, like violets, and her skin was fine and pale and also covered in freckles, except for her face which was almost flawlessly white.

Her child, though, was different. Her skin was sallow, not quite white, not quite brown. Her eyes were large and the colour of almonds; her hair was straight and black and divided into two bunches with green ribbons.

'Here, Kath! Have Beryl for me, would you? Take her down to Mum's or something.' The woman thrust her child into the arms of the girl.

Beryl protested briefly and clung to her mother, while staring intently at Jaspal and Marvinder. Then Kathleen extricated her, with soft cooing noises and promises to go to the swings, and finally the two of them left.

'I'm so sorry to intrude like this,' said Tom awkwardly. 'Let me introduce myself. My name is Tom Fletcher. I'm a teacher in India, but over on leave to see my parents. In India I met these two children, who are . . .' Tom paused, suddenly overwhelmed with uneasiness . . . 'who are . . . relatives,' he finally found a suitable word. 'Yes, relatives of Govind Singh. You may have heard that there has been terrible turmoil in India since Partition, with thousands dead and many families uprooted or separated. These two children, Jaspal and Marvinder, lost their mother and all other relatives are missing or dead. The only one left was Govind Singh. Am I right in believing that Govind Singh lives here?'

'Yes!' exclaimed the young woman with some bewilderment. ''Course he does. He's my husband. He'll be back in a minute. He only went out to get some Woodbines.'

Even as she spoke, they heard voices on the stairs. A man spoke to Kathleen and Beryl on their way out.

179

Tom moved over to Jaspal and Marvinder and put his hands on their shoulders. Jaspal was as still as a rock, but Marvinder was trembling uncontrollably.

The door flung open. A man strode in with a lit cigarette in his mouth. He was tall, his skin was brown, with short, sleek, greased black hair. He was wearing a dark grey suit which tried to look smart, but was really worn out. It was only his light, almond eyes which convinced Marvinder that she was looking at her father.

But his reaction at the sight of her was of intense shock. He staggered and looked as if he might faint. The cigarette fell from his mouth and lay smouldering on the carpet until Maeve, amazed at his reaction, stepped on it and put it out.

'Mother in Heaven, Govind! What's up with you? Are you ill? These people have come to see you.'

'Jhoti?' Govind stared at Marvinder. 'Jhoti? Is it you? Oh my God. Is it you?'

'No, Pa!' Marvinder spoke in Punjabi. 'I am your daughter Marvinder. We've lost our ma, so came to find you.'

Govind leaned up against the door and shut his eyes. 'Jhoti!' He kept saying the name over and over again, and suddenly, everything from the past came sweeping over him, and he remembered how they had galloped in bullock carts down the long, white road. The men had teased him mercilessly. Told him that he was marrying an old one-toothed hag without a penny to her name. Then he remembered the relief he had felt when he finally saw her. How he kept sneaking little looks all the way through the marriage ceremony, trying to see through her crimson veil. She was only thirteen but very pretty. Very pretty. Just as pretty as Marvinder looked now as she hid her face inside her veil. Marvinder was the very image of her mother.

Trouble was he had been too young to appreciate Jhoti then. He had neglected her; always put his studies and his friends before her. He didn't even turn up for Marvinder's birth. Well, he'd meant to, but when the baby was born early, and he heard it was a girl, he didn't bother. Someone had invited him to a party in Amritsar. He could feel shame about it now. He was older when Jaspal was born, and wiser. Wasn't he wise then? He opened his eyes and looked desperately round the room at everyone. Who was there who could tell him that he was ever a wise person? That he really cared when Jaspal was born; that for the first time in his life, he felt tenderness, even the first stirrings of love, for his wife Jhoti? She had borne him a son. He had a son. How had he managed to forget all that? Was it coming to England? Was it the war and the struggle to survive? The temptations to make money, to get big, to be somebody? For the first time, he didn't know why he hadn't gone home. Wasn't India really home?

With a terrible groan, he stepped towards Jaspal, his hands outstretched. 'Jaspal! My son. Are you my son?' he cried.

Jaspal recoiled away from him in horror and disgust and hid behind Marvinder.

Maeve rushed to Govind's side. 'What's this all about? Come and sit down, you look terrible.' She tried to hug him over to the armchair.

'He's not our father, Didi,' Jaspal suddenly shouted. 'Look, you can see! He's nothing like our father. He has no beard, he's cut his hair! He isn't a warrior or a scholar. He isn't even a Sikh! You've made a mistake, Didi!' He held up the photograph. The one and only image that Jaspal had had of his father all his life. 'That man's not my father!' he cried, and ripping the picture in two, he fled from the room.

They heard his feet clattering and stumbling down the dark stairs. Marvinder rushed after him, and Tom called out over the bannister, 'Marvinder! Stay with Jaspal! Stay outside while I sort this out.'

It was the sound of the violin which saved them. Jaspal had flung open the front door and crumpled up on the steps weeping. The neighbourhood children stared in alarm, disconcerted by such a show of emotion. Then Marvinder appeared. Where could they go to get away from the curious eyes?

It was like a miracle; from somewhere below them, she heard a distant high sound of a violin playing. It was so unexpected. It catapulted her in time back to a verandah in the Punjab, sitting huddled close to her mother, listening to the Chadwicks playing in a dark, sweetly-scented Indian evening. She realised that her whole life had been to the accompaniment of a violin and it resurrected everything that she could remember since the day she was born; her village, her friends and most of all, her mother. But at that moment, it did more. It came as a signal; as a message. Her father was upstairs, and here, down below was the thin, plaintive sound, filtering delicately up through all the grime and hardship of London poverty. It was as though Jhoti's spirit suddenly surrounded them to bring them comfort and courage.

She pulled Jaspal down the steps and then down the basement steps to the garden at the back, away from the staring children. The violin continued playing, and Marvinder held her brother close.

'Do you remember how we used to listen to the Chadwicks playing their music every evening? Our mother used to love it so much, and we had to sit with her on the verandah and listen until it was over. Do you remember anything of this, Jaspal?'

She held him until his sobbing stopped, and after a while, Jaspal said, 'Yes, Didi, I do remember. I remember our ma. I wish we had never lost her. I wish we were back home.' Then they sat on without speaking further, just listening, and allowing their own memories to fill their minds.

'Coooeee! Oi! You two!' Kathleen stood at the top of the steps with Beryl still clasped in her arms. 'Me mum says to come in and have some cake.'

'I don't want to go back in there. It smells!' snarled Jaspal aggressively.

182

'Come on, *bhai*! It's too cold to stay out here for long.'

Jaspal and Marvinder followed Kathleen back into the house and that foul-smelling hallway and climbed the stairs to the first floor. The door was open and to their relief the more pleasant smell of a freshly baked cake pervaded the air though it was mixed with tobacco smoke and stale cigarettes.

'Come on!' urged Kathleen, as Jaspal and Marvinder both held back shyly. They could hear the loud heavy laughter of men's voices and the clatter of cups and saucers. Then a woman appeared in the doorway, filling it up with her presence and her will.

'Come on in, you lot and get the door closed. Holy Mother of God, hurry up! We're letting all the warmth out,' she ordered in a voice which could have commanded armies.

It was Mrs O'Grady, mother of Patrick, Maeve, Michael and then later, as an afterthought, Kathleen. She was grandmother of Beryl, whom she now snatched from Kathleen's arms and on whose cheeks she planted a great loud kiss. She was wife of Gerry O'Grady, who had fought in the war until he had a leg blown off, and now sold newspapers on street corners. He sat there now, with his good leg up on the mantelpiece, sucking noisily at a cup of tea. She fed them all, laundered for them all, ruled them all and loved them all. She was tall and large, with her once red hair now scattered with silver and rolled up into curlers. Her sleeves were always up over the elbows, displaying her powerful arms and raw-red hands. But although she looked as though she could turn anyone of them upside down and smack their bottoms, her face was clear and kind and she looked you, no nonsense, straight in the eye.

'My God!' exclaimed Mr O'Grady. 'What have we here? A couple of little heathens by the look of it.'

'Mind your manners, Gerald O'Grady!' cried his wife with mock severity. 'We have guests from overseas. Relatives of our own dear son-in-law, Govind. So none of

183

your lip. Let's have a bit of decent hospitality, shall we?'

Patrick immediately jumped up. He was a strapping sort of fellow. Not much taller than five foot eight, but broad and muscular from heavy manual work.

'Please take a seat.' He bowed low before Marvinder, sweeping from his head an invisible feathered cap and looking at her with the same laughing, mischievous eyes.

'Here, and you can sit on this,' said Kathleen pulling up a stool for Jaspal.

Plates were pushed in front of them and they were offered a slice of the newly-baked cake they had smelled in the hall.

The table was a confusion of clean and dirty crockery, saucers of ash and half-lit cigarettes, a pack of cards and a piece of paper with lists of figures and IOUs scribbled on it.

'Do you drink tea? Or would you rather 'ave some milk, dears?' asked Mrs O'Grady.

'Milk, please,' Marvinder managed to squeak.

'Milk, please,' echoed Jaspal.

Mrs O'Grady took a bottle of milk off the shelf and poured out two cups.

They ate and drank and no one troubled them with questions. Michael and Patrick went on talking loudly, telling jokes and shouting with laughter, with everyone else joining in from time to time, and little Beryl was passed around like a doll. They all seemed to love her and wanted their turn at giving her a cuddle.

Suddenly, Michael handed her to Marvinder. 'Here! You hold her for a bit. She looks like you.'

Everyone turned and looked, but no one said anything, even though it was true.

Marvinder held her awkwardly at first, and bounced her on her knee without facing her. Then Beryl struggled to turn round. She wanted to play with Marvinder's long plaits. Kathleen laughed, and taking one of Marvinder's plaits she waggled it in Beryl's face and made her chortle.

Kathleen sat close to Marvinder. She too was entranced by her plaits.

'Can I undo one of them?' she asked.

Marvinder nodded, but was just as fascinated by Kathleen's red hair, so they took it in turns to do each other's hair.

Kathleen began chatting. 'What did you say your name was? Marvinder? That's nice, and your brother, what's he called? Jaspal? What kind of names are they? Are you from India like Govind? What's it like there? Have you seen lions and tigers and lots of wild animals like he has? Do you go to school? I do. I go to Grove Park. It's just down the road. Being a Catholic, I ought to go to the Convent, but it's too far. I don't mind. Are you a Methodist or something? Or nothing, like Govind? Maeve's trying to convert him! 'Course, Beryl's a Catholic. She was baptised an' all. Mum said, if she wasn't baptised and something happened to her, she wouldn't go to heaven. That's when she told Govind he'd better be quick and get baptised if he wanted to be in heaven with his daughter.'

Kathleen was quite happy to prattle on while she plaited and unplaited Marvinder's hair several times over, and didn't even notice that Marvinder hardly said a word.

Jaspal sat aloof, a little out of the circle. He refused to take Beryl on his knee when she tried to climb up and examine his topknot. He just solemnly ate several slices of cake and avoided meeting anyone's eye.

Mrs O'Grady put on the kettle to have warm water for washing up, and the table was cleared a little of all the debris that had been on it. Mr O'Grady swung his leg down from the mantlepiece and said, 'Right then, I'm off. Going to see a man about a job.'

'He always says that,' Mrs O'Grady winked at Marvinder, 'when he really means it's opening time at the pub.'

There was a knock on the door. Kathleen opened it, to reveal Tom and Maeve. Tom looked strained and they could see that Maeve had been crying.

Mrs O'Grady took things in hand. 'All right, you lot. I want you all out. Michael, Patrick, out. Gerry, you get off to the pub, and Kath, take Beryl down to the swings.' She turned to Tom and added, 'Do you want Kath to take them kiddies, too?'

Tom nodded gratefully. He leaned over quietly to Jaspal and Marvinder and said, 'We all need to talk a few things over together, but don't worry. Everything is going to be fine.'

When everyone had left, Mrs O'Grady presided over the bare wooden table and nodded to Tom and Maeve to sit down.

'Right, then!' she said. 'What's going on?'

'I'll tell you what's going on, Mum,' wailed Maeve bursting into tears again. 'That bloody Govind's a bigamist. I'm not even married to him, and Beryl's . . . ille . . . illeg . . .'

'Beryl's a bastard!' her mother finished off for her in a voice of deadly calm.

'What are we going to do?' Maeve sobbed loudly, and Tom got up and walked over to the window.

'Well, Mr Fletcher?' asked Mrs O'Grady.

Tom turned round, and to his surprise, the woman was quite cool and matter of fact. 'Well?' she repeated. 'What happens now? Do they go to prison or what?'

Tom came back to the table and sat down. 'I don't know the law, Mrs O'Grady. I think we should deal with that later. As I've been trying to explain to your daughter and Govind, we don't know if Govind's wife – I mean his Indian wife – if she's dead or alive. We may never find out. My first concern is Jaspal and Marvinder. These children have endured a major catastrophe. They have taken nearly a year crossing India alone, stowing away on a ship, coming to England – risking all sorts of dangers, in order to find their father. Now that they have found him I need your help so that we can do what's best. What are their

186

choices? To stay in England but be taken into care? To be sent back to India – but to whom? They have no known relatives. Or can they live with their father, here?'

'They must live with their father,' spoke a determined voice.

Govind stood in the doorway, red-eyed and dishevelled. 'They are my children. They will stay with me.'

Maeve threw herself at Govind, punching and slapping and kicking and crying. She screamed accusations at him; called him a liar and a cheat and threatened to have him thrown out. She told him he should clear off with his Indian children and never let her lay eyes on him again.

Tom leapt forward and tried to calm the situation, but suddenly Mrs O'Grady rose up and turned on him.

'All right, Mister . . . whatyoumecallits Fletcher. You've done your bit, and thank you very much, but we don't want no do-gooding outsiders interfering in our affairs. So I think it's time you left.'

Tom tried to protest. How could he leave without being certain the children would be all right? But Mrs O'Grady came storming up to him and took his elbow in a vice-like grip.

'Out! Out! You needn't worry your head about the children. They're our business now. They'll stay with us. They'll be all right, but I'll thank you never to show your face here again.' She opened the front door and all but pushed him down the steps. The door slammed behind him.

Then she turned and faced Maeve and Govind. They still confronted each other like battling warriors; Maeve, her chest heaving with emotion, and Govind standing with hunched shoulders and clenched fists. Mrs O'Grady led her daughter to an armchair and forced her down.

'Right then, you two!' She stepped back like a referee. 'Let's try and understand things clearly. It seems to me that what is past is past. We have to deal with the here and now. Do you get me?'

Maeve bowed her head, weeping silently and Govind nodded, his body suddenly sagging. He lit a cigarette and walked over to the window.

'We get you, Mrs O'Grady,' he said. 'What do you suggest?'

EIGHTEEN
A Sound from the Past

Kathleen had taken Beryl, Jaspal and Marvinder to the swings, which were a few streets away. She had pushed Beryl in one of those huge, black prams, with the hood up to protect her from a chilly wind. The same wind ruffled the thin cotton pyjamas, which Jaspal and Marvinder were wearing and it stiffened their limbs into a constant shiver.

It was a bleak playground containing a few basic items: an old, splintery slide, which was too high for safety, a roundabout, encircled on the ground by a well-worn track, a seesaw which had lost its buffers and a row of four wooden, seated swings hanging from a great height by thin chains.

They tried to play. Kathleen lifted Beryl out of the pram and plonked her on one of the swings.

'Hold tight now, won't you, Beryl. Ready?'

Marvinder stood in a dream. She couldn't keep her thoughts in one place. Now that she was farther away from home than she had ever been, memories of home seemed even clearer than ever. They swept over her wave after wave. First there had been the violin, whose thin, quivering sound had twisted in her mind like a key in a lock. Now the swing.

'Push me, push me!' She could hear Edith's demanding voice. Edith sat on the swing her father had rigged from the lemon tree, and Marvinder pushed her for a long, long time so that she could earn her turn to have a go on the swing. There was the yellow of the lemons and the warmth of the sun on her back and the soft cru-cruing of the doves, and Jhoti and Maliki chatting on the verandah . . .

189

'Why don't you have a go, Marv . . . whatever your name is,' cried Kathleen good-naturedly. 'I'll give you a push.'

Marvinder obeyed, and suddenly, there was the same sensation; the hands in her back thrusting her upwards; up and up and up, until suddenly, Kathleen gave an extra hard push and dashed right underneath her to the other side. Marvinder laughed.

Jaspal had gone to the seesaw. He jumped up and stood in the middle, aggressively tipping the ends up and down by shifting his weight from side to side. There was a scowl on his face. Failing to get any satisfaction from balancing, he jumped down and taking one end of the seesaw, thrust it upwards so hard, that it slammed into the ground on the other side, making the whole thing judder.

'Shall I sit at the other end?' Marvinder called to him.

'No!' Jaspal snapped, and continued thrusting the seesaw into the ground.

It was too cold to stay long. Beryl began to whimper, and no matter how hard Marvinder jumped around, she couldn't get warm.

'Come on, let's go back,' said Kathleen, lifting Beryl off the swing. 'I'm freezing half to death.'

Marvinder pulled her veil tightly round her head and shoulders and called her brother. 'Let's go, *bhai*! It's cold!'

'Don't want to,' snarled Jaspal turning his back.

'Jaspal, come on! We can't stay here for ever.'

'I'm not going back there,' shouted Jaspal.

'Hey, Jaspal *bhai*!' Marvinder ran over to him. She tried to take his arm, but he flung her off.

'If you want to go there, then go. I won't go back to that place.'

'But . . . our father is there . . .' Even Marvinder said the word 'father' with difficulty.

'He's not our father. Not any more. He's her father.' He gave a violent indication of his head towards Beryl.

They were speaking to each other in Punjabi, and Kathleen didn't understand. All she could see was the

190

anger in Jaspal and the way Marvinder pleaded with him.

'Come on, you two. I'm off!' Kathleen set off running, pushing the pram before her.

'Jaspal!' Marvinder tried again to grab his arm. 'Please, brother. We can't stay here. We must go back.'

'Get away from me! Get away! Don't you understand! I'm not going back there.'

Marvinder moved away and sat on a swing. Somehow, she no longer felt the cold. Just numb. She couldn't think any more. She pushed the swing listlessly with her feet, rocking herself to and fro, her head dropped down on her chest.

And that's where Mrs O'Grady found them when she came out later to look for them. She sat herself on the roundabout.

'Oi, you two. Come over here a minute. Come on.' Her voice was casual, but required obedience.

Marvinder got off the swing and sat a little distance away from her on one side of the roundabout, and Jaspal, with a surly shrug, leapt down from the seesaw and sat a little distance away from her on the other side.

'Want a sweet?' Mrs O'Grady held out a paper bag of boiled sweets. 'Go on!' She shook the bag at them.

First Marvinder took one, then Jaspal. Immediately, their mouths were filled with a warm, sugary, juicy flavour; an unbelievable sweetness.

They sat and sucked for a while without speaking. Then Mrs O'Grady got up and gestured towards home. 'Come on now,' she said gently. 'I think it's time we went home for tea. Couldn't you eat some nice toasted buns? Eh?'

Marvinder immediately got up to follow, but Jaspal stayed put. Mrs O'Grady fixed him with a hard eye. 'Come on now, fellow me lad. No more of this nonsense. Come on home. Your dad's waiting for you. Would another sweet get you there?' She held out the paper bag.

Finally, he got up, and slowly, slowly, began to follow them out of the play area.

★

191

'Where in heaven's name are we going to put them?' asked Mr O'Grady when he came home from the pub.

'I've worked it all out,' announced Mrs O'Grady, and at supper that night, she told them.

'For the moment, Kath can sleep up with Beryl, and Marvinder can have Kath's bed on the landing under the stairs.'

'Hey, Mum!' Kathleen protested with a wail. 'I don't want to leave my bed.'

'It's not for ever, I promise you,' said Mrs O'Grady. 'When Marvinder has got to know her family a little bit better, you can swap back, and she'll go upstairs.'

Kathleen sank back, placated but not pleased.

'Jaspal will sleep in with Michael and Patrick. I'll put him in that chair-bed. So, boys, you're going to have to watch your habits. No more coming home drunk in the middle of the night. All right. Settled?'

'Has to be,' grumbled Patrick. 'Don't look like we have no say anyhow.'

'The sooner we realise they're family, the better,' said Mrs O'Grady, clearing up the plates. 'I don't want no one from the Town Hall snooping round here, neither. All you tell anyone, plain and simple, is that these kids are relatives of Govind from India.'

Marvinder caught her father looking at her, and she lowered her eyes quickly with embarrassment. There were so many things to tell him, so many questions to ask, but she hadn't bargained on finding a stranger. Could this really be the same father who used to cycle down the long white road? The same father who comforted her when she thought that Basant was a witch and would eat her new-born baby brother? Was this the same father as in the photograph? Jaspal didn't think so, and yet – of course he did. Otherwise he wouldn't have torn up the picture.

'The children don't have much to say for themselves,' said Patrick mischievously. 'Aint yer got nothing to say to your dear old da? Eh, Marvinder?' He was sitting next to her and gave her a playful jab in the ribs.

'Leave her alone, Patrick,' cried Kathleen, defensively. 'Take no notice of him, Marv . . . whatever your name is. He's a rotten tease. Always has been.'

Marvinder looked up again at her father. Well, there was one question she wanted to ask. Perhaps the only question. Their eyes met and held, and she said in slow English so that they all understood, 'When are we going home?'

There was the silence of a held breath, then Mrs O'Grady immediately got up and began ordering everyone to clear the table. Maeve, who had gone as white as a sheet, said it was time to bath Beryl, and whisked her away upstairs to her own kitchen sink. Mr O'Grady and his sons got out a pack of cards.

'Are you joining us tonight, Govind?' asked Michael as he began vigorously shuffling the pack.

'Er . . . no. Not tonight. I'm meeting someone. Business.' He was looking at Jaspal.

'Jaspal?' Govind couldn't resist a further attempt to make contact. He stretched out to touch the silent boy, but Jaspal slid out of reach and turned his back on him.

'Well, I'll be off then,' said Govind, and left.

The whole house was breathing; the regular rising and falling of sleep. Marvinder, lying in the bed under the stairs, felt as if she were floating out in space. She wasn't sure if she was awake or asleep. She wasn't sure if she was thinking or dreaming. Thoughts, images, voices and sensations tumbled over and over, filling the odorous hallways and echoing up the stairs.

From time to time, she heard voices; Maeve and Mrs O'Grady, then later on, her father's voice. Somewhere, coiling up through the darkness, was the far-distant sound of the violin again and she thought about God. Where was God? she wondered, for deep inside her was a growing fear. Her father had disobeyed the Sikh law. He had cut his hair. God would surely be angry and punish him. But was God here in England? Did He know they were here?

Could He see her in this cubby hole? She curled herself up tightly and tucked her head into the thin blanket and hoped; she hoped that at least for a while, God wouldn't find them out.

Still the violin continued playing. She became curious. It seemed to be coming from below her head. She crouched on her knees and examined her space. Then she realised that there was a door, and that if she put her ear to the door, she could hear the violin more strongly.

She pulled back the mattress, and tried the handle. She hadn't expected the door to open, but open it did, and she fell back, feeling afraid. But now she could hear that the violin had been travelling up to her from behind the door.

She had noticed that Mrs O'Grady kept a box of matches on top of the gas meter in the hall. Electricity hadn't yet been installed in this building, so it was still lit by gas. Marvinder fumbled for the box in the darkness. With cold, shaky fingers, she struck a match, and briefly the whole hall lit up in the first flare of fire, then died down and went out. She struck another, shielding the flame this time from the draught. She went back to the door and holding out the match looked behind it. She found herself staring down a flight of stairs. The match went out. She struck another and stood at the top of the stairs. The violin sounded stronger than ever. She began to descend, one step at a time. The flickering match threw her shadow up on to the wall behind her like a giant silhouette.

After about twelve steps, she had reached a small landing, and there was a door to her right. She turned the handle. It opened, but was obstructed by something. Then she saw that it was Beryl's pram which was stored under the stairs on the ground floor. Marvinder was beginning to understand. She had found another stairway, narrow and dark and hidden from view. It was the servants' staircase, now forgotten. But still the sound of the violin came from below her, so lighting match after match, Marvinder carried on down, following the music.

At the bottom of a further ten steps, there was another door. She turned the handle, and as all the others, this one opened too. She stepped through.

She found herself in a narrow passageway. There was a row of pegs with a jacket and a raincoat hanging from it. There was an umbrella stand and a row of shoes. Opposite her was a door from beneath which sidled a thin shred of light, and the sound of music. It was so close and real and immediate, that Marvinder couldn't help reaching forward to the handle of the door.

She had to see, for in her mind's eye were Harold and Dora Chadwick . . . they played like this . . . it could be them on the other side of the door . . . who else ever made music like that? The notes of the violin rose and fell. She recognised the tune. Could it be Harold? She turned the handle and pushed open the door.

He didn't see her at first, he was so absorbed with his playing, but as he came to the end, and looked up, his bow hung from his hand in the air, frozen with astonishment.

The girl too seemed transfixed. Neither of them moved. Then he spoke quietly, as if she were a wild deer that he had come across unexpectedly in the forest and didn't wish to startle. 'Hello.' It was a simple word, but he uttered it gently and quietly.

'Hello,' she responded.

'Can I help you?' he said after a few seconds.

She didn't reply, but stood staring as though puzzled and uncomprehending.

She saw before her a thin, small, old man, with large, dark eyes which lay in hollows above his high, gaunt cheekbones. He had a long, fine, thin nose and a mouth, which though usually solemn, could suddenly smile with great friendliness. Everything about him looked fragile, as though he could be blown away, until she looked at his hands. The hands, which held the violin were long-fingered, strong and gnarled as old roots, with calloused tips from years of playing; his wrists were like the ends of iron chains; knobbly, strong and mobile.

'You're not Mr Chadwick,' she finally murmured.

Still not daring to move, in case this animal fled, he answered softly, 'No. I'm not Mr Chadwick. I am Doctor Silbermann.'

Her body was still poised, he could see, ready to go either way; to turn and flee or to relax and come nearer. There was a long silence. Then she said, 'Was it you, playing the violin?'

'Yes, it was me.'

'Do doctors play the violin?'

'If they are doctors of music, they certainly do,' he replied.

'I didn't know there were doctors of music.'

'In my country, there are.'

'Where is your country?' she asked. Her body, very slightly relaxed, and she clasped her hands in front of her.

'Austria,' he answered.

'I've never heard of Austria,' said Marvinder. 'Have you heard of India?'

'Of course! India is one of the great countries of the world.'

'Is it?' she said in a surprised voice. 'I didn't know that.'

Very slowly, the old man finally lowered his bow and placed the violin back in its case, which had been lying on a central table. He noticed that her eyes followed his movement, and rested almost longingly on the instrument as it lay in its blue velvet surround.

'Mr Chadwick played the violin.'

'Did he, my dear?'

'My mother loved hearing the music.'

'Then your mother had good taste,' said Dr Silbermann.

Marvinder moved, one step forward. Her eyes were still on the violin.

'Would you like to pick it up?' he asked.

She nodded. He would have lifted it up for her, but to his surprise, she seemed to know exactly what to do. She picked up the violin by its neck and tucked it under her chin, then she took up the bow, and held it, correctly within her fingers and thumb. She didn't draw the bow across the strings, but just stood for a while in a playing position, then put the violin back in its case, and returned the bow to the inside of the lid.

'Do you play, my dear?' asked Dr Silbermann.

'Oh, no. I only listen. I can hear you upstairs.'

'Come and see me again. I would love to have an audience when I play, and you can hold the violin again, if you wish, and maybe even make a sound.'

She didn't reply, though he could see impressions racing across her face like clouds across a sky. 'Yes,' she said, at last, and left.

NINETEEN
Unwillingly to School

The next thing to deal with was school.

They hadn't wanted to go, especially Jaspal; but Mrs O'Grady said, 'It's the law of the land, and unless you want to be taken away by the authorities, then you'd better go, and that's that.' She sorted it out the very next day.

Mrs O'Grady was that sort of person. She always made the best of a situation, no matter how bad. You wouldn't find her sitting around with her head in her hands moaning about how unfair the world was; they'd been bombed out twice in the war; lost everything, and had to start all over again. Goodness knows, she'd had her share of problems. But she was the kind of person to get on with things, and that's what she did now.

Once she had decided that Jaspal and Marvinder were here to stay, she got on with sorting them out; she went along to the Town Hall, fixed up ration books for them and she registered Jaspal at Christchurch Junior School and Marvinder at Grange Park Secondary Modern, where Kathleen went. She went to every jumble sale in the district looking for clothes. She bought trousers and skirts and shirts and blouses and socks and vests, all for a penny or twopence or threepence. Her family called her the queen of jumble sales, because she always came back with lots of bargains.

Tom Fletcher had also wrapped up the clothes they had been given on the ship, and which they had left behind in Hampstead. He popped in a few extra and parcelled them off to Whitworth Road, with a note to say he hoped he could visit them on his next leave home from India.

So on that first day of school, Jaspal and Marvinder were suitably dressed; Jaspal, in a pair of grey kneecap-length trousers, with a white shirt and grey pullover, and Marvinder had a navy blue box-pleated gymslip over a blue-and-white-checked blouse and a red cardigan buttoned up the front. It's true that some of the woollies had patched elbows and the clothes had traces of stains which hadn't washed out, but no one could say that any child who had passed through Mrs O'Grady's hands, hadn't always looked neat and as well turned out as was possible in the circumstances.

Mrs O'Grady accompanied them on their first day. Govind had wanted to take them, but Jaspal turned his back and refused to be in the same room as his father, let alone walk to school with him.

'Give him time,' Mrs O'Grady advised.

Marvinder had plaited her hair into two long, neat plaits, and helped Jaspal to brush his hair and tuck it up into a topknot under a neat, white handkerchief.

They felt strange and conspicuous, as if they had gone to school wearing dressing-up clothes, and as they walked along with Kathleen and Mrs O'Grady, they kept glancing around, certain that everyone was looking at them.

Everyone was looking at them, especially the other children. But not at their clothes. They were looking at them. No one had ever seen people like that before; brown children; one who wore boy's clothes yet had his hair piled on top of his head in a topknot, and the girl, with long black plaits which nearly touched her bottom. But if anyone seemed tempted to pull them or make rude remarks, Mrs O'Grady was there to glare fiercely with a look that said, 'Don't you dare . . .'

Jaspal's school came first. Already they could hear the shrill chorus of children's voices. On the other side of some iron railings, was a high, grimy red-brick building, with long, church-like windows and a pitched roof. The building was surrounded by hard, grey concrete on which a hoard of children chased and ran.

It was the first time that Jaspal and Marvinder had seen so many English children together. Because it was a cold late autumn, they all wore coats or blazers, scarves and gloves. Some of the girls covered their heads with hoods or berets. They ran about vigorously with bright red cheeks; they played ball games and chase; skipped with skipping ropes and even did handstands up against the wall; and all the time, their voices hung in the air in one long, endless, exuberant scream.

Jaspal hung back terrified and clung to Marvinder. Mrs O'Grady had to drag them apart.

'Come on! You'll be all right. It's bound to be scary first day, but by the end of the week, you mark my words, you'll be running to school, you will. Now then,' she stopped and drew them close within her arms. 'I've got something for you lot from Govind.' She pressed two pennies into each of their hands.

'Ooh good!' cried Kathleen, appreciatively. 'We'll go to the sweet shop after school and buy some sherbet. Do you like sherbet?'

Jaspal didn't respond, but Marvinder nodded eagerly to make up for him. They had no idea what sherbet was, but Kathleen's eyes glowed with such pleasure that they could only believe that it must be something truly delightful.

A fierce whistle blew. Mrs O'Grady waved at a teacher, then pushed Jaspal through the iron gates. It was better to leave him now.

The schoolchildren stopped their games, and skilfully crisscrossing each other like flocks of starlings, quickly formed lines in front of their class teachers. The screaming stopped, and an awesome hush fell over the playground. The children stood with straight backs and hands by their sides. If anyone wriggled or giggled or whispered to their friend, a teacher pounced with ruler in hand, and thwack, struck the offender across the backs of the legs.

Jaspal stood and shivered, partly with cold, but partly with fear. An icy wind blew in sharp gusts around his bare legs and seemed to penetrate to his very bones. He looked back at the railings, but Mrs O'Grady and the girls had gone.

He wondered what he should do. Join one of the lines? If so, which line?

Suddenly dozens of eyes silently turned on him. The teachers turned too, aware that something else had caught the children's attention.

'Ah! This must be the new boy,' said a sharp voice. 'I'll see to it.'

A suppressed outburst of sniggers rippled over the children, instantly ceasing when the teacher whirled round on them with her ruler raised threateningly.

A woman strode over to Jaspal. Everything about her was fawn; a fawn skirt, fawn jersey, fawn stockings. Even her skin seemed a sallow fawn colour; but Jaspal was mesmerised by the pair of bright red-rimmed spectacles, behind which her hard, brown eyes fixed on him, like a hawk about to pounce on a rabbit.

She stood so close, that Jaspal took one step back, and wondered if she would strike him. 'Are you Jaspal Singh?' she demanded.

Jaspal nodded.

'Come with me then,' and with a sharp, long-nailed finger prodding into his back, she marched him over to one of the line-ups.

'Class 6,' announced the teacher. 'This is a new boy. He comes from India. His name is Jaspal Singh. I rely on you to look after him. Graham Shepherd, come here!' she called.

From somewhere in the middle of the line, a boy stepped out and came up to his teacher. 'Yes, Miss Marsh?'

He was a round-faced, pasty boy, almost podgy, with lank, dark brown hair which he kept shaking nervously back from his eyes. He was bigger and taller than the rest, but with the ungainly look of the overgrown child.

'I want you to look after Jaspal. Show him the cloakrooms, lavatories and classroom. I've moved your desk so that you will both be sitting together, and I expect

201

you to ensure that Jaspal knows exactly what to do at play time and dinner time. Now both of you go back into line please.'

Graham cast a silent look which ordered Jaspal to follow him. They walked down the line. The children had maliciously closed the gap that Graham had left, so they had to walk right to the very back.

'Pig-face! Smelly bottom!' Low voices hissed abuse as they passed by.

'Who's your black friend? Ask him why he's got a hanky on his head.'

'Shut up!' snarled Graham.

'Who's talking!' bellowed Miss Marsh.

No one answered. She strode down the line, tapping the ruler on the palm of her hand. The children bowed their heads and tightened their lips.

'March in!' ordered Miss Marsh.

The children marched into school.

Marvinder's school was bigger. It was called a secondary modern for boys and girls. Mrs O'Grady left them at the gates and told Kathleen to take Marvinder to the secretary's office.

They first had to cross a broad courtyard to a side door marked 'Girls', which immediately plunged them into a forest of cloakrooms, with hooks and pegs and coats and smelly gymshoes. Other girls were pouring in and quickly surrounded them with stares and questions. 'Hey, Kath! Who's that?'

But Kathleen managed to drag Marvinder through the throng and lead her up some stone stairs to a polished, wooden-floored entrance hall.

Marvinder got the impression that Kathleen looked a bit nervous herself. She straightened her back, and her hand clutched Marvinder's as if she, too, needed reassurance.

They approached a large oak door marked secretary, and knocked.

'Enter,' instructed a severe female voice.

Kathleen opened the door and said, 'I'm Kathleen O'Grady.'

'Yes, Kathleen!' intoned the grey-haired woman sitting in front of the typewriter. 'What can I do for you?'

'I've brought in the new girl, Miss,' said Kathleen, pulling Marvinder alongside her. You know, the Indian girl who's living with us now. Me mum's been in touch. She's expected.'

'Ah yes!' The secretary took off her spectacles and pushed back her chair. 'Your name is Marvinder, isn't it? Marvinder Singh?' She surveyed her with narrowed eyes.

Marvinder nodded, briefly raising her head, then shyly dropping it again.

'Yes, we are expecting you. You will be in Kathleen's class for the time being, so I think the two of you can get along now to your classroom. Kathleen, tell Miss Clements that you've seen me.'

'Yes, Miss,' replied Kathleen dutifully.

Once outside the door again, Kathleen heaved a sigh of relief, and then said to Marvinder, 'Follow me!'

Marvinder followed her down a gloomy, green-painted corridor and up some stone steps to another green-painted corridor. There was little designed to lift the spirits.

She glanced longingly out of the windows as they hurried by. Ever since they had arrived in England, not a day had ever gone by when Marvinder wasn't reminded of India. It might be the distant bark of a dog or the early morning caw of a crow; it might be a patch of pure blue sky caught suddenly in the branches of a tree, or the colour of wintry grass in the park recalling the fields of wheat around her village.

Today, she saw the church – or rather, what was left of it. It was beyond the grey, concrete playground and over a broken-down boundary wall. The blast of a bomb had ripped off its roof, shattered all its windows and left it an empty shell. Now, all it had for a congregation were the weeds and wild flowers which had immediately seeded themselves, and filled the aisle and pews with their long, tangled fingers. But Marvinder remembered All Saints Church in Deri and the congregation singing hymns; how she used to pump the bellows for the church organ; and she and Edith playing round the gravestones and the day the war began.

Miss Clements came panting up behind them. 'Ah! Kathleen! Is this the new girl who's joining the class?

'Yes, Miss. Marvinder, Miss!' answered Kathleen.

'Marvinder! Nice name,' exclaimed Miss Clements. 'Come on now, girls. Hurry! We're late.'

Marvinder would discover quickly that Miss Clements did everything in a hurry. She walked in a hurry, spoke as though she were out of breath and rustled through her desk in a constant state of fluster. Her face was kind, but always anxious.

As the girls scurried along behind her, Kathleeen chattered amiably. 'Are you good at Arithmetic, Marvinder? I'm not. I'm always getting whacked for mistakes. Not blooming fair. What's your spelling like? You'd better watch out for Mr Bartington. He makes you write words out a hundred times during play time, if you get them wrong. I hope you sit next to me, then perhaps we can help each other.'

Marvinder felt herself flush with nervousness. What would they do when they found out that she had never been to school?

Now, as they approached the classroom, they could hear uproar and Miss Clements became even more agitated. Through the glass-panelled door, they could see some girls and boys climbing across the desks and others engaged in throwing things at each other.

Miss Clements flung open the door. 'Children, children!' her voice wailed. 'How could you behave like this the minute my back is turned. Return to your places this instant.'

For fifteen seconds there was a scurrying round while

children scrambled back to their desks. The restoration of discipline was swifter than usual, because they were consumed with curiosity about the new girl.

'That's better,' sighed Miss Clements, knowing that she was weak. Most other teachers would have declared an immediate detention for the whole class and kept them in at play time; especially Mr Bartington, in the next door classroom, who would be bound to have heard the rumpus, and would berate her for it in the staff room at break. But Miss Clements couldn't wage war on her pupils, perhaps because she had no confidence that she would win.

'Who's that, Miss?' a voice called out cheekily.

'Hey, Kath! Does she really live with you?'

'Is she going to be in our class, Miss?' cried another.

'Where does she come from, Miss?'

Marvinder looked round at all the faces who scrutinised her. Standing uneasily before this class, she felt nervous and vulnerable.

'Sit down, Kathleen,' said Miss Clements, and Marvinder watched Kathleen as she took her place in the third row from the back, her red hair looking even more red against the shades of brown and blonde heads around her.

The desks in the class were set out in rows; six or eight deep and eight across in groups of two with an aisle between each group so that the teacher could walk up and down. There was an empty desk in the very front row right in the middle, as far away from Kathleen as possible. Marvinder knew that it would be hers. She looked at her companions on either side. To the left was a solemn, bespectacled, rather prim-looking girl and on the right, a boy with a not-unpleasant expression, who looked earnestly up at Miss Clements as he chewed the end of his pencil.

'Sitting with the teacher's pet!' hissed a voice as Marvinder was told to sit down.

Marvinder cast a despairing look at Kathleen who

shrugged at her sympathetically. She watched all the children lifting up their desk lids and getting out their exercise books and pens ready for writing. A boy went round with a long-spouted jug, filling up the ink wells. What would they do when they found out about her?

Then suddenly, she heard her name. Miss Clements was explaining to the class that Marvinder had never been to school, though she spoke a fair amount of English; that everyone must help her to catch up and be very kind to her while she was here.

As the morning lessons were first English and then Maths, Miss Clements gave Marvinder some work she had prepared especially for her. Marvinder needed to start from the very beginning. Even holding a pencil was strange to her, and she spent the whole morning copying out letters of the alphabet and eventually writing her name.

At breaktime a group of curious children surrounded Marvinder in the playground. She was flanked by Kathleen and Josephine, who seemed keen to bask in her reflected glory, and stood by protectively as the interrogation began.

'Are you a princess?' asked one.

'Do you ride on elephants?'

'Have you ever seen a tiger?'

'Why don't you have a dot in the middle of your forehead? Were you born without yours?'

One boy said, 'Do you go round with bows and arrows?' And everybody jeered at him. 'Silly idiot,' they laughed. 'She's an Indian from India not a Red Indian from America who fights the cowboys!'

The boy blushed and felt foolish.

These children had heard a lot of stories about India but they had never ever seen a real Indian before, and they touched her brown skin, wonderingly; admired her long, black plaits and gazed upon her as if she were precious.

Marvinder couldn't yet read or write, so in most subjects she was at a great disadvantage, but in the afternoon, she came into her own in the needlework lesson, and not even the teacher was more advanced than Marvinder. Just in one lesson, she produced a beautifully embroidered sampler, skilfully using all the different coloured threads, to create a design of flowers and leaves. It was immediately put up on the wall for display.

At the end of the day, feeling pleased and stimulated, she and Kathleen raced out of school. Jaspal had been told to wait at his school to be collected by them. He need only do this for a day or two until he was more confident.

He was there, alone, walking up and down rattling a stick on the railings. He looked sullen and didn't greet his sister as she approached. Marvinder tipped his face up in the palm of her hand and said, 'Well, little brother, how was school for you?'

Jaspal wouldn't answer, and pushed Marvinder's hand away. Marvinder was taken aback. 'Hey, Jaspal! What's with you then? Is that the way to greet your sister?'

'Come on!' cried Kathleen. 'Remember, I got some money for a treat.'

They caught up with a group of children all intent on the same destination; the sweet shop on the corner. Fingers delved inside pockets, fishing out farthings, halfpennies and pennies. They eyed the huge jars of sweets stacked on the shelves; humbugs, peppermints, Liquorice Allsorts and lemon somethings.

'Hey, Blacky, do you want to try some?' It was Josephine who sat next to her in school. She held out a yellow-stained palm on which she had shaken out some lemonade powder from a paper bag.

'Don't call her "Blacky",' Kathleen admonished her, 'she's called Marvinder.'

Marvinder looked curiously at the vivid yellow substance, into which the girl was dipping a licked finger and then sucking vigorously.

'Try some of mine,' said Josephine pushing forward and generously holding out her palm.

Marvinder licked her finger and dipped it into the

powder. Then, tentatively, she touched the tip of her tongue. Immediately, a sharp, sweet, lemony taste flooded in. It activated her taste buds and made her mouth water for more. She looked up with an expression of wonderment.

'Aint yer never had lemonade powder before?' asked another girl.

Kathleen bought a packet of sherbet powder for herself with a long liquorice stick for a straw.

''Ere! Have a suck of this,' she said, offering it to Jaspal, but he just ignored it and turned away.

Marvinder chose a penny sherbet with the liquorice stick, because she found she really liked liquorice and enjoyed nibbling off a piece after every suck of sherbet.

'Is he your brother?' asked Josephine.

'Brother,' Marvinder confirmed.

'He looks like a girl, doesn't he, with his hair being long an' all that.'

Marvinder shrugged and muttered, 'We must never cut our hair.'

'Who says so?'

'Guru Nanak,' Marvinder mumured, her voice dying away as she saw the puzzlement on their faces. Nobody here had even heard of Guru Nanak, the great founder of the Sikh religion. She wondered if they had even heard of God.

'Is his hair as long as yours?' persisted another child.

'Go on, show us! Let it out. Let's see. Cor! What a lark!'

They jostled round, the mood suddenly becoming too boisterous.

Kathleen called out, 'Look, there's Govind.' She sounded relieved.

He was waiting for them over the road.

The school children dispersed in a flash. Jaspal looked as though he wanted to disappear, too, but Marvinder grabbed his arm and held it tightly.

'I see you've already been in the sweet shop,' said Govind eyeing their packets of sherbert, as he came over to join them. 'Except you, Jaspal. Nothing for you, son?'

Jaspal wouldn't answer and turned his head away, though Marvinder still held on to him tightly.

'He didn't want anything,' explained Kathleen.

'I've brought some stale bread with me.' Govind held up a brown paper bag. 'Thought we could go to the pond in the park and feed the ducks. Shall we?'

'Yes, yes!' exclaimed Kathleen, enthusiastically. 'I like doing that, and seeing them swans, too. There are great big swans. Quite scary. Me mum says they could kill you if they attacked. I've seen these get angry – especially with dogs. They really hate dogs. Did you know that? I wonder why.'

Kathleen was already skipping on ahead to the park, not bothering to know whether Jaspal and Marvinder wanted to go. 'An' I'll introduce you to Polly,' she chattered on. 'Polly's an African parrot, and she's seventy years old! Isn't that amazing? She talks and says rhymes, and she swears too, just like her keeper. "Bloody poor show! Bloody poor show!" and things you can't repeat. Terrible really, but it makes you laugh.'

They followed her awkwardly, aware of their father trying to keep pace.

'How was school?' asked Govind. He addressed the question to Jaspal, but it was Marvinder who answered.

'I had a good day, Pa. They gave me special work to help me to learn to read and write, but no one was better than me at needlework!' she said proudly.

Govind looked down at her and smiled. 'That's good. That's very good. Now, what about Jaspal? What kind of day did he have?'

'Come on, Jaspal,' Marvinder urged him. 'Tell Pa about your day.'

But Jaspal stayed stubbornly silent.

When they reached the pond, Kathleen grabbed the paper bag from Govind's hand. Jaspal followed her to the water's edge, where she willingly tore off a chunk of the bread for him, and the two soon moved further and further away as they got absorbed in enticing the ducks close enough to feed from the hand.

Govind and Marvinder stood alone, side by side. For a while they just watched in silence. Then Govind said, without taking his eyes off Jaspal, 'Tell me about Ma.'

TWENTY

A Man in a Riley

A car drove slowly down the length of Whitworth Road. When it reached the bottom, it did a three-point turn and drove back again, slowing down to a walking pace as it passed Number 18.

At the end of the road, it stopped, and the driver turned the engine off.

The car had already caught Jaspal's attention. Cars were still a novelty for him, and for the moment, had become a passionate interest. He identified this car as a Riley 1947. It was a nice dark maroon colour, with a fine yellow and brown double stripe all the way round the centre of the bodywork. He made a mental note of its registration number; ARG 482.

He wondered if he dared approach it. He had skipped school today, and spent all his time hidden in his hideaway on the bomb site, where Number 23 used to be. But he wanted to come closer to the car; to touch it and admire the gleaming aluminium headlamps, the radiator and the silver figurine on the bonnet.

The driver was well-dressed, as far as Jaspal could make out. He seemed to be wearing a grey overcoat and a trilby hat, so it was hard to see his face, but he got the impression that the man was middle-aged. He certainly didn't belong to these parts, and now Jaspal began idly to speculate what he could be doing.

Five minutes passed. Still the man just sat there. He didn't get out to stretch his legs, and he didn't read, to pass the time while waiting. He didn't even seem to be specially keeping watch, so he was not a private detective.

Jaspal began to get stiff. He was crouched behind a

mound of earth which disguised a door – the door to Jaspal's own secret den.

Suddenly, he saw the driver sit up and look straight ahead through the windscreen. His eyes were fixed on a man walking down the road. Jaspal frowned with puzzlement. It was his father, Govind. It was Govind coming down the road. The driver seemed to be studying him with intense concentration, then he started the car and began to drive very slowly towards him. Govind had almost reached Number 18, when the driver accelerated in order to draw level with him and catch him before he entered the house.

Jaspal saw his father stop with a look of surprise. He saw the driver wind down the car window and reach over to talk to him. Then, to Jaspal's amazement, Govind opened the car door and got inside and the two men drove away.

The street was empty once more. The Town Hall clock was striking three. Jaspal had an hour before he could go home. He slid back down the mound and sat thoughtfully for a moment, like a fox planning his next move. Then he opened the door of his den and went inside.

Jaspal came to his den when he was playing truant from school. It was better than wandering the streets or hiding in the park, especially when it was raining. He never came when there were other children around. He just didn't want to risk anyone finding out about it.

Today, he had played truant from school. Not for any reason in particular. Just that he hated school. He hated the buildings, hated the teachers and hated the children, and anyway, his den was the only place he could go to have complete privacy and feel that he was in charge. It was an amazing find and Jaspal was proud to know that it was his secret. He had been wary at first, for it seemed impossible that no one else knew about it. But gradually, as he watched and listened, he became more and more confident that this was his discovery and he could claim it as his own den.

He was always careful to camouflage the entrance when

212

he went away again, by scraping back the earth, and pulling the brambles over with a long stick. He had to be careful, because most of the children in the street played here on the site of Number 23. It was a great playground – full of old beams, partly propped-up floors; bits of stairway; piles of rubble and bricks and timber and wrecked furniture. There had once been a council notice up saying, 'DANGER – KEEP OUT', but it had been pulled down and thrown on to a bonfire on Guy Fawkes night.

Most of the girls and boys had already made their own dens on the other side. They'd done a good job, using corrugated iron, bits of wood and old curtains to drape around and create a room. They had found charred pieces of broken chairs, which sometimes they patched together, and one lot had managed to drag in a saggy settee.

Jaspal had found his hideaway when he was being chased by a bunch of boys from the next two streets away. They were a gang who called themselves the Spitfires. All the children in Whitworth Road were afraid of them, but there was nobody among them quite big enough or strong enough to stand up to the gang. Jaspal hadn't known about them at first; nobody warned him, so he found out the hard way.

Walking home from school, he had stopped at the park to see the ducks. He'd kept some bread all day in his pocket for them. He reckoned the ducks were his best friends, and he loved feeding them and watching them scrabble about in the water, chasing after his offerings with gleeful quacks. He had just emptied the brown paper bag, when he heard voices behind him:

'Quack, quack, quack! Ducky, ducky, ducky! Is that a little girly with her hair on top? Or is it a sissy boy who'd like to be wearing dresses!'

They had advanced mockingly towards him, led by Charlie Saunders and Jonnie Gladwell. They were the leaders of the Spitfires.

'I wonder how long his hair is?'

'Why don't we find out?'

It took just half a second for Jaspal to realise that they were serious. He backed away, looking around to see who was about, but there was nobody on this bleak December day, except an old lady walking her dog, so he turned and ran.

As he ran, he could hear their sarcastic shouts and jeers and their heavy feet pounding after him. 'Don't let him get away! Catch him! We'll get the scissors and cut all his hair off.'

He was a good runner, Jaspal. But he knew they wouldn't give up. He reached the top of Whitworth Road, but didn't think he could make it to Number 18. So he dashed into the bomb site. First he hid in one of the dens Marvinder, Kathleen and their friends had made. But when he heard the gang spreading out all over to look for him, kicking aside sheets of tin and timber, he knew that was no good.

Desperately, he crawled about on his hands and knees, dodging them this way and that, until, finally, he was cornered, though they didn't know it. Jonnie was coming towards him from one side and Terry, another of the gang, from the other. Between them was a large clump of brambles and stinging nettles. Jaspal began to edge himself deeper and deeper into this painful hole, biting on his lips as the thorns tore at his skin and the nettles stung like a swarm of bees. Then half-fainting with agony, he lay utterly still.

'He's gone! The bloomin' so and so!' Terry and Jonnie had said to each other with annoyance.

'You let him get away, you blithering idiots,' snarled Charlie.

'No we didn't!' they protested vehemently. 'You didn't do no better yourself.'

They began to quarrel among themselves. Then Billy said, 'Well I'm bored with this anyway. We'll get him another time.'

'Oh yes! We surely will! He can't hide from us for long.'

And suddenly, they had gone.

It was then that Jaspal had noticed what looked like the top part of a door. Despite his burning, stinging skin, he scraped the earth away with his hands, and exposed the full door, which after further scraping and prodding and levering, he managed to open.

He found himself staring at a flight of steps descending into pitch darkness. There was an overpowering smell of dank walls and mould, as he tentatively edged his way down two or three steps. Nothing impeded him; no rubble, no fallen beams, no clogged-up earth. The closed door had protected its space, as if it were a tomb, from the chaos of the outside world. But as it was too dark to see even his hand in front of him, he decided to return another time with a torch, or some matches.

What Jaspal had found was the back cellar of Number 23 and it was crammed with stuff. They must have stored most of a household to save it from the bombing, but all trace of the cellar had been buried under the rubble of a direct hit. There was a lot of furniture; the usual things like chests of drawers, chairs and tables, lamps and crockery, but the most fantastic discovery of all was a windup gramophone and a cupboard absolutely full of black, breakable, but perfectly intact 78 records.

Jaspal now lit a candle which he fixed into a saucer. It threw out a dim, wavering light. He needed to stay hidden for at least another hour. He lifted out one of the records and put it on the turntable. Taking the handle at the side he wound up the machine until it would go no further. He pulled a lever marked go, and the turntable began to spin. The dog on the red HMV label went round and round so fast, he was just a brown blur. Jaspal carefully took the silver arm of the gramophone and with a steady hand, lowered the steel needle on to the grooves of the record.

A light lilting introduction from the Palm Court Orchestra filled the air; a high, melancholy tenor voice entered, singing, 'Have you ever been lonely? Have you ever been blue?' Jaspal sank huddled into one of the armchairs and began to think about his father.

For the first time, he began to think about him without his insides twisting with rage; without the burning sense of betrayal, blame and overwhelming disappointment. Instead, he was suddenly curious. He still felt hatred, but it was cooler, and for the first time, instead of not wishing to know anything about his father at all, he wanted to find out more about him. He wanted to know how he knew the man in the Riley car and where they had gone together.

Where did Govind go each day? What did he do? He certainly didn't have the same sort of job as Michael and Patrick. They worked on building sites, setting off each morning in rough corduroys and donkey jackets, and coming back covered in grime and dust. But Govind always put on that same suit and tie and set off to catch a bus, like a man going to the office.

Up until now, Jaspal had never asked and never cared. Now he began to imagine and he began to wonder.

The candle spluttered. It had burnt down to a pool of wax on a broken plate, and any minute now it would extinguish itself. Jaspal sighed with annoyance. The record ended, and he quickly returned it to its brown cover. Then he replaced the gramophone arm and closed the lid.

Well, he wasn't going to stay down here in the pitch dark. Best thing would be to go up and crawl into one of the other dens. Surely it would be four o'clock soon. He opened the cellar door and cautiously peered through the brambles to see if it was safe to come out.

The bomb site was empty, except for a blackbird hopping in the soft earth and a faint breeze teasing at a bit of torn material. But although it was not quite four o'clock, it was almost dark, and it made him feel safe to go out.

He could see the bright lights of the High Street. They drew him towards them. Christmas was coming, and the shop windows were full of decorations and lights and

216

offers to meet Santa Claus. He was intrigued; spellbound at all the wonderful things which were on sale. He couldn't believe that anyone in the world had enough money for that beautiful painted toy yacht, or the silver-studded cowboy outfit with a holster and shiny, metal guns; and then there were the rows and rows of little model cars, all perfect miniatures of the real thing. He looked and looked and longed with a hopeless longing.

Jaspal had been edging along the street, window-gazing. He had stopped in front of Pemberton's and was looking at the magnificent bicycle on display in the window, when he caught the reflection of Charlie Saunders staring back at him. He turned, his body braced to run, but it was no use. He was surrounded by the Spitfire Gang. Three or four of them came steadily towards him, shutting off all means of escape. Then the taunting started.

'Look who I've found,' cried Charlie.

'We've been looking for you.'

'Oi, Blacky, whatchya doing on our patch?'

'Hey, show us your hair.' A hand reached out and flicked at his topknot.

Jaspal tried to move out of reach, but only found himself hemmed against the shop window.

'Why don't you wash, Blacky! Or are you so dirty it won't come off?'

'Na, it's all God's fault. He left them Blackies in the oven too long and they got burned.'

And the ugly voices burst out laughing and jeering.

Now they had come so close, he could smell their breath and their hatred. They began to tug at his clothes and rip off his topknot. Jaspal struggled and lashed out with his hands, but they gripped him tighter.

Suddenly the shopkeeper ran out angrily. 'Oi! You lot! Clear off before I call the police! Go on, you bunch of hooligans, trying to wreck my shop, are you? Go on, scram, the lot of you.'

Briefly, they turned their jeers on the shopkeeper, and in that split second, Jaspal made a dash for it, but he hardly

217

got two paces away, when a boy stuck out a leg and tripped him up. Jaspal crashed to the pavement with two boys on top of him. He rolled around and kicked and struggled and managed to scramble to his feet. Again, they advanced upon him. He faced them, crouching like a wild animal at bay.

'Where's your mummy, little boy – or is it little girl? We can't tell, can we, fellas?'

They broke out into mock sobbing. 'He ain't got no mummy! Ain't got no mummy!' The words pierced Jaspal to the heart like a thousand arrows. They made his eyes burn, his stomach sicken, his fists clench, till suddenly, it was more than he could stand. With a piercing cry, he flew at Charlie Saunders, his fists flying, his legs kicking and his head butting.

There was a gasp of surprise, and a shout of excitement. 'They're fighting! They're fighting!'

Spontaneously, they formed a circle and created an arena for them there on the pavement. Other children, on their way home from school, stopped and joined the cheering crowd, even adults paused to watch the spectacle, as the two boys struggled and sparred, danced around each other and threw out punches.

'Go on, Charlie, let him 'ave it!' voices shouted.

'That's it, go for the jaw. Knock 'im out! Show 'im he can't mix with the likes of us and get away with it.'

But suddenly, there were other voices, more impartial. More interested in the quality of the match. Jaspal was putting up a good fight. He had both fists up, lashing out with his right or his left, equally.

'Hey, that Blacky's not bad!' exclaimed a man's voice in the crowd. 'That's it, sonny, give him a hook.'

Suddenly, Jaspal caught Charlie right on the nose. With a cry of pain, the boy staggered and fell, with blood pouring from his nostrils. But Jaspal had now got so carried away with his fury, that he leapt on top of him and continued punching.

Then, a forceful hand came out of nowhere. It reached

down. He felt gripped by the collar and hauled off. A loud commanding voice said, 'Right, that's it. You can all go home. It's over.'

Charlie got to his feet, humiliated, shaking off the helping hands of the rest of his gang. He clutched his nose painfully and gasped, 'I'll get you, Jaspal Singh! I'll get you. Just you wait.' He staggered off down the street. The crowd dispersed reluctantly, continuing to discuss the finer points of the match.

The grip on Jaspal's collar didn't slacken. He felt himself frogmarched down the road for a while, and then the walking stopped. He felt dizzy. His topknot had been torn off, and his hair cascaded down his shoulders. A car was parked, and he leant on it weakly, panting to catch his breath.

'Right, get in, lad,' the voice was gentler, and moved him aside to open the door.

Jaspal had a brief impression of a maroon car, then he was sitting inside, in soft, leathery seats. The driver went round to get in. Jaspal could see his grey overcoat, and as the stranger slipped into the driver's seat, he saw the trilby hat.

'I'll drive you home,' said the man.

Yes, he knew where home was. He drove to Whitworth Road, and stopped outside Number 18.

'It's here, isn't it?' he asked.

Jaspal nodded. The man got out and opened the rear door for him.

'You've got a good left hook, my boy, but I should stay out of trouble if I were you. You won't remember me, but I'm a friend of your father's. I'll be seeing you again soon.'

Then he got back in the car and drove away.

Jaspal couldn't get rid of the feeling that he had heard that voice before. He stood for a moment staring after the car. It was the same car which had picked up his father. He saw the registration number, ARG 482.

He went up the steps and rang the buzzer twice. Marvinder opened the door. She had Beryl in her arms.

'Jaspal! Brother! What's happened. What have you been doing?' Marvinder cried with alarm. She put Beryl down and pulled Jaspal into the hall.

'Just look at you! There's blood on your shirt! And look at your hands and knees and your hair all down!'

Jaspal, feeling suddenly weak and shocked, flopped on the stairs. Beryl came and stood before him.

'Jaspal hurting?' she lisped with sweet concern. She sat down on the step next to him and gave him a hug.

'What happened, *bhai*?' asked Marvinder sitting on the other side of him.

'I got into a fight,' muttered Jaspal. He wanted to cry. Suddenly his head was aching and his grazed knees felt stiff and sore.

'You idiot!' cried Marvinder.

'But I was winning! I was the one that was winning. I made his nose bleed. You should have seen him – that Charlie Saunders.'

Kathleen came clattering down the stairs.

'What's going on down here?' she demanded. Then she exclaimed, 'Mother of God! What happened to you?'

'Jaspal's been fighting,' announced Beryl.

'Jaspal said he was fighting Charlie Saunders,' added Marvinder.

'You what?' cried Kathleen, awe-struck. 'You never went and got into a fight with them Spitfires, did you?'

'Yeh! And I won him, too!' Jaspal was suddenly beginning to feel quite proud of himself.

Kathleen was clattering back up the stairs, shouting out, 'Mum! Maeve! Jaspal's been fighting Charlie Saunders.'

Mr Rayner, who lived in the ground floor flat with his invalid wife, stuck his head grumpily round the door.

'Clear off!' he shouted angrily. 'How many times have I told you blooming Paddys to stop hanging around outside my door. I'll get you with my stick, if I catch you again.'

He was always threatening them and shaking his stick at them. He never did anything except shout, but the children didn't take any chances and followed Kathleen up the stairs.

'What's going on?' asked Maeve leaning over the upper bannister.

'It's Jaspal,' Kathleen informed her. 'He got into a fight with Charlie Saunders.'

'Oh goodness. Are you all right, Jaspal?' she asked sympathetically. But she could see from his grim upturned face, that he wouldn't talk to her, any more than he would talk to his father, so she sighed and withdrew.

For the moment, the only family he was prepared to be a part of was Mrs O'Grady's. They all pushed inside, Kathleen calling out, 'Mum, Mum, look at Jaspal.'

'God in heaven!' cried Mrs O'Grady when she saw the state he was in. 'They didn't half lay into you. What were you up to? How come you bumped into them at that time of day.'

Then she looked at him suspiciously. 'You did go to school today, didn't you?'

'Sort of,' muttered Jaspal.

'What do you mean, sort of? You should get it through your thick head. If you play truant, them school inspectors will be round. They'll cart you off. I'm telling you. So watch it!'

Jaspal hung his head silently.

When she had fully appraised him, she said, 'I'll get Patrick to take you down the baths tonight. He usually has one on a Friday. I reckon you could do with a long hot soak. Here now, sit over there on the settee and I'll make you a cup of tea while we're waiting for him to come home.'

Beryl climbed up and snuggled close to him. Jaspal tried to move away from her, but every time he shuffled some distance between them, she wriggled up and closed the gap.

'I love you, Jaspal,' she said putting her chin on his arm.

'Get off!' snorted Jaspal impatiently, and moved over to the armchair.

'Come on, Beryl,' cried Marvinder sweeping up the little girl. 'Let's go upstairs. We can cut out those dolls from the book and dress them.'

'Marvi!' Jaspal called out. He wanted her to stay. Wanted to tell her about their father and the strange man in the Riley.

'What?' she cried, giggling as Beryl pulled at her plaits.

'Didi!'

'Yes, *bhai*?' She didn't call him *bhai* quite so much these days. How he wished sometimes it was just the two of them out on the road.

He was interrupted, as Michael and Patrick came in, and Mrs O'Grady packed the girls off upstairs.

The boys were always covered in dust and dirt after a day's work on a building site, so every day, Mrs O'Grady made sure that a big saucepan and a kettle full of water were heated and ready for whoever got in first. The brothers usually went to the public baths on Friday night, so that they were clean for the weekend, but tonight Michael was going to earn a bit of extra money doing an inside painting job. He would have his proper bath tomorrow and then take his girlfriend dancing at the palais.

So Mrs O'Grady told Patrick to take Jaspal along to the baths tonight. 'He's been in a fight, and needs cleaning up.'

'Have you now?' said Patrick. 'Shaping up for Madison Square?' he teased and went off to haul his motorbike up from the shed in the back garden.

'What's Madison Square?' asked Jaspal.

'It's in America. New York. It's where all the prize fighters go and bash each other to bits for hundreds of pounds,' said Michael.

Mrs O'Grady popped upstairs to see Maeve and finding that he and Michael were alone, Jaspal suddenly asked, 'What does my dad do?'

'Why don't you ask him?' retorted Michael. He was at the kitchen sink, stripped down to the waist, washing his body with water from the kettle.

'Don't want to,' mumbled Jaspal.

'Well, it's about time you did want to,' said Michael, soaping under his arms and round his chest. 'He is your dad, whatever he's done.'

'Does Maeve know?'

'No more than the rest of us. She knows what we know.'

'Why can't you just tell me?' persisted Jaspal.

Michael sluiced handfuls of water all over his face and neck, and then with a flannel, mopped up the soap, before finally saying, 'Well, I think he's some sort of salesman. I can't say that I know more than that meself! All I can tell you is that he never seems to be short of a penny or two. He's generous with it, too. I'll give him that. Pays Mum a fair amount and Maeve and Beryl never go short.'

'What does he sell?' asked Jaspal.

'God knows!' Michael grabbed a towel and began rubbing himself dry. 'If you ask your dad, he'll tell you,' he said with a grin.

Patrick called out, 'Are you coming, Jaspal? Let's get off to the baths then.'

Patrick had one of these great old heavy motorbikes with a sidecar. Jaspal had never had a ride before, and was thrilled. 'Can I sit up behind you?' he begged.

Patrick chucked a bag of clean clothes for both of them into the sidecar, then strapping on a helmet, he sat astride his machine, and nodded to Jaspal to climb on behind.

They roared down Whitworth Road at great speed; turned so sharply left at the bottom that Jaspal thought his knee would touch the road, and then they streaked along the High Street, weaving in and out of the traffic until they came to a large old, red brick Victorian building, with the words Town Hall engraved in stone over the top of the entrance. Across a forecourt to the side, was an adjoining building with the words, Municipal Baths and Public Swimming Pool.

They paid sixpence each, and for that were given a

large, white fleecy towel and a bar of green soap.

It was all hot and steamy, smelling of carbolic and soap and swimming pools. But it was nice. They went into neighbouring cubicles and turned on the taps. Torrents of wonderful green, hot water rushed in, and they filled the baths right up to the top, as hot as they could stand it.

'Will you be all right, lad?' asked Michael.

Jaspal had already stripped off, and was stretched out in the bath, almost floating because he had run it so deep.

'I'm right next door then,' grinned Michael.

'Heaven is a long hot soak!' sang Michael through the partition wall. 'When I'm rich, I'll build myself a big house with lots of bedrooms, so that everyone has his own bedroom, and each bedroom will have its own bathroom – just like you see at the pictures! It will be tiled from top to bottom and have fleecy rugs to stand on, and potted plants in the corner.'

'Is my pa a rich man?' asked Jaspal.

There was a silence from next door for a moment, then Patrick replied, 'He's richer than me.'

'What does he do?'

'Well, he buys and sells things, somewhere down the East End – I don't know. In Stepney or somewhere. He used to live there, and has connections.'

'We looked for my father in Stepney. That's how we got your address in Clapham. We got it from an old woman there.'

'Yeh! Well, I reckon Clapham's a better district to live in than Stepney,' laughed Patrick.

'There's some man who knows my father. He drives a Riley. He brought me home after my fight. He knew where I lived. How did he know that, eh?' queried Jaspal.

'Yeh, strange!' agreed Patrick. 'But then, your dad knows a lot of people, and after all, what other Indians live round here? He would guess you lived at the same address as your dad, seeing as how you look like him.'

'I don't look like him at all,' protested Jaspal, sitting up in the bath. 'He's cut his hair and beard. He's like an Englishman.'

'That doesn't mean to say you don't have the same coloured skin, the same shaped face, the same broad nose, the same light brown eyes and even the same way of looking and walking.'

'Hmm.' Jaspal sinking back in the water. 'Do I?'

'Don't forget,' added Patrick, 'it's not only your outside looks which you have inherited. You've probably got a lot of his character too!'

By the time they returned home, Govind had come back. He looked anxiously at Jaspal as he walked in through the door.

'I hear you got into a fight today,' Govind said with concern.

Jaspal nodded and didn't meet his eye.

'Were you hurt?'

'No,' Jaspal spoke the one word almost defiantly.

'Have you thought about maybe cutting your hair like an English boy? You would have an easier time with the boys if you did.'

Jaspal looked up at his father. He looked him squarely in the eyes, his expression filled with contempt. 'Never,' he declared. 'No matter what they do to me, I will never disobey the Sikh law.'

PART THREE

Just as in the Wheel

'Just as in the wheel
The rim is joined to the spokes
And the spokes are joined to the hub,
So all Life and Intelligence is joined
With the Lord of All.'

The Upanishads

TWENTY-ONE
Finding Out

'Tell me about Mr Chadwick,' said Doctor Silbermann.

Marvinder had called to see him after school, as she often did, these days.

'He lived in India, where I lived,' Marvinder started slowly.

She thought about those days so often; but the thoughts stayed locked in her head, because there seemed to be nobody to talk to. She wanted to make friends with her father, despite the fact that he had changed so much; she tried to talk to him. At first he had asked her about Jhoti, and life back home, and what had happened to everybody, but he seemed to go into a daze and not really connect his past life with himself in England.

Yet she loved him; he was her father and she longed to be loved by him; but Govind hardly seemed to see her. She felt invisible. She and Jaspal lived, ate and slept on the first floor with the O'Gradys, partly because Jaspal was still so hostile and partly because Maeve always seemed to have excuses. There was never room for them upstairs, even just for a meal, so Marvinder only went up from time to time, with Beryl or Kathleen. But if Govind came down to the O'Gradys, he only had eyes for Jaspal, and if Jaspal wasn't there, he would just give Marvinder a pat and go away again.

'Mr Chadwick played the violin and Mrs Chadwick played the piano . . .' said Marvinder, as Doctor Silbermann lit up a pipe, and then blinked at her encouragingly through a blur of smoke.

It was like opening the flood gates; starting slowly, at first, but then as the force of her memories piled up, everything that she could remember in the whole of her life rushed out in one big torrent.

He learned of how her world had disintegrated; first with the deaths of the Chadwick twins, then the war and the splitting of India to create Pakistan, the loss of Jhoti, their mother, and their flight to England to find their father.

When she had finished, she curled up in a chair watching the yellow spluttering of a flame in the gas fire. She felt strangely relieved, as though someone else was sharing her burden now.

She had told him things that she hadn't told people on the ship or Tom Fletcher, or even her father, when he had asked. Somehow, she felt Doctor Silbermann would understand; he would understand how important trivial memories were; smells and sounds, small actions, like squatting on the verandah next to her mother while she rocked Jaspal; pushing Edith on the swing; the sound of the bucket clanking in the well; and then, all of a sudden she told him of her guilt.

'They asked me to keep an eye on the twins. They told Edith and me to play with them, because Dora Chadwick, the memsahib, had a big party that night and asked my mother to help her. Edith wanted to play at the palace. She didn't want the twins to come. We ran away from them. We left them unguarded. I should have stayed. It's all my fault! What will God do?'

Doctor Silbermann walked over to the window, and gazed out into the wilderness of the back garden. No one was interested in cultivating it, not even he, so there was an anarchy of weeds and flowers, all dying down now because of the winter.

'What will God do?' he repeated almost to himself. 'Which God? Your God? My God? The Chadwicks' God? Does God DO anything?'

Doctor Silbermann picked up his violin and began to play a slow, haunting melody.

When it ended, he put down the violin and went to the piano. There was a jumble of music, papers, bills, a metronome and bits of worn resin. His long fingers flicked among the items and finally he turned, holding a collection of faded, dull photographs. They were just the sort of out-of-focus family photographs which usually mouldered away in albums. These looked as though they had been hastily ripped out and thrust into a bag, for they were bent and fingered. They should by now have been framed to preserve them, instead of lying around gathering dust on the top of the piano.

'This was my family.' His voice was harsh. 'I, too, had twins. They were both girls, Anna and Rebecca, see here!'

He held out a photograph of two young girls. They had long, dark curls, and pretty round faces with mischievous eyes.

'I had a son, Felix, and a wife, and sisters and brothers, cousins, uncles – just as you did, my dear; see here, and here and here . . .' he held out one photograph after another with trembling hands.

'Where are they?' asked Marvinder, fearfully. Doctor Silbermann suddenly looked old and crumpled as he turned his face away to hide his tears.

'Dead, my dear. All gone. In India, Hindus, Muslims and Sikhs were killing each other; in my country, the Nazis were slaughtering Jews. You see, we both have something in common. We have both been through a holocaust.'

He picked up the violin again. 'You know, even your friends, the Chadwicks, endured a kind of holocaust. They lost their twins, and the grief they feel about that must be as bad as the grief I feel for my children, and you for your mother; and we all feel guilt, because we are alive and they are dead. I don't know what God will do, my dear. All I know is that we, who are alive, have to go on living, and find a way of living. I play the violin to heal my pain. It sounds as though the Chadwicks did too.'

'Yes, yes! They never stopped playing, even after the twins died,' agreed Marvinder. She suddenly got up and went over to him.

'Doctor Silbermann!' She touched his arm, gently. 'Do you think I . . . do you think I could ever play the violin?'

Doctor Silbermann turned and, although his eyes were brimming with tears, looked at her with great joy and said, 'My dear, of course you could; and I will teach you! I could tell you were meant to be a violinist the minute you picked up the instrument.'

Then Christmas overwhelmed them. It didn't matter whether you were Catholic, Protestant, Sikh or Jew, Christmas was hard to avoid. It beamed enticingly out of every shop window, it dominated activities at school, what with making Christmas cards and decorations and learning a part in the nativity play. And the carol singers were beginning to call. Little huddles of bundled-up children, sometimes clutching a carol book and torch, while endeavouring to sing through six verses of 'While Shepherds Watched Their Flocks By Night' and trying not to be silly by singing instead, 'While shepherds washed their socks by night all seated round a tub . . .!'

'What's the money for?' some canny householders challenged them, and wouldn't give a penny unless the answer was, 'for the children in Africa' or 'the RSPCA', and this was even though the carol singers were themselves as poor as church mice, and had really hoped to collect enough money to pay for their Christmas presents.

Jaspal hung in a shop doorway. The shop window was warmly lit with fairy lights and Christmas decorations. Its friendliness drew him in out of the cold.

He had been watching a model steam train go round and round a track. It had everything, this train set; a perfect model station, signals, a tiny model train driver, a signal-man and even trees and bushes along the side. But now, his attention was elsewhere. He was determined to follow his father, and find out where he went each day.

The Town Hall clock had just struck nine. He should be in school, but . . . 'too bad', he thought. For once, he had a couple of shillings in his pocket, collected from carol singing, so he knew he could follow his father on to the Underground. The desire to know what his father did each day had been growing and growing.

Jaspal would have looked conspicuous, what with his topknot and brown skin, so it was just as well that he was wearing a hooded duffle coat which Mrs O'Grady had bought him from the army surplus stores, and a scarf which he wrapped round half his face. Then he waited in the shop doorway, with one eye irrestistibly on the steam train, and the other on the High Street and the entrance to the Underground.

It was a bitter, murky morning, with a thick, yellow smog hanging in the air, too heavy to disperse easily. This suited Jaspal, because most people were hurrying along with their heads tucked down into their collars and their eyes fixed only on the ground in front. The lack of visibility seemed to increase his awareness of sound. He could hear the clip clop of the huge shire horses pulling the milk cart round the streets, and the milkman's cry of 'Milko! Milko!' The trolley buses sounded almost eerie, as they whirred along the cables, and he could hear the conductor begging his passengers to 'Hurry along there, please! Everybody hold tight!' and then the 'Ting, ting!' as he rang the bell to go.

Strangest of all were the people's feet. Somehow, he had never been aware before of such a sound of shoes, just walking down a street; the clicking of high heels, the thudding of leather soles, or the regular tread of the sensible shoe. But today, as he stood in the doorway, straining not to miss his father, he found himself listening to the footfall of hundreds of different, invisible individuals, passing to and fro, their feet carrying each of them to their own private destination.

Jaspal knew that his father usually left for work a little after they had all gone to school. He could just see Mr

O'Grady through the gloom, standing on his one leg on the far corner of the street, with a pile of newspapers under one arm, and a single newspaper held out with the other, as he yelled 'Mail and the Mirror! "Royal Couple Return Home!" Read all about it!'

Jaspal knew to avoid Mr O'Grady. Because if Mr O'Grady saw Jaspal when he should have been at school, he would have bellowed at him and waved one of his crutches, and told him to get himself off to school, or one leg or no, he would get him by the collar and take him there himself.

But now, suddenly, he saw a figure. He was walking briskly. From his blurred outline, Jaspal knew from the height, and the set of his square shoulders, that it was his father.

He watched, as Govind went up to Mr O'Grady and bought a paper from him; they exchanged a few words, then Govind crossed the road, jay-walking between the trolley buses and the cars, which were creeping their way along the street, their dipped headlights scouring a path through the gloom. He leapt agilely on to the pavement at the far side and carried on to the Underground.

Jaspal slipped out of the shop doorway and hurried to the Underground entrance. This was the tricky bit, to follow and not be seen, and to know to which station he was going.

There was a short queue at the ticket office. Jaspal joined it, keeping his back mainly turned away from his father, who was three or four people ahead of him.

As his father asked for his ticket, Jaspal risked edging closer to try and hear his destination, but he couldn't. His father bought his ticket and walked briskly away towards the escalator.

Jaspal's heart was beating furiously. He mustn't lose him.

But he had to wait for a man wanting a ticket to Ealing, who fumbled for the change; and a woman, who needed

234

to know the best route to get to Earls Court, and seemed keen on holding a conversation rather than getting directions. Finally, it was Jaspal's turn.

'Yes?' The ticket man asked him.

'Er . . . I should have been with my father, but I was late, and he's gone without me.' There was a hint of panic in his voice as he tried to see which way his father had gone. 'Did you just sell a ticket to an Indian man?'

'Well, yes, as a matter of fact I did. I often sell him one. He goes to Stepney most days!'

'Me too, then!' cried Jaspal, desperately. 'A half to Stepney, please.' He pushed the money through the counter, snatched his ticket and fled.

'Change at Monument!' The ticket man yelled after him.

As Jaspal reached the top of the escalator, he just saw his father step off at the bottom and disappear round to the left for trains which were northbound.

He careered down the escalator, his feet flying. He could hear a train coming in. The doors were opening. He reached the bottom and dashed round the corner. He looked up and down the platform, then Jaspal saw his father boarding the train several carriages up, too far away for him to get closer, so he just flung himself through the closing doors immediately opposite.

He couldn't relax and sit back. At every stop, Jaspal jumped up and looked out, just to check that his father didn't get out.

The stations passed by; Elephant and Castle, London Bridge, Monument. Monument! Jaspal remembered. That's the stop the ticket man had said he must change at. He leaned out of the open door and looked up the train. He instantly drew back. His father had got out and was walking down the platform, straight towards him. The doors were beginning to close. Jaspal put his foot in the way. The doors opened again and the instant Govind passed by, Jaspal fell out of the train, as the doors attempted to close for the second time.

His father didn't look back. He was following signs for the District Line. Jaspal kept pace behind him. When they reached the District Line platform, there were quite a lot of people, and Jaspal mingled without being noticed.

He got into the next carriage from his father, but was able to keep his eye on him through the intervening door. Tower Hill, Aldgate East, Whitechapel, and, at last, Stepney Green.

Govind got up and stood at the doors waiting for them to open; Jaspal did the same. Govind strode out. He looked like a man in a hurry. Jaspal had to run to keep up with him. When they reached the exit, Govind turned left, and began striding down the road through the fog. Jaspal hardly had to worry about being seen, for Govind never looked back.

It was a bleak and blasted landscape; street after street had been erased by the bombing, and now, tall cranes loomed like long-necked herons through the fog, as the slow task of rebuilding continued day by day.

Suddenly, Govind vanished. Jaspal ran to the point where he had last seen him. There was a pub, a low row of abandoned and boarded-up terraced houses, a bomb site with a lot of open rubble, and at the bottom of a *cul de sac*, a large, partly-bombed warehouse. When Jaspal saw a Riley parked outside the warehouse doors, he was certain this was where his father had gone.

Then there was the sound of another car, coming up behind him. Jaspal's heart jerked with fear, he didn't know why. He leapt into the rubble of a front garden, and hid behind a hedge. It was a large, posh car. He had only ever caught a glimpse of one or two of that make, for it was definitely not the sort of car you saw around Clapham. It was an Armstrong Siddley Sapphire; a high, carriage-like saloon, almost fit for royalty, with walnut panels and light leather seats, and the bodywork painted two-tone – black and bottle green. It came looming down the narrow street, somehow sinister; too big, too opulent and gleaming, parading too much wealth for this poor, beaten-up area.

Jaspal watched with awe, as it pulled up alongside the Riley. Two men wearing heavy, fur-collared coats and Homburg hats, got out and went inside the warehouse.

Then the street was empty and a dull, wintry silence was not broken, even by the few birds who perched motionless on the leafless trees.

Jaspal stepped out from the garden and walked towards the warehouse door. Where before it had been slightly ajar, now it was firmly closed. Very quietly, he leaned his weight against it, turning the knob, but then he realised it was bolted from the inside.

There was an alley running along the side. Jaspal walked the length of it and round to the back. It was full of rubbish; rotting newspapers, tin cans, beer bottles and cardboard boxes. But, there was a window. It was grimy, it was broken, it was quite small and high – too high for him to see inside, but it was there.

Jaspal looked around for something to stand on. The cardboard boxes were too soft and rotted to be of any use. Then he noticed a rusting petrol can lying among some brambles. Trying not to make any noise, he pulled it free of the thorny tentacles and manoeuvred it into position under the window. He threw off his duffle coat. It was too cumbersome, and then he climbed, carefully placing his weight evenly on the tin barrel. He gripped the window frame and looked inside.

There were five or six men at the far end; the two men who had just arrived in the Armstrong Siddley Sapphire, three others, wearing raincoats and trilbies and Govind, trying to keep up his appearance, although he couldn't diguise the worn patches of his second-hand navy overcoat.

They were examining crates and boxes and making lists and handing out instructions. Jaspal longed to get closer and hear more. On the other side of the window was a whole row of crates. Jaspal swung one leg inside and then the other, so that he was sitting on the window ledge with both legs inside resting on the crates. Gripping the top of

237

the window for safety, he allowed some weight to test out the crates. They felt solid, so he eased the rest of his body through. For a moment, he just crouched there, like a cat, then sprang down to the ground. His feet made the slightest of sounds on impact, and one of the men said, 'What was that?'

But no one else had heard, so they carried on talking.

'Right, Govind, you can take the consignment of silk ties. Try selling them in West London.'

'Oh, come on, Mr Elmhirst. I've been with your lot now for nearly five years, and all you ever give me to sell are ties and shirts and ladies' stockings. When am I going to have some of the bigger stuff? You've let Alfie there have cigarettes and booze, and maybe soon the petrol. I could do with more money. I've got two kids come over from India now, and they need things. Give us a break, Mr Elmhirst.'

The two men in the Homburg hats glanced at each other. They didn't look very pleased, but Mr Elmhirst said in an oily but civil voice:

'Be a good fellow, Govind. Just get rid of this lot today, and when you check back here tonight, we'll discuss it. All right?'

Govind shrugged. 'I really do want to discuss it, Mr Elmhirst. I mean, I think it's time I did a little better out of all this.'

'Govind, I've told you,' said Mr Elmhirst sternly. 'We'll talk about it tonight.'

Govind sighed with defeat. 'Where shall I go today?'

'We thought, Ealing, didn't we, Wilfrid? There's a good class of person in Ealing, who might be partial to a silk tie. After all, Christmas is nearly with us.'

One of the men in a raincoat handed Govind a largish suitcase. Govind propped it on his knee and opened it briefly.

'How many ties in here?'

'Two hundred.'

'Two hundred!' Govind whistled. 'Crikey, I'll never get

rid of all those. How much do I ask for them?'

'Five shillings and sixpence. Three for fifteen bob.'

Govind picked up the suitcase. It looked heavy, and he already seemed weary although the day had hardly started. He opened the door, and paused.

'Well, tonight then.'

And he let himself out.

Jaspal dropped down into the alley. He grabbed his duffle coat and scurried round to the front. Govind was walking back down the road, a little less briskly than he had started out. He walked for a fair distance, not back to Stepney Green tube station, but on to Mile End, where he picked up the Central Line for Ealing Broadway.

Jaspal followed his father all day long. Up and down the streets he paced, knocking upon door after door after door.

It was usually women who answered his knock, and Jaspal heard him say over and over again, 'Good morning, Madam!' Or, 'Good afternoon, Madam. May I interest you in a beautiful Indian silk tie? It is the best possible quality. We are just beginning to import them, so you can't find these anywhere else in the shops. Have you men in your household? A husband perhaps, a father or son?'

And if Govind thought the woman open to a bit of flirtation, he would wink and add, 'or a lover, maybe – lucky fellow! Could you think of a better Christmas present than a silk tie? Just let me show you my range.'

Then Govind opened up the suitcase and brought out one glittering tie after another; extolling the beauty of their design, the high craftsmanship and the rarity of finding such quality in a silk tie, in post-war Britain.

'Buy three!' he suggested. 'And you can have the lot for fifteen bob.'

Well, now he knew the truth. Outside on the hard, chilly pavement, Jaspal stared through the misted-up windows of the ABC cafeteria, and felt disgust. After hours of plodding the streets, Govind slumped at a table, drinking a cup of tea. He looked shabby, beaten, a failure, sheltering in the cafés for warmth like some old tramp. He was nothing but a con man. He had conned his family back home, and even conned the O'Gradys. Everything about him was a lie. Now he could prove it. Govind was no scholar, no soldier. He wasn't even a businessman. He was hardly better than a beggar, trudging from door to door, almost beseeching people to buy his ties.

By three o'clock, it was already dark because the sun had never managed to break through the smog all day, and with a look of dejection, Govind decided to pack up and head back for Stepney. It would be over an hour before he got there. Jaspal followed him.

The sun had set behind the smog, so that by the time they got to the warehouse again, the dark had become like night.

The Riley and the Armstrong Siddley Sapphire were there, parked in the street.

As Govind went in through the front door, Jaspal once again slipped round the back and climbed up to the window.

He wriggled inside. It was totally black, except for a ring of kerosene light in a hurricane lamp, which hung from a beam. The same men stood around within the circle of the light. Their shadows crouched like giant conspirators, folding into each other like a many-headed monster, as they leaned inwards, talking.

Suddenly, Jaspal felt afraid. The men looked menacing. They looked fed-up with Govind. They didn't like what he was asking. Their voices became dangerous, hissing like snakes.

'You know what, Govind?' uttered one of the men in the Homburg hats, who had come in the Armstrong Siddley Sapphire. 'You know what? I'm beginning to get sick of the sight of your black face and your whining voice. I'm not sure that I trust you, any more. That last consignment of ladies' stockings; I told you to sell them at five shillings and sixpence a pair. Some little birdie told me you've been adding a penny or two, and pocketing the extra. Have you, or have you not? Now look at these ties. Didn't exactly sell many of them, did you? Perhaps you were asking more than we told you to. Trying to pocket a bit of extra profit, were you? Search him, Sid.'

A man lunged forward, and even though he was shorter than Govind, grabbed him by the lapels and thrust his face within inches of his.

'Getting greedy, are we? Trying to do some wheeler-dealings on the side, are we?'

He thrust his hands into Govind's pockets, pulling them inside out. Not caring that he scattered his keys, tube ticket, coins on the floor. But he found nothing.

'Probably stashed it away somewhere before coming here,' suggested Sid.

Mr Elmhirst studied Govind like a cat sizing up a mouse.

'You make me nervous. It's sneaky people like you, who start doing their own thing. It's scum like you bring trouble for the rest of us, and I don't like trouble.'

Jaspal wondered why his father didn't hurl the man off him. He was just a small little rat. Why, with one flick of his arm, Govind could have sent him flying. Why did he just stand there taking all those insults? Jaspal began to quiver with outrage.

'I told you we shouldn't have taken him on in the first place,' said the other man in the Homburg hat. 'He's too conspicuous, and he's not one of us. We've never been sure we can trust him.'

'How can you say that?' protested Govind. 'Name me one day, one deal, one job where I've ever let you down.'

The other men seemed to be forming themselves into a circle around Govind, while Mr Elmhirst went on talking.

'I've given you an example. You've been selling ties and stockings above the agreed rate, and pocketing the difference, haven't you?'

'Well . . . I . . . just once maybe. I needed some extra cash. I was going to give it you back – tell you . . .'

'Then there were the pants and vests. Did you think because it was Uxbridge I wouldn't find out about it? Well, I've even got dicky birds in Uxbridge, Mr Blackface-Singh, and I heard about the way you double-crossed me, you lying coolie.'

There was a resounding slap, as Mr Elmhirst struck Govind across his face.

'Pa!' Jaspal couldn't resist the choked cry.

'Who's that! Has he brought someone with him?'

'I thought I heard someone here, before!' cried Sid, and suddenly a knife glinted in his hand.

Govind lashed out and made a run for the door. Another man leapt in front of him and hurled him away.

For a moment, no one knew where to focus, on Govind, or the intruder? Jaspal fled into a corner behind some packing cases. On hands and knees, he began crawling down the back of them towards where his father was sprawled on the floor. Suddenly, he felt a strangling grip round his neck, and he was hauled out, choking and spluttering.

He saw the raised knife and shrieked, 'Pa!'

As Govind threw himself forward to protect Jaspal, he tried to push away the man who clung to his back.

The knife came down. There was a fearful shriek. An arc of bright red blood fountained up.

They fell back in horror.

'You got Dave, you idiot. You went and got Dave.'

The two men in the Homburg hats stepped back coldly, and looked at Sid who still held the bloodstained knife.

'Well, he looks done for. You'd better see to Govind. Get rid of him,' Mr Elmhirst indicated Govind, who was still sprawled in a daze, while Dave's blood streamed all round him.

As everyone stared in shock, Jaspal gave a sudden wriggle, and in his moment of freedom, grabbed the hurricane lamp and hurled it with all his might to the back of the warehouse. For a brief second, there was pitch darkness; then a soft, muffled 'boom' as the flame ignited some cardboard boxes. A second later the whole place was ablaze like the centre of hell.

There were panicked shouts of, 'Quick! Get out! Run for it!'

The men fled through the warehouse door, locking it behind them. Jaspal hammered frantically.

'Let us out! Let us out!'

'Jaspal, it's no use.' It was Govind. He had staggered to his feet. 'Which way did you get in? Quick? Before it's too late.' The smoke was billowing all around and beginning to choke them, and the heat was searing their skin and scorching their hair.

'Over there, Pa. The back window,' gasped Jaspal.

'Help me with Dave.'

The flames were shooting all around them. Govind grabbed Dave under his arms and dragged him to the back. Then he climbed on to the crates, and Jaspal had to somehow help to heave Dave to his knees so that Govind could get a grip of him, and drag the dead weight up to the window. Then Govind got out first, so that he could pull Dave through. He let the body drop into the piles of leaves and rubbish, and then reached for Jaspal. As they dragged Dave round to the front, away from the burning building, they could hear the raucous jangle of fire engines.

'Come on!' Govind put an arm round Jaspal and made him run.

'Where are we going, Pa? What about Dave?'

'We're going to a friend. They'll look after Dave.' Govind jerked his head in the direction of the fire engines.

'But they'll say I did it. That I killed Dave.'

'Is Dave dead?' Jaspal was filled with dread.

'I don't know. He looked it. He'd lost of lot of blood. Come on, Jaspal. Run, if you can, boy, run!'

They ran and stumbled and paused; bent over in the shadows to catch their breath, then ran again; down this street, then that street, and finally stopped at a house. Even in the darkness, the street looked vaguely familiar to Jaspal. His father urged him down the steps of a large building, down into the basement. He didn't knock on the door. He went to a side window, and tapped a special rhythm as in morse code. Nothing happened, he tapped again. At last, the window opened, just a crack, then was flung wide and an incredulous woman's face looked out.

'Govind!' she exclaimed. 'Oh, my God, Govind! Is it you?'

'Hush woman, hush! For God's sake. Don't disturb your mother. Can you let us in without her knowing? We're in trouble.'

She shut the window, and a moment later had opened the back door.

She took them into her bedroom. It was safer there. Govind and Jaspal collapsed on the bed, gasping for breath.

'So, you come back to me when you're in trouble, just like you always did,' said Edna Gardner.

'I told you I'd written, Edna, and I did. It's not my fault you never replied, so naturally, I thought we were over,' Govind explained.

'Yeh!' Her body flopped, as she conceded the truth of his words. 'You did write; once; only I never knew till a month or so ago, when your children,' she spoke the word bitterly, 'came looking for you. Me mum got to the letter first and never gave it me.'

'Then, Edna!' Govind got up and gripped her arms. 'Will you help me? I'm in terrible trouble. I need to hide out for a bit.'

She took a match and lit all four sections of her gas fire. Then she turned and saw them properly.

'My God!' She gave a stiffled shriek. 'You're both covered in blood. Oh, my God!' She went as white as a sheet and looked as if she might faint.

'Edna! It's all right. A man got stabbed. We helped him, I promise you. We made sure he would be all right. That's why we're covered in blood. That's why you must help us. Please, Edna. We're innocent, I swear.'

244

She studied them, while her fingers nervously clutched her neck, and her thin chest heaved with anxiety.

'Look, get my boy something to eat, could you?' said Govind in a calm voice. 'A glass of milk, some bread – something. Then I want him to go home.'

'But, Pa!' Jaspal protested. 'What about you?'

'Jaspal, I'm in trouble, but I'm not having you involved, too, do you understand? You're not to tell anybody what happened tonight. Go home. You may be in trouble for playing truant, but that's all right. You can get over that. They won't throw you into prison for playing truant. But this might be murder . . .'

'Murder? Oh my God, Govind! What the hell have you done?' Edna began sobbing quietly.

'He didn't do it!' cried Jaspal. 'I was there. He didn't do nothing. They were trying to kill him!'

Govind gently took Edna's arm and led her to the door.

'Edna, get the boy some food, and let him go. The sooner he goes, the sooner I can decide what to do, and leave you in peace.'

Edna nodded, choking her sobs into her apron, and left the room.

TWENTY-TWO
Missing

When Jaspal turned into Whitworth Road, the first thing he saw was the Riley, parked outside Number 18.

Half-collapsing with fright and fatigue and despair, he leaned within the shadows of a side alley. The men from Stepney had come to the house – Mr Elmhirst, Sid and the others. They must have found out that he and his father had escaped from the fire. Now they were waiting for them. Probably they wanted to kill them both, because he and his father knew who had really killed Dave.

Panic flooded his brain, drowning out all clear thoughts, except one – he couldn't go home. He had to stay free. He retreated further down the alley. It ran along the backs of the houses, and he knew that if he followed it, he would come to the bomb site and the security of his own den.

His legs seem to have lost all their strength and power. He kept stumbling and falling to his knees. As he passed the back of Number 20, a dog began barking furiously. It raced up the fence on the other side from him, snarling into the cracks, as if it smelt his fear and despised him for it.

He reached the bomb site and realised that the heavy smog of the day had suddenly lifted. A moon hung full and free, lighting his way across the rubble. Yet still, in his distress, he wrong-footed, and crashed heavily into a crater full of sharp-edged bricks and broken glass. Clutching a bruised knee, he rolled over on to his back. He stared through streaming eyes, up at a sky as black and vast and star-spangled as an Indian sky. He opened his mouth and gave a long, piercing howl.

'Ma! Oh, Ma! Take me home! Please come and take me home!'　★

Harold Chadwick wound down the window of his Riley.

'Did you hear something?'

'No,' said his daughter, Edith. She sat stiffly beside him, in her warm, school coat and velour hat. Her gloved hands dutifully held a large Christmas parcel on her lap.

'If we were in the country, I would say it sounded like a rabbit or a fox caught in a trap.' He listened for a few moments, his breath spiralling upwards into the chilled air, then wound the window up again.

'Why don't we just go in, Daddy,' she said impatiently. 'It's so cold here, and we've been waiting for at least fifteen minutes. I want to get home for *Dick Barton* on the radio.'

'I'm sorry, darling.' Harold Chadwick patted his daughter affectionately. 'It was good of you to come with me. I just felt that it would be easier for Jaspal and Marvinder, if you were there while I spoke to Govind. You used to be such friends, you and Marvinder. I just hoped that maybe . . .' Harold hesitated, unsure how to express his hopes. The deaths of the twins had hung like a reproachful cloud over their lives. Not one of them had been able to talk about the twins. Yet Harold knew each of them carried an intolerable burden of guilt and shame and sorrow; too much for each to carry alone, and yet, up until now, it was a burden which they had not shared with each other.

'Govind really should be back now. He told me this was the time he usually got home. You see, Tom Fletcher warned me, that the O'Gradys can be a tough lot especially Mrs O'Grady. They're terrified of anything that smacks of officialdom or the law. She gave Tom very short shrift, I can tell you. So I didn't want to knock on the door without Govind being there, or it might be slammed in my face. But I'll only give it a few more minutes, then we'll have to take the risk. We can at least leave the parcel.' He glanced sideways at his daughter's face, trying to identify some emotion, some clue as to what she was feeling.

'I suppose so,' said Edith stonily, and stared out of the window.

'I wonder if you'll recognise Marvinder. I wonder if she'll recognise you,' murmured Harold.

Edith took off a glove and held her hand up into the dull light from the lamppost, shining in through the windscreen. The ring on her finger was inset with one small orange stone, yet it glowed with the intensity of an Indian sun. It was the ring Marvinder had given her. She gazed at it for a long time, without saying a word, then put her glove back on again.

Harold noticed her action; waited for a comment, and when none came, continued talking, just to keep the atmosphere light.

'Jaspal had really changed. Shot up. I only deduced it was him when I dragged him out of that fight, otherwise, had we been in India, I wouldn't have recognised him. Oh, come on, Govind! Where are you!' Harold's fingers drummed the steering wheel impatiently.

Finally, after a few more minutes, Harold opened the car door.

'All right then, darling. We'll just have to brave it. Perhaps we'll be lucky and Marvinder will open the door.'

Edith got out. They both stood side by side looking up the battered steps to the front door. There was no light on in the hall, although they could see the lit windows of the O'Gradys on the first floor, all steamed-up from cooking.

Though neither of them could tell each other, they were both afraid. They knew that meeting Jaspal and Marvinder would be painful.

Suddenly Edith's body jerked with surprise, and she gripped her father's arm. 'Listen, Daddy! Listen! Someone's playing the violin! Perhaps that's the sound you heard earlier!'

They stood transfixed as a Mozart melody drifted forlornly up the basement steps. It enticed both of them down to the garden at the back. Doctor Silbermann often didn't draw the curtains, so Harold and Edith, standing in the darkness, were able to gaze inside his room without being seen.

'It's Jhoti! . . . Or . . .' he looked again disbelievingly, 'Marvinder!' exclaimed Harold. 'It's extraordinary! It's . . . a miracle! Marvinder!'

Once, it had been he and Dora playing each evening, in India, while Jhoti and her children had listened out on the verandah. Jhoti had once shyly told him how the music comforted her. Now, like a mirror image; or a wheel that has turned in time, here was Marvinder in a room in England, playing the violin, while he listened from the outside.

Doctor Silbermann stood at her elbow, with his own violin under his chin. From time to time, he stopped her; played a phrase; pointed out some bowing and then played with her.

'Marvinder!' Edith whispered, and suddenly, something snapped inside her. She dropped the Christmas parcel and rushed to the window. She beat on the glass, shouting, 'Marvinder! Marvinder! Marvi!'

They saw Marvinder stop with astonishment. The old man put down his violin and left the room. Moments later the door opened. He and Marvinder stood blinking into the darkness.

'Is it one of your friends, my dear?' asked Doctor Silbermann.

'I don't know,' Marvinder sounded puzzled.

Harold was about to make their presence known, when Edith ran into the light of the doorway. 'Marvinder! It's me! Edith!'

Upstairs, in the top flat, Maeve looked anxiously out of the window. She could see down the length of the street to the main road. Govind hadn't returned, and she felt a pang of worry. She, too, saw the Riley parked below and wondered whose it was.

On the bed behind her, Beryl lay tossing and moaning. Her temperature had suddenly gone up through the day and her cough was sharper. Kathleen sat with her. Every now and then, she dipped a flannel into the bowl of cold water and patted the child's burning forehead.

'Poor Beryl,' she murmured softly. 'Poor little baby.'

'Kath!' Maeve called her younger sister. 'Do you know whose car that is down there?'

Kathleen got up and moved over to the window.

'Dunno,' murmured Kathleen. 'Looks a bit like the car which brought Jaspal home after that fight he had. Perhaps he's home now. I'll go and see.'

'Don't be long!' wailed Maeve as Kathleen clattered down the stairs to the first floor. 'I need your help with Beryl.'

'Jaspal! You back?' Kathleen burst into the flat. The place was full of steam because all four hobs of the gas cooker contained saucepans of boiling water for Patrick and Michael and there was a large saucepan of rabbit stew which her mother was stirring.

'Is Jaspal home yet?' she asked again.

Patrick had just finished his wash and was towelling his chest vigorously. 'Nope! Ain't seen the boy since I left this morning.'

'Did he go to school today?' asked Michael, as he leaned over the kitchen sink, rinsing and flannelling his face.

'We set off together, this morning,' said Kathleen. 'Me and Marvinder told him we was going to do some Christmas shopping. We went to the Christmas bazaar at the Church Hall. We didn't see him there, though he said he might come.'

'He's getting out of hand, that boy,' commented Mr O'Grady, shifting his leg on the mantelpiece. 'You should be firmer with him, Mother. He's becoming too much of a handful, playing truant all the time, and being rude to his dad. You're going to have to put the wooden spoon to him.'

'I know, I know!' muttered Mrs O'Grady. 'But the boy's not settled. He hasn't made any friends yet, what with all the ragging he has to put with. I don't want him running off, or anything daft like that. It's just a question of time, till he suddenly realises on which side his bread is buttered.'

'Perhaps he's down with Marvinder and Doctor Silbermann,' said Kathleen looking out of the window. The Riley was still there. 'I'll go and see.'

'Well, don't be long, my girl. You and Marvinder be back in five minutes. This stew is just about ready.'

'Righty ho, Mum!' and Kathleen dashed away, slamming the door behind her.

'Govind's late, isn't he?' remarked Patrick, combing back his hair in front of a steamed-up mirror.

'Up to one of his so-called business deals, I suppose,' snorted Michael.

'Jaspal asked me, in the baths the other night, what his dad did for a living. Didn't know what to say. How could I tell him he was a spiv, up to his eyes in black marketeering?' Patrick used a finger to rub away the steam on the mirror.

'Not that he'd know what that was anyway,' said Michael.

'Yeh, but all the same . . . that Govind takes a risk hanging out with a bunch of sharks, and I reckon, he'll get his head bitten off one of these days if he's not careful.'

Maeve came in holding Beryl. The child was red in the face from coughing.

'Mum, I'm worried about Beryl. She's never had a cough like this before. Where's Kath? She said she'd be back quick. She knows I need her help.'

'She's gone down to old Doctor Silbermann to see if Jaspal's back yet. And where's Govind? He's late, isn't he?'

'Yeh! He should have been back an hour ago,' Maeve said fretfully. She smoothed the damp hair from her child's perspiring forehead. 'I think I ought to take Beryl to the doctor's. She don't half look bad. Does she to you?' Maeve held out Beryl for her mother to examine.

Beryl sucked in her breath and coughed, a choking, spluttering, lung-draining cough, which made her face go red.

'I thought it might be the smog 'an all that, but she didn't cough when we was out shopping. It was the minute we got indoors; then she began. Had me up all last night, she did.'

'Yes, I heard her!' murmured Mrs O'Grady. She took Beryl in her arms and rocked her.

'Give her whisky and honey!' advised Mr O'Grady from his corner. 'That's what me mother always gave us! Warms the cockles of your heart, and it makes you sleep.'

'Oh, Dad!' Maeve gave a shaky laugh. 'You'll always find a reason for a drop of alcohol, won't you!'

'But we could try lemon and honey,' said Mrs O'Grady. 'I'll make it up for her after supper. If she's no better in the night, you can take her to Doctor Macarthy in the morning.'

'Hey, Mother! When are we eating?' demanded Patrick. 'I'm bloody ravenous.'

'I'm putting it out. I'm putting it out. Jesus Mary, I 'aven't got six arms. One of you go and get them two girls. I don't know. Everyone's disappearing. Where the hell is Jaspal and where's Govind?'

'I made him a curry tonight,' said Maeve, taking Beryl from Mrs O'Grady.'

'Yeh, I can smell it,' growled Michael. 'It pongs for days after.'

'No worse than stewed rabbit or boiled cabbage,' retorted Maeve.

'Except that I happen to like stewed rabbit and I can't stand curry,' answered Michael.

'That's too damned bad,' snapped Maeve.

'Hey, you two! What the hell?' cried Mrs O'Grady, exasperated. 'Squabbling like a pair of babies. Will one of you please go down and get the girls! Patrick! You go!'

'Why is it always me?' exclaimed Patrick, throwing up his hands. 'I'm fixing me wireless. Send Michael.'

'My God! To hear you all, no one would believe you were adults. I reckon it's you lot still need the wooden spoon.'

252

'Patri . . .'

'All right, all right! I'm going!' He boxed the air and pretended to take a swipe at Michael. 'Make sure little brother doesn't get more stew than me!'

Mrs O'Grady had put out seven bowls and began ladling rabbit stew into them. When she had served five, she stopped and turned round looking harrassed.

'For pity's sake, where are these children? First Kath disappears, now Patrick – and where the hell are Jaspal and Govind?'

Maeve went to the window. 'Hey! You know that car that's been out there all this time? It was visiting Doctor Silbermann. Oh, there's Marvinder and Kath and Patrick. Come and see!'

Michael and Mrs O'Grady hurried over to the window.

'Well!' she exploded. 'Well, I never! They look like toffs, don't they!' and her eyes narrowed, as she watched Harold Chadwick and Edith emerge from the basement.

'Marvinder seems to know them. Look how she's holding that girl's hand!'

This was too much for Mr O'Grady. Usually, nothing would make him stir from his corner by the mantelpiece, once he had got in from selling newspapers, but his curiosity was too much for him, and grasping his crutches, he swung over to the window.

'I wonder if it's anything to do with the young man who brought them kids here – Fletcher,' he grunted. 'Could mean trouble. In my opinion, Maeve should take Beryl and go back to Ireland and live with my sister in Cork. That Govind's no good. I always said so.'

'Don't you go on about that again,' exploded Maeve, turning on her father. 'Govind's all right. At least he brings in the money . . .' she bit her tongue, as she saw her father's face redden with rage, but she added, 'He fought in the war too. You never give him that.'

'Yeh – we all know how some people fought!' sneered Mr O'Grady.

'What do you mean?' screamed Maeve, furiously. 'Are

253

you trying to imply that . . .'

'Shut up, Maeve!' snapped her mother. 'Drop it!'

'Yeh, but Mum! Dad's always been against Govind. It's not fair. Govind's doing his best, same as everyone else.'

'Huh!' snorted her father. 'Best at what? That's what I'd like to know – him and his city suit. What does he get up to? You're afraid to ask, my girl!'

'Gerry O'Grady, you've said enough,' berated Mrs O'Grady. 'Belt up and get to the table. Me rabbit stew's being ruined by the lot of you.' Then she went to the window, pulled it up and leaned right out.

'Kath! Michael! Marvinder! For the love of God, get yourselves up here and eat your supper, otherwise you can just go to bed hungry,' and she thrust the window down again with a slam that made the pane rattle.

'At last!' exclaimed Mrs O'Grady, when Kathleen, Michael and Marvinder came back. 'What was going on down there? Who were those people?'

'They were the Chadwicks, Mr Chadwick and Edith, my friend. We knew them in India.' Marvinder's voice trembled. She wanted to tell them more; tell them that the Chadwicks had known her and Jaspal ever since they were born; they had known her mother and father; they were part of India – her India, and the sight of them had sent waves of longing, anguish and homesickness rushing over her. 'Oh, Ma, oh, Ma!' she cried inside herself.

When she and Edith had talked, the memories which flooded back were almost too much to bear. The sentences had jerked out, short and stilted. Each knew that the other wanted to remember India. Could either of them have ever been so happy, as in those early days of childhood, playing on the swing or exploring the palace? But it was also in India that their lives had been shattered by tragedy. Ralph and Grace . . . Ralph and Grace . . . their names tolled like bells in all their memories; and then Jhoti.

'Is your mother alive?' Edith had whispered.

'I don't know!' The words seemed wrenched from Marvinder's throat.

'Will you go back and look for her?'

'Yes . . . I . . . if my father will take us . . .' Marvinder stretched out her hands in a gesture of helplessness. 'And your mother?' Marvinder asked. 'Is she well?'

Edith shrugged. 'Yes. Well.' There was a long pause, then she commented under her breath, 'She doesn't love me. She'd rather be back in India caring for the twins' grave. She always loved them more than me, alive or dead.'

Edith spoke so bitterly, that Marvinder couldn't reply. Then Edith asked whether she still had the locket. Marvinder opened the top buttons of her blouse, and joyfully revealed the locket which, she told her, had hung round her neck, since the day Edith gave it to her. Then Edith had removed her glove, and shown Marvinder the ring.

'Whenever anyone sees this ring, they want to know where I got it! I always have it with me. We're not allowed to wear any jewellery at school, but I manage to get away with it!' She smiled.

Too soon, Harold Chadwick said they had to go. They couldn't wait any longer for Govind and Jaspal as Mrs Chadwick would worry. He gave Marvinder six pennies and a piece of paper with his number written on it.

'As soon as Govind and Jaspal come home, I want you to phone me. Will you do that?' he asked her earnestly.

Marvinder had clung to Edith's hand. 'Please don't go,' she had cried.

'We'll see you again soon – all of us together, and have a long, long time to talk,' Mr Chadwick reassured her. 'Mrs Chadwick is longing to see you.' Then they had all hugged, said goodbye and driven away.

'Come on, eat up! The dinner's practically ruined.' Mrs O'Grady's irritable voice pushed aside Marvinder's thoughts.

'And what about that brother of yours? Where the devil is he?' Mrs O'Grady sounded angry and worried. 'God knows, I've done my best to be patient and understanding, but the saints themselves would be driven to distraction by his behaviour.'

'I don't know where he is,' stammered Marvinder. She stared at her plate of stew, vaguely wishing it were the curry she could smell upstairs. 'I wish he'd been here to see Mr Chadwick and Edith.'

'There've been complaints from the school, you know, and the truancy inspector's been round. That boy will have the council on to us.'

'He's a chip off the old block, is Jaspal. Him and his father, they're nothing but trouble,' grumbled Mr O'Grady.

Marvinder hung her head. Her joy at seeing the Chadwicks turned to misery. Kathleen kicked her leg sympathetically under the table. 'Take no notice,' her grin said.

'And your father. He's not back either. Thoughtless, I call it, what with Beryl being ill and Maeve half worried to death.' Mrs O'Grady's usually cheerful face was stiff with anxiety.

They fell into silence, eating uneasily. Upstairs, they could hear Maeve pacing up and down, and Beryl coughing incessantly. She seemed to cough in hollow spasms, sucking her breath in with a strange whistling sound.

Suddenly, Marvinder was afraid.

TWENTY-THREE

Have You Ever Been Lonely?

'What's that rattling?'

'Sorry, Mum,' muttered Marvinder. She had slipped into calling Mrs O'Grady 'Mum' because everyone else did. 'They're pennies Mr Chadwick gave me so I could call him when my dad and brother come home.'

'Yes, well!' Mrs O'Grady frowned. 'Where the dickens are they, I'd like to know.'

They had finished eating, and cleared away. Outside it was dark and gloomy and felt like the middle of the night, although it was only seven.

'Boys!' Mrs O'Grady addressed her sons. 'You two better go and look for Jaspal. I don't want him out this late.'

Patrick and Michael scowled. 'We've a darts match in the pub tonight,' protested Michael. 'Really, that boy needs a whipping, the trouble he gives us these days.'

'He already gets plenty of the cane at school,' cried Marvinder. 'Please, please don't whip him here. I'll give him a good talking to, I promise.'

'Shall me and Marvinder go looking, too?' asked Kath excited by the situation. 'We can split up. It'll be quicker.'

'You will do no such thing. I'm not having young girls wandering the streets at this time of night. No, you two'll stay here. Marvinder, you help me wash up, and Kath, go on up to Maeve and give her a hand with Beryl. The poor kid's coughing like a drain.'

Mrs O'Grady began to stack the dirty plates, when suddenly three sharp, fierce raps declared unmistakably that someone was at the front door. For a moment, they all looked at each other with alarm. Mr O'Grady instinctively straightened himself up and reached for his crutches. Patrick and Michael went to the window.

'God in heaven! It's the cops.'

'What!' Mrs O'Grady rushed over with alarm.

They could hear Maeve coming rapidly down the stairs. She burst in, looking terrified. 'The police! The police are here! Oh, God! It must be about Govind! Oh, Mum!'

'Calm down, calm down, the lot of you!' shouted Mrs O'Grady. 'Gerry, for God's sake, sit down. You all look like a bunch of guilty criminals, with something to hide. Kath and Marvinder, go and look after Beryl, she's all on her own up there.'

The two girls, wide-eyed with anxiety, did as they were told.

'Right, Patrick, go and let 'em in.'

Mrs O'Grady wiped her hands on her overall, then took it off, and straightened her hair. No one spoke. They listened to Patrick's feet, almost counting him down the stairs. They heard him open the door, and then an exchange of deep voices. Two pairs of footsteps mounted the stairs.

Patrick nervously ushered in a policeman. The policeman removed his helmet and asked if he could speak with Mrs Govind Singh.

Maeve looked bewildered, as if she didn't recognise her own name.

'Go on, Maeve,' said her mother firmly elbowing her forward. 'That's you.'

'Is he d . . . dead . . . Has he been in an accident . . .?' she stammered, and burst into tears.

'Oh, Maeve! Come on, my girl,' begged Mrs O'Grady. 'Why go on so before we've heard what the policeman has to say? You can tell us all, Officer. We're all one big family here. We don't have secrets from each other.'

'Huh!' snorted Mr O'Grady. 'Except Govind. He's one big mystery, he is. We don't know what he gets up to.'

'Shut up, Gerry!' snarled Mrs O'Grady, and Maeve cried even louder.

'The fact is,' said the policeman, 'we've arrested Govind Singh for the attempted murder of one Mr Dave Greatorex.'

'You what?' There was consternation. Maeve stopped crying, and there was a low murmur of exclamations.

'Murder?' demanded Mrs O'Grady. 'Dave Greatorex? Who the hell's he?'

'A petty criminal. We've had him up before for black marketeering. There's quite a gang of them. Govind Singh got mixed up with them. Selling black market underwear, ties, and other such-like items.'

'Oh, my God!' Mr O'Grady slapped his knee with joyful contempt. 'Selling underwear! Our Govind. Our city gent, who always told us about his business deals – ha!' and he broke out into wheezy laughing.

'Shut up, Gerry, will you!' Mrs O'Grady remonstrated with him again. 'What happened?' she asked.

'There was some argument in a warehouse. A fight broke out. Dave Greatorex was stabbed. Govind Singh was known to be present at the time and involved in the fight. He hid out at the house of an old girlfriend, I understand – excuse me, Mrs Singh,' he nodded sympathetically at Maeve. 'It was the mother who rang the police and gave him away – a Mrs Gardner. There seems no doubt about it. He was covered in blood when we picked him up. But he says his son was with him. He says his son was a witness and he knows what happened, so naturally we've come to interview him. Mrs Singh, may we have a word with the young lad. Jaspal, is it?' He looked at his notes.

Maeve sat down and began to cry softly. 'He hasn't come home. We don't know where he is.'

'We was just about to send the boys off looking for him,' explained Mrs O'Grady. 'He should have been home hours ago, but he's a right tearaway, this one. Always playing truant and coming home all hours, so we didn't think too much about it.'

'What on earth was he doing with Govind!' muttered

Michael. 'The boy hated his father. Didn't get along with him at all. Can't think how he got involved with all this.'

'So he's not here, then?' said the policeman. 'Well then, when he comes in, I'll thank you to bring him along to the police station straight away, no matter how late. We need a statement from him.'

'You said attempted murder, officer?' asked Patrick.

'Yes. So far. The man's still alive, but unconscious. We'll need a statement from him when he wakes up. If he wakes up.'

Marvinder lay in her bed under the stairs. There was trouble. She knew it was bad. They didn't tell her exactly what but it involved her father and the police. All her brain could think of was Jaspal. Nothing else mattered to her now, except to know that Jaspal was safe. Never before had she felt such fear in her stomach. Even during the worst of their struggles, they had always been together. Now, not knowing where he was, she was frantic with worry. She tossed and turned and sat up and lay down. Every sound that reached her made her react. Was it he?

She spoke his name out in whispers. 'Jaspal, where are you? Come home, Jaspal!'

Upstairs, she could hear Beryl coughing. It sounded frightening. The child would cough again and again, and then there was a long pause while she sucked in her breath, until it seemed she would choke, then she finally coughed, a reverberant, echoing cough, which released the breath so that she could take another one.

She could hear Maeve pacing up and down, trying to soothe her.

'Jaspal, Jaspal!' Marvinder felt overwhelmed with fear for her brother. How could she sleep while he was still missing? Patrick and Michael said they had looked everywhere. They had cruised the streets on the motorbike; they had asked various children in the neighbourhood if anyone had seen Jaspal. They went to

260

the park where they knew he liked to go and feed the ducks. They combed the bomb site, where so many children had made dens. Michael said they had searched everywhere and called his name, but to no avail.

Finally, they had come home.

'Well,' said Mrs O'Grady, 'there's no reason to believe any harm has come to him. He's run away, but he'll be back. The minute he gets hungry, you mark my words, he'll be back. You've all done it – remember? Patrick and you, Michael, you've both run away in your time. You came back. He will too.'

She spoke confidently, but it was not enough to reassure Marvinder. Something was wrong, she felt it in her bones. Something was very wrong. He needed help, she was sure of it. She sat up in her bed, her head leaning on her knees; then, suddenly, she knew she couldn't stay put any longer, she must go out herself. Hastily, she pulled her clothes over her pyjamas. It was very cold out there, and she wanted to wear everything she could. She lifted her mac off the peg and wrapped a scarf round her head and neck, then she decided to go down the back stairs to Doctor Silbermann's flat and leave by his door. She knew he never locked it. No one could hear her leave by that door.

She took the box of matches from the top of the gas meter and, in short bursts, lit her way down, leaning against the wall for support, feeling for each step with her foot, before treading.

Even though it was the middle of the night, Doctor Silbermann, too, was awake. He was playing his violin very softly. Marvinder paused to listen. It sounded unbearably lonely. She wondered whether to go in, but then decided not to. But the sound gave her courage as she opened his back door from the passage, and stepped out into the night air. The moon glistened silver along the damp pavement. She looked up and down the street like a wild animal, sniffing the air as if to pick up a scent. She turned right, and began to walk towards the bomb site. Suddenly, a car came driving slowly down the road

261

towards her. She recognised it. It was the Chadwicks' car. She ran towards it waving her arms with joy. The car's headlights caught her in full beam and slowed down almost to a stop. She ran to the driver's window, and cried, 'Oh, Mr Chadwick! I'm so glad you came back, I . . .'

She recoiled with horror. It wasn't Harold Chadwick at the wheel. It was another man, who scrutinised her with a hard expression. He wound down the window, as she withdrew step by step, backwards.

'Hey, you! Are you connected, by any chance, with Govind Singh, or his son?'

A man in the shadows of the back seat leaned forward and peered up at her. 'We should take her, Sid. You don't get many blackies round these parts. She's probably related.'

'The driver began to open his door. 'Hey, you!' he called. 'Don't go away.' He was trying to sound friendly. 'We can take you to Govind Singh.'

Now Marvinder began to run. She heard the man swear. He got out of his car and began to run after her. Marvinder looked round desperately. The man was between her and home. She fled across the road. She could see the outlines of the bomb site. She knew every ditch and crater, every pile of rubble, every half-fallen wall. Sometimes crawling, sometimes running, sometimes just lying very, very still, she managed to escape the men. She could hear them cursing and swearing as they stumbled, tripped and groped their way across the rough ground.

Suddenly, one of them fell heavily with a sharp yell of pain. 'Darnation! My ankle. I think I've twisted it. For pity's sake, Sid, let's get the hell out of here. We'll never find the kid in all this. We should watch the house. That's where they'll come back to sooner or later. Come on.'

The two men staggered away, and after a while, Marvinder heard the car start up and move off.

She was lying sprawled flat on her stomach close to a thick patch of brambles and weeds. Even though they had gone, she didn't move immediately, but lay there with her head on her arm. She could hear something. At first she thought she must be dreaming. It seemed to be music, coming very faintly to her from beneath her head. She got to her feet, but then, she couldn't hear it any more. So she lay back down with her ear to the ground. Yes, there it was again. Music coming from below. She crawled along, trying to trace its source. Her pyjamas, day clothes and raincoat protected her from the tearing thorns and stinging nettles. She thrust a path through them, staying only where she could hear the music. Then she saw the door. It was not quite hidden within the very middle of the bramble patch. It was a simple door, an ordinary wooden door with an ordinary door knob.

Slowly, she gripped the knob and turned. The door swung silently inwards, and as it did, the music welled upwards from somewhere beyond the flight of steps. 'Have you ever been lonely?' sang the tenor voice.

Marvinder crept down, down, down. There was the faintest light glimmering from within, to light her way.

She stepped forward. Somehow, she hadn't been afraid, and now she wasn't surprised when she saw her brother, curled up in a large, high, winged chair. On a tall-legged table at his elbow was a flickering candle, and near it, an old gramophone with a record going round and round.

She called out softly, so as not to startle him.

'Jaspal, *bhai*! It's me, Marvinder!' she spoke in Punjabi.

With the instincts of a hunted animal, Jaspal leapt to his feet, his eyes wide with anticipation, instantly appraising his options in the face of danger. Marvinder ran forward so that he could see properly. 'Jaspal, *bhai*, it's me. Didi! I'm so glad I've found you.'

As though every last vestige of physical and emotional strength had gone, Jaspal crumpled into his sister's arms.

How many times during their flight across India, had Marvinder nursed, rocked and soothed her younger brother? Now, once again, she held him in her arms and stroked his brow and whispered to him that everything would be all right; that he was safe and nothing would happen. Just hearing his sister speaking to him in Punjabi, as she used to before, comforted him, and gradually his shoulders stopped heaving, and he began to breathe with the evenness of sleep. She eased him back into the chair, and looked around for something that would make a bed. There was no going home tonight, while those men were around.

There was a crate containing curtains. They were old and musty, and as she dragged them out, she disturbed some spiders and beetles which scurried away. The candle was getting very low and was beginning to waver in its last flickers of life. Marvinder worked fast. She found some cushions, cardboard and piles of old newspapers. She spread them out to create as much padding as possible, then coaxed Jaspal to lie down where he could stretch out and sleep.

Then she lay down beside him, and arranged some curtains over them as a blanket.

They were together again. Jaspal was safe. Nothing else mattered for the moment. She lay with her arms around him, watching the ceiling fade into black as the candle went out.

TWENTY-FOUR
On the Run

When Harold Chadwick and Edith returned home, Dora was hovering anxiously in the bay window of their suburban semi-detached house. They were much later than they said they would be, and because it was still foggy, she had begun to imagine that they had crashed or had some mishap.

She opened the front door to them, looking pale and agitated. 'Thank God, you're back. I was getting so worried, and I wouldn't have known where to look for you.' She pulled them both in, and helped Harold off with his coat.

They went thankfully into their warm, elegant sitting room, with its grand piano in the window, its Wilton carpet and Indian rugs; its comfy Chesterfield sofa and easy-chairs, and its chintz curtains and cushions to match. Superimposed over all this were the Christmas decorations, which looped in colourful paper chains from one corner to another, and the mantelpiece already crammed with Christmas cards, and the Christmas tree in one corner, adorned with lights and tinsel and stars.

Dora had put on all four bars of the wooden-encased gas fire, with the warm red glow of the artificial coals which gave that extra impression of cosy comfort.

'I suppose I've missed *Dick Barton*,' muttered Edith, going over to the wireless and switching it on.

''Fraid so, darling,' replied Dora, 'but, tell me, please! Did you actually meet Govind, Marvinder and Jaspal. Oh, darling, how was Marvinder? Was she pleased to see you? Do tell me, how are they?' Dora's questions tumbled out eagerly.

'We only saw Marvinder,' said Edith. 'Govind and Jaspal were late home, and we couldn't wait any longer.' She fiddled with the tuner, turning it through the different stations. Harold sat quietly, and lit up a pipe. He looked withdrawn and thoughtful. While Edith continued to tell her about Marvinder, Dora went over to a cocktail cabinet and poured out a whisky and soda.

'Here, darling!' She put it in her husband's hand. 'You look as though you could do with this. Is everything all right?'

'They live in such a dreadful slum, Mummy!' said Edith. 'The smell was almost unbearable. I wanted to hold my nose. But do you know what? She plays the violin. She's learning from a man who lives downstairs. We heard her, didn't we Daddy?'

Harold nodded. 'Yes, it was quite extraordinary to see Marvinder playing the fiddle.'

'Who's this man?' asked Dora, intrigued.

'A Doctor Silbermann,' said Harold. 'He's a Jewish refugee from Vienna. Lost his whole family in the Nazi concentration camps. He had been a professional violinist, he told me. Actually played with the Vienna Philharmonic. Now here he is, living in a slum in South London, teaching another little refugee, our own Marvinder, no less, how to play the violin. He says she's good. Got talent. I mean she's only been learning a matter of weeks, and already she knows her positions and is playing tunes. He was so pleased to meet me, because Marvinder had told him that she had learned to love the violin from hearing you and me play in India!'

'I've heard you both play all my life, and it didn't make me want to play the violin, or the piano,' cried Edith, her voice edged with jealousy. 'I expect you would have liked a child who did.' She was being cruel, and she knew it. Ralph had often fretted to be allowed to touch the piano, and he had shown every promise of wanting to learn.

'I think it's time you were in bed, now,' said Harold hastily.

'Yes,' said Dora. Her voice was brittle. 'I'll go up and run your bath.'

'Dearest Edith.' Harold drew his daughter on to his knee. 'We love you as you are. We grieve for our twins, of course we do, but you were our first, and now you are our last, and we love you extra specially. We need you extra specially. Don't you see?'

Edith's body was stiff and unforgiving. 'Yes, I do see. Goodnight, Daddy,' and she put her face forward for her goodnight kiss, then went upstairs.

When Dora finally came downstairs, Harold had got out his violin and selected some music which lay open on the piano. 'Do you know, Dora,' Harold suddenly spoke with anguish. 'I could almost blame myself for everything that has gone wrong in the world. I feel like some kind of evil jinx; an avenging angel. Wherever I've gone, I've left disaster behind me. Yet – I didn't mean it. I've only ever wanted good.'

'Harold, what on earth do you mean? What are you saying?' Dora took the violin from him, put it down and led him to the sofa. She sat close, putting her arms round him. For the first time, she felt the stronger one as she could sense him shuddering.

'If I hadn't gone to India, I wouldn't have met Govind. If I hadn't met Govind, he would have stayed in India and been the farmer that his father had been, and his grandfather before that. If I hadn't gone to India, you wouldn't have either. We would have had our children in England. Don't you see? Ralph and Grace might still have been alive; Jhoti, Govind and their children might still have been together. Jaspal and Marvinder wouldn't have come to England – to live in . . . yes, Edith was right – an awful slum. Somehow, poverty here seems so much worse, so much more degrading; and Edith, Edith might have felt more loved. I feel responsible for everything.' He bowed his head in his hands. 'Please forgive me, Dora. Please forgive.'

★

There was nothing to tell Jaspal and Marvinder that it was dawn. No natural light penetrated the cellar. So they just slept and slept, until their bodies no longer required any more sleep, and they finally awoke in the darkness.

Marvinder felt the box of matches lying close to her fingers. She sat up and struck a match, and Jaspal opened his eyes, blinking with pleasure that he was not alone. 'Are we going to go home?' he asked.

'If the men have gone,' said Marvinder. 'I'll creep up and see.'

Another match lit her way up the steps where she opened the cellar door. More pleasurable than the grey daylight, which met her eyes, was the rush of sweet-smelling air; the smell of dew on grass and brambles, Michaelmas daisies and ragwort; the smell of damp, clean earth. She listened. The birds whistled so sweetly. In the distance, she could hear a faint roar of traffic from the main road, and that particular whine of the trolley buses; and coming down the street was the steady clip–clop of the milk cart, and the tinkle of bottles, as the milkman made his deliveries. The thought of a glass of milk brought an ache of hunger to her stomach, and she knew that Jaspal, too, must be famished. She still had Mr Chadwick's six pennies in her pocket. Should she risk being seen in the road to buy a bottle of milk? She could buy half a pint and still have threepence left for a phone call.

Stealthily, bending low, she made her way across the bomb site. The huge shire horse was standing patiently, harnessed to a large milk cart which was stacked high with bottles. Beyond the horse she could see down the road to Number 18. There was no sign of any car. Now that she had heard Jaspal's account of what had happened in the warehouse, she understood who those men must have been, and the danger her brother was in.

Perhaps, they should just go home. After all, Michael and Patrick were there. They would protect them. All she and Jaspal had to do was cross the road and run a few yards down. Marvinder hesitated, then ran back to the cellar.

'Jaspal, *bhai,*' she called. 'Come on out, quickly. There's no one around except the milkman. We should go home. Come! Hurry! Everyone will be so worried.'

Jaspal emerged like a dishevelled field mouse, his hair muffed up, his eyes not yet accustomed to the light.

'Are you certain?' he asked warily.

'I looked and didn't see anything,' she assured him.

'Well, be careful anyway. Stay hidden, until you are absolutely sure.'

The brother and sister crept towards the road. The milk cart had moved down a bit, and the horse was snorting great clouds of warm breath into the early morning air. There were no such huge horses in India, with their great hooved feet and clumps of hair around the ankles, so Jaspal and Marvinder were a little nervous of getting too close, but they used the horse and cart as a shield and checked that their way was clear. The street was empty. Even the milkman was out of sight.

'Let's go!' whispered Marvinder. They moved out, walked down the pavement a little way; began to run, their eyes fixed on Number 18. They started off across the road, but as they reached the middle, a car suddenly accelerated out from nowhere. The children froze with horror. It was the Riley. They turned and ran, back towards the bomb site, but now they knew they dared not hide out there any more. They stumbled across the rough ground and out into the alley on the other side, where the men couldn't drive. They ran and ran towards the main road. They would be safer there with all the people around. On the corner, Marvinder saw a red telephone box.

'I'll telephone Mr Chadwick. He'll come and get us,' Marvinder gasped. 'Keep a look out!'

She pulled open the heavy door and fumbled for her pennies, and laid them out on top of the phone box. She had never made a phone call before but she had stood next to Mrs O'Grady while she telephoned her brother in Kilburn. Now, with shaky fingers, she went through the

269

process. She pulled out the envelope on the back of which Harold had written his number. RIC 4492. She put in her three pennies, dialled the number and waited. She could hear the ringing at the other end. It was still early, perhaps everyone was still asleep. As she waited, she could see Jaspal, nervously looking up and down the road, keeping a look out for the Riley. Suddenly, he began to wave and gesticulate desperately. At that moment, the phone was picked up. It was Edith who answered, but before Marvinder could press button A, Jaspal had flung open the door and pulled her out, leaving the telephone dangling from the cord.

'They're coming! They've seen us! Where do we go?' Jaspal's voice rose with panic.

Marvinder dragged him along towards the tube station. They had to cross the road, zig-zagging between the cars and buses. There were three men now. Two of them had got out and were advancing on them. Jaspal and Marvinder stood paralysed in the middle of the main street, with the traffic pouring round them. Suddenly, they heard a fierce tooting and an angry voice bellowed at them.

'You crazy or something! Get off the road this instant!' It was a furious-looking taxi driver leaning out of his cab window waving a fist at them.

Marvinder would never know how she dared, or where she got the inspiration from, but quick as a flash, she pulled open the taxi door and bundled herself and Jaspal inside.

Before the taxi driver could protest, she said as authoritatively as possible, 'Take us to Hampstead. Number 26 Heath Drive.'

The taxi driver turned round suspiciously. They looked like nothing but a couple of ragamuffins and he was all ready to throw them out. But there was something so desperate and urgent about their faces, that he just mumbled, 'I hope you can pay for this, for believe me, if you can't, I'll be driving you to the police station.'

'Please, hurry,' begged Marvinder. 'We'll pay when we get there,' and the children crouched low, as they glimpsed the men hunting up and down the street for them.

'Marvi! How are we going to pay?'

'You don't have to give any money until you arrive,' explained Marvinder, 'and we're going to Aunt Gertrude's. She'll pay. I'm sure of it. She can lend us the money and one day we'll give it her back.'

It was only when they had crossed the river and were heading north towards Hampstead, that Jaspal and Marvinder felt relaxed enough to sit back comfortably in their seats, though they both kept looking out of the rear window to ensure that no one was following. It was twenty minutes later that the taxi climbed the hill to Hampstead, and turned left into Heath Drive. He came to a stop outside Number 26. Both children got out. The taxi driver did, too. He wasn't going to risk them scarpering off on to the Heath without paying. He stood guard while they went to the front door and rang the bell. He couldn't imagine what a couple of beggars like these could be doing at a house like this.

Annie opened the door. When she saw the children, she squealed with amazement and left them standing on the doorstep. She ran back into the house, yelling, 'Madam! Madam! It's them Blackies. They've come back.'

Two cats came sliding out of the doorway and entwined themselves around the children's legs as they waited. Cook appeared from the kitchen. 'Well, come on in then, don't just stand there with the door open,' she cried, but beaming all over her face.

'We need to pay the taxi,' said Marvinder fearfully.

'Oh, gracious me! Lord and Lady Muck now, are we, going round in taxis?' joked Cook.

Aunt Gertrude came hurrying out of her study, full of exclamations. 'Why CHILDREN! How WONDERFUL to see you. Come in. COME IN.'

'Aunt Gertrude, we had to take a taxi, and I haven't got

the money to pay him,' quavered Marvinder, now wondering how she had ever dared take the taxi in the first place.

Aunt Gertrude went out and saw the taxi driver leaning on the garden gate, his engine still running and the meter ticking over.

'My goodness,' she cried. 'Just a minute, I must find my handbag.' She rushed back inside, and then came out again a few moments later, pulling open a purse and anxiously demanding how much was owing.

The taxi driver checked the meter. 'That's ten shillings and sixpence,' he said.

'Oh, well,' murmured Aunt Gertrude, 'I SUPPOSE there's no choice. HERE you are, my man,' and she handed him a ten shilling note and a two shilling piece. 'Just give me back a shilling,' she said, 'and THANK YOU for bringing them.'

'Thank you, ma'am,' he doffed his cap. 'I'm just glad they weren't a couple of hooligans trying to trick me.'

'I promise we'll pay you back, Aunt Gertrude,' said Marvinder earnestly.

'Don't worry about it now. Let's go in and find out what on EARTH has brought you here. Now, have you had breakfast?' Her keen eye had already detected Jaspal leaning weakly against the wall, and noted their unbrushed hair and their clothes all covered in earth and dust.

The children shook their heads. Cook was instantly despatched to make a hearty breakfast, and while they were waiting, Aunt Gertrude gave them a glass of milk each to drink, and listened, while they told her the extraordinary story of their father.

'Dear, oh dear, oh dear!' exclaimed Aunt Gertrude from time to time. 'What a to-do!'

'I was trying to telephone Mr Chadwick,' said Marvinder, 'but then the men came back and nearly caught us.'

When Aunt Gertrude heard the Chadwicks' name, she smiled with relief. 'THEY'LL know what to do! Oh

EXCELLENT! I must telephone them immediately. Have you their number, Marvinder?'

Marvinder felt a surge of panic. She had left all her pennies and the number in the telephone box. She closed her eyes. She had dialled the number. What was it. She said it slowly, 'RIC 4492.'

From where they were seated in the kitchen, Jaspal and Marvinder couldn't quite hear what Aunt Gertrude said on the telephone. There was a lot of, 'Yes, they just turned up in a taxi . . . yes . . . hmmm . . . yes . . . no . . . all right . . . whatever you think . . .'

Cook presented them with a king's breakfast. They had a steaming bowl of porridge, followed by boiled eggs, lots of toast and lashings of butter, even though it was severely rationed; then an apple and another glass of milk. 'Gracious me! Anyone would think you hadn't eaten in a week,' observed Cook, as the children gobbled up their food.

Aunt Gertrude came in and told them that the Chadwicks were coming later, about midday. 'I suggest that you go and play on the Heath with Annie. Take a bat and ball. I know it's hard to tell with your kind of colour, but I would say that you were both rather pale underneath that brown skin! A good dose of fresh air and exercise is the best answer!'

Annie looked pleased. It got her off having to do the washing up and peeling the potatoes. She pulled on her coat, and soon the three of them were racing across the wintry Heath.

What Aunt Gertrude didn't tell Jaspal and Marvinder was that the Chadwicks were first going to call by at Whitworth Road and tell the O'Gradys that the children were safe, and then Harold was going to the prison, where Govind was being held on remand. It was on a smaller charge of black marketeering, but with the threat that he would later be charged for attempted murder, or even murder, if Dave Greatorex died.

★

273

Harold dropped Dora and Edith off at Dora's friend's flat in Maida Vale, where they could wait comfortably while he went to the prison.

'Here, but for the grace of God go I.' He remembered the words with a shudder as he passed through the prison gate. Once more, he was overwhelmed by a sense of responsibility. It was his fault that Govind was here. His fault that this man could be charged with murder, could be found guilty, and hanged by the neck until he be dead.

Briefly, his courage failed him. He hesitated and felt sick. The warder asked him if he was all right. Harold nodded and straightened himself, and followed him into the interview room.

When Govind was led in between two warders and seated on the other side of the glass, Harold had to force himself to raise his eyes and meet Govind's. He wasn't sure he would recognise him any more. What should he expect? Would he see fear, anger, defeat, weakness? Instead, he looked up and saw a face brimming with relief and friendship; a face which he didn't instantly recognise, without the beard and turban, but whose eyes and voice were instantly familiar.

'Mr Chadwick, Sahib!' Govind's voice broke slightly as he spoke his name. 'I am so happy to see you.'

'Govind!' Harold held up a hand in salute. 'My dear fellow. I am so sorry to find you in this mess. I have come to see how I can help.'

There was a long silence, while each man struggled with memories and emotions.

'If only the war hadn't broken out . . .' Harold shook his head with guilty despair. 'Could things have worked out differently, Govind?'

'I don't know, sir. I . . . England disturbed me. And then the war, too. It changed my values. It made me forget India – even my wife and children . . . They stopped being a part of me. They belonged to another life, and I couldn't imagine ever going back to it.' Govind dropped his head in shame. 'Now,' he continued, his head still lowered, and his voice almost at a whisper, 'Now, I am about to bring shame again, on my other . . . wife . . . Maeve, and my other child Beryl . . . and it's no wonder that my son Jaspal hates me. Whatever punishment they give me, I will deserve it – even death.'

'No, no, no!' Harold cried passionately. 'You will not face death. Your son is safe and free to tell the story; and this man, Dave Greatorex, may not die, and he too will tell the truth. Have courage, Govind, and do not take all the blame for what has happened to you. I share it with you. If it hadn't been for me, you would not have come to England and got into this mess, so share your guilt with me, and we'll fight this together.'

'Sir,' Govind said quietly. 'You and your missus have already suffered too much. Marvinder told me about the deaths of your children. She and Jaspal feel guilt. It seems our lives are all connected and intertwined.'

'Yes, Govind, they are.' Harold got to his feet. 'I am now going to see Jaspal and Marvinder. I expect they will come and visit you in a few days, if you wish.'

'Oh, God, no, no! I couldn't bear them to see me like this. I have already disgraced them so much. Please preserve them from this. Preserve me from seeing the disappointment in their faces.'

'As you wish, Govind,' said Harold quietly. 'In any case I will return in a day or two.'

Annie, Jaspal and Marvinder were wandering slowly back across the Heath. They had chased and played and the brisk, fresh air had brought colour back into their cheeks. Marvinder said that being so high up on the Heath and looking across over London was like being on top of the world. 'It's as good as the Himalayas,' she cried, and they all laughed.

As they came over the rim of the hill and saw Heath Drive winding up before them, Jaspal and Marvinder suddenly stopped dead in their tracks, clutching each other with fear. A Riley was cruising slowly up the road.

275

'Hey, you two! What's up?' demanded Annie.

'It's them – the men! The ones looking for Jaspal!' cried Marvinder. They dropped to the ground, lying flat on their stomachs in the long yellow grass.

Marvinder turned her face towards Jaspal and said, 'The Chadwicks have a Riley, too!'

'Do you remember their number?' asked Jaspal.

'Of course not,' said his sister.

'ARG 482,' murmured Jaspal. 'That's the number of the men's car.'

'Are you sure?' asked Marvinder.

'I read it the first time I saw it, waiting outside our house in Whitworth Road. It must have been one of them who brought me back after the fight.'

'Then we must run. We must get away again,' cried Marvinder. 'Annie, Annie! Those are the men who are after us. We must hide again. Where shall we go?'

Annie looked puzzled. 'Are you sure? I've just seen a lady get out, and a girl. Now there's a man getting out. He doesn't look like a crook to me. He looks like a proper gentleman. Are you sure it's them?'

Marvinder and Jaspal risked a little peep.

'Jaspal!' Marvinder leaped joyfully to her feet. 'It's the Chadwicks!'

'Is that Mr Chadwick?' Jaspal stared intently at the man in the grey overcoat and the trilby hat. He stared again at the Riley as the truth dawned on him. 'So it was Mr Chadwick who took me home after the fight!' exclaimed Jaspal wonderingly. 'And I thought he was one of them crooks because they had a Riley too. I remember now, there was something about him . . . I recognised his voice . . . but he didn't look anything like what he looked in India, so I didn't realise . . . Come on!' He gave a shout of excitement. 'Let's go!'

As they went racing down the hill towards the road, Edith saw them. She laughed and pointed, then came running, running, running, to meet her old friends once more.   ★

276

Dora was waiting for them. She stood, half in the shadows of the wintry room, and half-lit by a pale light which filtered in from the bay window. It was as though she had halted time in its tracks. Nothing about her had changed. Her slim body was still tense and schoolgirl-straight, clasping her hands nervously in front. The skin of her face, seemed if anything, even smoother, drawn tautly over her cheekbones and across her brow; and her eyes, though blue, burned hot like an Indian sky waiting for the rains.

There was a smell of lemons and temple flowers; a sweet fragrance of cloves and cardamom and cooking rice and the coconut oil which Jhoti used in her hair.

There were doves cru-cruing and quarrelling crows, and the fever bird monotonously climbing the scale over and over again. She could hear the creak of the rope as someone sat on the swing, and children's voices invaded her ears calling, laughing, arguing and protesting.

The sun, streaming through into the living room, was the same sun which had etched shadows of ferns and hanging flowers across the stone verandah, and during hot afternoons, had prised its burning way between every slit and chink: between the frets of the bamboo blind, or the Indian curtain wafting in the doorway, or the shuttered windows of a darkened bedroom.

When Dora saw Jaspal and Marvinder standing before her, it was as though they all turned slowly on a wheel, backwards through time; her twins came alive. She saw them, their bare limbs burnishing under the Indian sun, golden as temple idols; Jaspal glided past on his buffalo; Marvinder sidled down the hibiscus hedge towards the swing and Jhoti and Maliki chatted on the verandah.

They came into the living room, hesitantly, their cheeks rosy from playing on the Heath. Marvinder was holding Jaspal's hand – protecting him, just as she used to.

Dora held out her arms and silently embraced them.

That afternoon in Hampstead slid slowly by, as they all sorted out past from present and lost dreams from reality, and when it was over, each knew for certain, that the past was the past. There was no going back, except in fleeting memory or hazy nostalgia. The dead were dead, and there was nothing for it but to go forward.

TWENTY-FIVE

Deep and Dreamless Streets

'Is Jaspal home?' The boy bent down and pulled up his over-stretched, grey socks as he spoke.

Kathleen had opened the door to his knock. Down the steps beyond him, she could see a cluster of other boys. They all lived in Whitworth Road or in a neighbouring street, and most went to Jaspal's school.

Kathleen turned and bellowed up the stairs, 'Jaspal! You're wanted!'

Jaspal appeared at the top.

'Who is it?' he asked.

'Phil Potter and his mates,' she said.

'Oh, yeh!' said Jaspal casually. 'That's all right then, I'm coming,' and leaning over the bannister, he slid all the way to the bottom on his stomach.

Jaspal went outside to the top of the front steps and looked down on them. He stood with his legs apart and his hands in his pockets. Instead of having his hair tied into a topknot, Jaspal was wearing a black turban, bound in tight, neat folds round his head in the Sikh style. It made him look tall and formidable.

Phil Potter had returned to the gate and joined the others. There was Fatty Roberts and Graham Shepherd; the twins, Bobby and Derek; there was Teddy Boyle, thin and pale from TB, and Bill Horton with his round, National Health glasses, which earned him the name of Spekky Four Eyes. They all stared up at him, expectantly. He sensed their awe. Word had got round. The boy they had all called a sissy had beaten up Charlie Saunders, the gang leader of the Spitfires – and made his nose bleed. More than that, he had fought with real crooks; he had

279

seen murder – well, nearly murder – the man was expected to live, but Govind could have gone to the gallows! There was going to be a trial, and Jaspal would have to give evidence to save his father from going to prison for a long time.

They had all seen Jaspal being collected by a police car and driven away to make a statement. The stories abounded, and in all of them, Jaspal was a hero. He had even got into the evening papers.

They weren't a very tough-looking lot, Phil's mates, in their grubby grey pullovers, and their socks wrinkling down their legs, but with Jaspal on their side, they felt they could walk down the High Street with their heads held high, and so what, if they met the Spitfires? They would never again slink down the back alleys like cowardly rats.

'You coming, Jaspal?' asked Phil.

'Yeh, I'm coming.' Jaspal jumped the whole flight of stone steps and landed with a spring before them. 'Why don't we go up Mattock Woods?' he suggested. 'I feel like climbing some trees, and there's good places to hide there, and we could make bows and arrows.'

The boys swaggered off, and Kathleen went back up to the top flat, where Marvinder had taken her turn in looking after Beryl.

The doctor had diagnosed whooping cough.

'There's no cure,' he said. 'You'll just have to sit it through and hope she's strong enough to take it. It's other infections you have to watch for now. I may have to give her penicillin. Don't let her temperature get too high. Dampen her down with a cold cloth if it does. The main thing is to make sure she catches her breath when she's in the middle of a coughing fit. Keep her room cool, but draught-free.'

It was the whooping that terrified them all. Mrs O'Grady said it was like waiting for the German buzz bombs when the war was on. When you could hear them buzzing, you knew they were on the move, and with luck

would pass right over and miss out your house; but it was
when the noise suddenly stopped, and there was that
silence; that's when you knew you were in danger and the
bomb was about to drop. It was the same with Beryl.
When she coughed, at least you knew she was breathing,
but when she whooped as she took in her breath for the
next cough and then there was silence, that's when they
rushed to her side, because it meant her breath had got
trapped and she was in danger of choking.

Marvinder was massaging Beryl's feet. It soothed the
child more than anything else, and when she lay propped
up against three pillows, relaxed and calm, she didn't
cough so much.

As Marvinder massaged, she told her stories. She
described the games she and Edith used to play in India;
how they used to dress up in sarees and pretend they were
princesses. She told Beryl about Rani, Jaspal's buffalo, and
how they used to ride on her back and take her into the
river to bathe.

'Oh, Marvi, can I go to India and do that?' sighed Beryl
longingly.

'I'll take you, one day,' Marvinder promised her.

'Me, too,' breathed Kathleen. 'I'd like to go too.' Then
she looked at Marvinder with genuine puzzlement. 'Hey,
Marvi, were you really friends with that girl, Edith? I
mean, she's so posh-like, and stuck-up.'

'Oh, she's not really. Not with me, anyway,' said
Marvinder. 'I've known her all my life. We were born on
the same day in the same village in India. She's almost like
a sister.'

'I'm your sister, aren't I, Marvi?' declared Beryl,
snuggling up close.

'Yes, my little darling, you are my sister and I love you,'
cried Marvinder hugging the child and covering her with
kisses.

'What does that make me?' asked Kathleen. 'I'm not
your sister. Beryl could look like an Indian girl with her
dark skin and black hair, but me . . .?'

281

Marvinder shook her head as she once again gazed with wonder at Kathleen's bright red hair, and pale skin with the ginger freckles. 'You – I've never seen anyone in India who looked like you – never!'

The two girls looked at each other with glee and burst out laughing at how different they were.

'But,' said Kathleen, becoming very solemn, 'I could be your aunt. After all, I am Beryl's aunt, and if Beryl is your sister, then I must be your aunt too.'

'Really?' asked Marvinder looking thoroughly mystified. 'Shall I call you "Aunty", then?'

'Don't you dare!' exclaimed Kathleen. 'You'd make me feel old,' and they all broke into laughter again.

'Are you going to live with Edith? I heard Mum saying you and Jaspal might, 'cos the Chadwicks suggested it, and there's too many of us in these flats.'

Marvinder became serious and turned her head away. 'I don't know,' she said at last. 'It's nice here with my dad and my sister and Jaspal . . . and you and Mum . . . and Doctor Silbermann downstairs . . . and Patrick and Michael . . . and,' then her face brightened with merriment again, 'even your dad! And I don't want to leave this school. Miss Clement says I'm getting on like a house on fire with my reading and writing, and I like it there, being with you and Josephine and all of them, and I like playing the violin in the music section for the nativity play.'

'What about Jaspal?' asked Kathleen.

'I'm not sure. He misses India,' murmured Marvinder.

Then Marvinder told Kathleen, that if she wanted her bed back under the stairs in the hall, she'd be quite happy to sleep with Beryl now.

'Did you hear that, Maeve? Marvinder says I can go back to my bed under the stairs.'

'That's grand, then,' said Maeve wistfully. These days she lived in a daze, what with Govind in prison awaiting trial, maybe for murder, and Beryl ill with whooping cough. Sometimes, in the middle of the night, when the coughing was worst, she was terrified to sleep in case Beryl choked and silently suffocated. But she realised that Marvinder, too, was listening attentively, and sometimes had appeared in the night to help to soothe the racked child. Kathleen usually slept through it all. Grudgingly, Maeve had got used to Marvinder coming into the flat more and more because she loved helping with Beryl.

'I always wanted a sister,' explained Marvinder.

But whatever their problems, nothing stopped Christmas closing in on them. It was now only a week away. One evening, Patrick and Michael came home jubilantly carrying a Christmas tree. They had saved the money up between them and brought some decorations as well. Kathleen, Jaspal and Marvinder were thrilled. Mrs O'Grady found an old bucket for it to stand in, which they filled with earth and covered round with red crepe paper.

'We'll put it in the window,' said Michael, 'then it can be seen from outside as well.'

Beryl cried and said she wanted a Christmas tree up at the top where she could see it. So Michael chopped off some of the lower branches and made a little tree all for her, and put it upstairs by her bed.

Marvinder thought Christmas was like one of those huge ocean liners. It seemed to come gliding towards them from a great distance, all ablaze with light. And everyone seemed to fix their eyes on it as though, somehow, they could be one of the passengers up there on the decks, dining and dancing. As it came closer, they were all absorbed by it – even if it was just to stare into the dazzling windows and watch the beautiful people; even if it was just to bob around in its wash. Everyone felt the spirit of it; the putting on of a white dress with a silver tinsel head band, singing carols for the nativity play, or the traipsing round Woolworths with piles of saved-up pennies to buy a present, and trying also to afford the festive wrapping paper – just like Edith's present, so that when it was put round the tree, it looked like part of the decorations.

And it didn't cost anything to go and visit Father Christmas in Pemberton's, even if they knew he couldn't possibly give them that shiny bike that was in the window, or the train set, or the beautiful, new unbreakable doll, with eyes of glassy blue. It didn't cost anything to ask.

But Marvinder wasn't sure what it all meant – all this greed and need; the aching desire to have as well as to give. She wasn't sure that she could ever be on that Christmas liner – up there with the merriment, the singing and the eating. Everyone, no matter how poor, was creating a performance; making the effort. They all knew the play and the script; they all spoke the same words. The great ship came closer and swamped them with carols and music and prayers and stories and food, and everyone tried harder to live up to the expectations.

Mrs O'Grady said they wouldn't be able to afford a chicken for Christmas day, but she was hoping for some boiled ham. Maeve had already set to and made a Christmas cake. 'It has to be made early,' she explained, 'so that it has time to soak in and get really fruity.'

Two days before Christmas, Kathleen, Josephine and some others went on a last desperate tour of the neighbourhood doorsteps, carol singing. They needed the money; there was still Granny's present to get, or Cousin Joe's or something for those best friends at school.

Marvinder stood in an empty street. On either side of her, the windows of the houses rose up, brightly-lit, with the glow of Christmas decorations glimmering through the grime. Kathleen and the others had rushed on ahead to gather in a tight cluster on a doorstep, trying to make democratic decisions as to which carol to try next. They chose, 'O Little Town of Bethlehem', and Marvinder wondered about the deep and dreamless streets, and the silent stars and found herself remembering the long white road which ran past her village in the Punjab.

She slipped away to go and see Doctor Silbermann.

'Aren't you celebrating Christmas?' she asked, noting

the lack of Christmas decorations.

'Oh, yes,' he said. 'How could anyone not celebrate Christmas if it means celebrating new life and new hope. My celebration, as a Jew, is really Hanukkah. But even we Jews in Vienna, we all loved Christmas. We would go down to the cathedral to see the Christmas tree, and how we loved the Christmas markets where we could buy our presents.'

'Were they better than Woolworths?' asked Marvinder.

'They were magic. Can you imagine lots of stalls lit by hanging lanterns, and piled with all sorts of crafts for sale that people have made? Beautiful things, made by potters and carpenters, tailors and embroiderers. They were fairy markets.'

'Sounds like a bazaar in India,' sighed Marvinder.

Then Doctor Silbermann went to an old wardrobe standing in the corner of his room. He opened the door and brought out a large object all beautifully wrapped in Christmas paper.

'I'm glad you called round, my dear,' he said smiling. 'I wanted to give you your Christmas present quietly. Here. Take it.'

Marvinder's eyes opened with astonishment. 'A Christmas present? For me?' She took it wonderingly. 'Should I put it under the tree upstairs?'

'I think you should open it now,' he said, 'and while you do that, I'll go and get out the chocolate biscuits.'

Marvinder undid the red ribbon and folded back the bright wrapping. She knew what it was. She knew before she even revealed it. You can't easily disguise the shape of a violin. There was a black case, and when she undid the clasps, and opened it, there, lying in a soft, yellow interior, was a shining violin. Its bow was fixed to the inside of the lid, and in a small compartment at one end of the case, was a piece of resin for rubbing on the horse hair of the bow and a chin rest to support the instrument.

'Is this really mine? Mine to keep and take away?'

Doctor Silbermann beamed with the pleasure he had

285

caused. He watched her lift it out and hold it between her chin and left shoulder. She took out the bow and tightened the hair with the little knob at the end. Then using the resin, she rubbed it up and down the length of the hair on the bow and prepared it for playing.

'Is it tuned?' she asked.

'I tuned it yesterday, before wrapping it up for you,' he said. 'Try it and see.'

So Marvinder drew the bow up and down all four strings. 'It's wonderful, wonderful!' she cried. 'Oh, thank you, Doctor Silbermann, thank you!'

'I thought perhaps you could do an exam by next spring, and then maybe enter a music festival in the summer. It would do you good to play before people. What do you think?'

'I would be like a real violinist!' cried Marvinder.

On Christmas Eve, a Riley came cruising down Whitworth Road. Jaspal saw it, and couldn't avoid that stab of fear, even though he knew that all the men had been arrested and that no one could harm him any more. But then he saw the number plate ARG 482. He raced down the stairs shouting at the top of his voice. 'The Chadwicks are coming!'

He flung open the front door. The car stopped. Harold Chadwick got out and opened the door for his passenger.

'Pa!' Jaspal cried, his feet rooted to the ground; but it was only for a moment, and then with a shout of joy, he hurled himself into his father's arms.

Dave Greatorex had regained consciousness and would live, but because the gang had left him in the burning warehouse, not caring whether he was alive or dead, he had told the police everything he knew.

Word spread that Govind was home. Soon the O'Grady flat was crowded out with people, all eager to find out what had happened, and asking, now that he was cleared of murder, what about his black marketeering?

'It's good to have "friends",' some people muttered,

when they heard that Harold Chadwick had stood bail for him.

'Yeh, but he did save a bloke's life,' argued others, defending him. 'That had to count for something, and it's not as though he was carrying on with gold or petrol or even tobacco. I mean, to keep a man in gaol for selling ties and ladies' underwear is a bit much!'

So they gossiped on. Marvinder came up from Doctor Silbermann with her own violin, longing to show it off. She saw her brother standing proudly next to his father, while they once again told the gathered assembly how they got themselves and Dave Greatorex out of the burning warehouse.

Marvinder stood in the doorway, unseen by everyone, except Harold Chadwick. How like her mother she looked, so tall and upright, and straight as an arrow.

'If only Jhoti could see her now, she would be so proud,' thought Harold.

There is a long white road which runs from one horizon to another. It seems to have no beginning and no end, but emerges out of one heat haze only to disappear into the watery distance of another.

The villages along that road, which were razed and ploughed back into the soil like stubble at the end of a harvest, had now reseeded themselves; grown up again in the furrows of war, with new life and a new generation.

Displaced people, those who had survived, were offered their land back; and some returned in dribs and drabs, fearfully, in case they met up with the ghosts of loved ones and memories too painful to live with.

Tom Fletcher wrote to Govind and told him his land was there to claim, if he wished it. Perhaps he would want to hold it for Jaspal.

Jaspal was staring out of the window, across the jagged ocean of London roofs. He thought he had forgotten India. He thought he had forgotten Rani, his buffalo, and the path across the fields to school where he and Nazakhat used to run. The colours came back to him now – the mustard and green, the blue and the orange; the layer upon layer of smells and sounds.

Did he want this back, they had asked?

'Yes,' he said turning round. 'Yes.'